# THE
# SHIPBUILDER'S
# WIFE

OTHER BOOKS AND AUDIOBOOKS
BY JENNIFER MOORE:

*Becoming Lady Lockwood*

*Lady Emma's Campaign*

*Miss Burton Unmasks a Prince*

*Simply Anna*

*Lady Helen Finds Her Song*

*A Place for Miss Snow*

*Miss Whitaker Opens Her Heart*

*Miss Leslie's Secret*

*My Dearest Enemy*

# THE SHIPBUILDER'S WIFE

A novel by

## JENNIFER MOORE

Covenant Communications, Inc.

Published by Covenant Communications, Inc.
American Fork, Utah

Printed in the United States of America
First Printing: September 2018

24 23 22 21 20 19 18    10 9 8 7 6 5 4 3 2 1

ISBN: 978-1-52440-7209

*For Julie, Becky, Wendy, and Holly—*
*because you know where to find the olives*

# Acknowledgments

WHEN A BOOK IS FINISHED, I feel a strange mix of emotions: a bit of pride in the work, relief that it is finished, sadness to leave behind characters who've become friends, and overwhelming gratitude for the people who helped me along the way.

First, of course, so many thanks to my husband, Frank. He's my anchor and holds his scatterbrained wife and our family together with his steadiness. My boys, James, Ben, Andrew, and Joey, are the joys of my life. They are supportive and helpful, and I couldn't be more grateful for their help as I put together a story.

Thanks to Josi Kilpack, Nancy Allen, Ronda Hinrichsen, and Becki Clayson for help figuring out this plot, especially the romance.

Thank you, Margot Hovley, for making me accountable.

Thanks, Carla Kelly, for sending me research books and giving advice.

Michelle Lucas and Wende Moore, thanks for your expertise on Virginia and for your help with setting.

Thank you, Laurie Lewis. I love your *Free Men and Dreamers* series, and your source notes are so helpful.

A huge thanks to the girls of the Great England Writing Adventure 2017 for a writing retreat to beat all others, and the world's best birthday party.

Thank you to my parents, Penny and Ed Lunt, and my grandma Gladys Tidwell, for their family history research that makes this story personal and close to my heart.

Thanks, Kami Hancock, for your edits and for being patient when I needed "just a few weeks longer." You're the best, matey!

Thank you, Toree Douglas, for making another beautiful cover.

And I would be remiss if I didn't thank the History Channel, biographers, journal keepers, documentary makers, historical cartographers, war reenactors, and the other recorders of history. Thank you for not letting this war be forgotten.

# CHAPTER 1

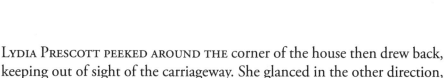

LYDIA PRESCOTT PEEKED AROUND THE corner of the house then drew back, keeping out of sight of the carriageway. She glanced in the other direction, but none of her parents' guests had noticed that she'd slipped away from the garden party. A coach had just arrived at the plantation, and she recognized the four black horses pulling it. Jefferson Caraway was here at last.

She pinched her cheeks to heighten their color and moved along the garden path to the spot she'd chosen. Jefferson would have to pass this opening in the hedge, and of course a gentleman like Mr. Caraway wouldn't ignore a lady in need of assistance. It was the perfect excuse for a moment alone, which was certainly the only thing that had prevented him thus far from proposing marriage.

Months of dancing, visits, and flirting had made it obvious that Jefferson preferred Lydia, and, for her part, she was smitten with the man. Her father's insistence that Lydia settle upon a suitor by the end of summer had changed Lydia's approach to her social engagements. She no longer had the luxury of stringing along a line of suitors. She was determined to marry Jefferson, and once Lydia set her mind to something, nothing prevented her from achieving it.

Jefferson Caraway was an accomplished rider and a graceful dancer, and he always paid a compliment when she arranged her hair differently or wore a new gown. He had also recently become a landowner when he inherited a large cotton plantation on the James River, slightly farther than twenty miles from Lydia's home at Rosefield Park.

She smiled, satisfied that her future was unfolding exactly as she intended. Before the end of summer she would be Lydia Caraway of Elmswood Manor. Her mother would plan the grandest wedding Virginia had ever seen, and

Lydia would have the life she'd always dreamed of. Not to mention, she'd be the envy of every young woman from Charleston to Boston.

Footsteps crunched on the gravel path, and Lydia tugged on the ribbon that tied the sleeve just above her elbow, pulling apart the bow. She faced away from the opening and waited until the steps drew closer.

"Oh dear," she said, fussing with the ribbons she couldn't quite reach with both hands.

The footsteps stopped.

Lydia drew in her breath, waiting.

"Might I be of assistance, miss?"

The low timbre of the voice startled her, and she turned quickly. The man standing before her was a stranger.

Lydia took a step back. "Who . . . ?" With some effort, she regained her composure, drawing in her breath and pushing down her shoulders. "Do you mind, sir? It is not polite to startle someone . . ."

"I beg your pardon." He inclined his head. "I didn't mean to invade your privacy. Your words led me to assume you were distressed."

Again she was taken aback by the deepness of his voice and the overall largeness of the man. He was at least a foot taller than she, and twice as broad. Though the cut and the fabric were of good quality, his coat was not of the latest fashion. And the way the wool stretched across his shoulders gave the impression that the garment was making an effort to contain him. Her impulse was to cringe away or hide.

She raised her chin. "As you see, I am perfectly well."

The focus in his eyes grew keener as he studied her. His gaze lit on the loose ribbons, and the corner of his mouth pulled to the side. "Very ill-mannered of me. I apologize again. I should have realized you did not intend to be discovered."

His tone held no sarcasm, but that pull of his lips—did he realize she'd come here deliberately? Was he smirking?

Lydia was not certain how to react to this man, which was unusual. She typically read people well and knew precisely what to say.

"Yes, well, if you will excuse—" She spoke in a dismissive tone and started to turn away.

"Oh there you are," a woman's voice said as two other people stepped through the opening in the hedge and joined the man.

Relief relaxed Lydia's muscles. She was glad she and the large man were no longer alone.

The woman who'd spoken was older, possibly the man's mother or aunt. She was quite tall, and an elegant blue promenade dress with silk embroidery complimented her slender frame. The gown was of the latest fashion and very likely French, and since the British had blockaded every American harbor, such a garment was expensive and quite difficult to come by.

The woman looked somewhat familiar, and Lydia thought they must have met before. She was likely a friend of Lydia's mother. With her was another man, closer in age to the first.

"Wondered where you'd gotten off to, Jake," the new man said, slapping the other on the shoulder. He wore a coat much like his friend's. Well made, but a few years out of fashion. Not uncommon during wartime but still an indication that the man's status was inferior to her own. "Worried you'd fled the premises—" He stopped short when his gaze landed on Lydia. "Oh. I beg your pardon, miss. I did not see you there. How do you do?" He swept off his hat and bowed.

Lydia lifted a brow. Neither of the men was acquainted with her, and more importantly she'd not given her consent for them to become so. They were very brazen, acting so comfortably with a woman to whom they'd not been introduced. Apparently these common men did not know the first thing about proper manners.

The woman turned as well, and when her gaze landed on Lydia, she smiled. "Oh, Lydia Prescott." She placed a hand over her heart. "How lovely you've become." She stepped forward and took Lydia's hand with her long fingers. "Let me look at you, my dear."

That greeting was more in the manner Lydia was used to. She gave her prettiest smile, tipping her head the slightest bit and opening her eyes wide, in just the way she knew older women found endearing.

"You may not remember me, dear," the woman said. "Mrs. Elnora Hathaway. We met two winters ago at Mrs. Madison's ball in Washington City."

"Of course, Mrs. Hathaway." Lydia curtsied. No wonder she didn't remember Mrs. Hathaway. Dolly Madison's party was by far the grandest gathering she'd ever attended. Sophisticated ladies and stylish gentlemen from as far away as Boston had filled the president's richly decorated house. The food, the music, the dancing, all of it had been so extravagant. As a young girl of seventeen, Lydia had been overwhelmed, to say the least. "I am so glad you arrived safely." She smiled. "Mamá will be pleased to see you."

The woman gave her hand a squeeze. "And allow me to introduce my companions." Seeing Lydia's nod of assent, she gestured with her folded fan toward the large man who'd first come upon her. "Mr. Jacob Steele of Annapolis. Miss Prescott, you have, undoubtedly, heard of Steele Shipyard."

"Of course." Lydia nodded, even though she certainly had not heard of Steele Shipyard. Why would a debutante from one of the most prosperous plantations in Virginia give a fig about something so banal?

"Mr. Steele was apprenticed to my husband in Washington when he was young, and now here he is, a national hero, building warships to fight against the British." Mrs. Hathaway beamed at Jacob Steele as if he were an adorable puppy instead of a looming titan.

"We are all indebted to you for your service to America, sir," Lydia said.

Jacob Steele bowed. "Pleased to make your acquaintance, Miss Prescott." His voice was so deep it was practically a growl. His chin was wide, his strong jaw covered with a shadow caused by the sort of thick whiskers Lydia imagined sprouted back a moment after they were shaved. Neither his appearance nor his mannerisms were the least bit refined.

"And Mr. Alden Thatcher." Mrs. Hathaway held her fan toward the other man with an elegant motion. "Mr. Thatcher commands a merchant ship."

Why would her parents have invited a shipbuilder and a sailor to their midsummer garden party?

Lydia curtsied again, finding it much easier to smile at Mr. Thatcher. He seemed kind, with a cheerful countenance and brown eyes sparkling as if they held a joke. He was certainly more pleasant than his companion and much less intimidating.

"I imagine the British blockades are even more of a frustration to you than to those of us wishing to sell tobacco and cotton or hoping for decent tea, Mr. Thatcher," Lydia said. She widened her eyes and blinked to emphasize her lashes. "I do hope the redcoats don't impress you into their navy."

"As do I, Miss Prescott." His smile turned into a scowl. "Those lobsterbacks are guilty of far worse offenses than disrupting shipments and harassing sailors, however."

"Oh yes." Mrs. Hathaway opened her fan and waved it in front of her. "The plantation raids. Horrifying." She looked at Lydia and seemed to regret her outburst. "But, of course, you have nothing to fear, my dear." Her eyes rounded and she glanced to the others as if hoping for their support in reassuring the younger woman.

Mrs. Hathaway's words made resentment swell inside Lydia's chest. She was very aware of the dangers the British posed to the river plantations and didn't appreciate being spoken down to as if she were a child. "We are not in danger here. Papá says the redcoats won't find Rosefield. The house is too far away from the river, and the dock is difficult to see if one doesn't know where to look."

"And he's absolutely right." Mrs. Hathaway snapped the fan closed and gave a brisk nod that didn't quite agree with her uncertain smile.

Lydia glanced at Mr. Steele. The man's full attention was directed upon her like a stage lamp on an opera singer. He seemed to be considering what she said, and she wondered if he agreed or not. His face gave away nothing.

She glanced away, arranging her face into a teasing expression. She wagged her finger at Mr. Thatcher as if scolding him. "I must say, this is very serious talk for a party."

"I express my deepest apology," he replied, a smile lighting his eyes. "I shall endeavor to stick to socially appropriate topics."

Lydia wagged her finger again, giving a scowl and then followed it with a smirk to show that she was teasing. "See that you do, sir."

"How boorish of me not to have inquired after your health or commented on the weather." Mr. Thatcher put a hand over his heart. "I am hopeless."

"Very uncivilized." Lydia shook her head as if his lack of manners were a true pity. She gave another smile to Mr. Thatcher then turned to include the others. "Come. My parents will be happy to welcome you. You'll want iced tea on this hot day, and you must try our cook's famous lemon cake."

"That sounds lovely," Mrs. Hathaway said. She slipped her hand into the crook of Jacob Steele's elbow.

Lydia took Alden Thatcher's offered arm and the pair started up the pathway with the others following. They'd only taken a few steps, however, when a hand tugged at her elbow, stopping her.

She looked back and met Jacob's gaze. His very close gaze. "If you please, Miss Prescott." He removed his gloves and took hold of the ribbons hanging from her sleeve.

Lydia watched as he pursed his lips, and with careful movements she would have thought impossible for such large hands, he retied the bow into a wrinkled, lopsided knot.

Jacob stepped back and tipped his hat, the small pull at the corner of his mouth seeming this time more like a smile than a smirk.

She released her breath. "Thank you," she said, but the words came out as a whisper. She cleared her throat and turned, grabbing on to Alden's arm, and walked with quick steps toward the party.

The hedge ended, and the pathway emerged into a grassy field upon a gentle hill, giving a full view of the elegant gardens surrounding the Great House at Rosefield Park.

Lydia glanced at Mr. Thatcher's face and saw his eyes widen at the sudden prospect. The exact reaction her father and his father before him had intended with the design of the hedge-lined pathway.

She gazed with pride at her home. Thick pillars supported the porch roof, running the entire length of the house and giving shade to a group of string musicians. Above, potted flowers hung from the white wrought-iron railing surrounding the second floor balcony. The gardens spread out from the house in orderly fashion, crisscrossed walking paths and shaped hedges dividing the park into sections and showcasing the prized rose collection for which the plantation was famous. Grand oaks, tall pines, and blooming magnolia trees provided shade and fragrance at the edges of the gardens, and beneath these, tables were laden with delicious refreshment for the Prescotts' guests. Beyond the house was a stream that led to a pond.

Groups mingled throughout the park, admiring the roses, listening to the music, and visiting with the most prominent members of American high society. It was often said summer didn't truly begin until the Prescotts' annual rose-garden picnic. The event was a tradition going back generations, and to receive an invitation signified one's status among the wealthiest landowners in the southern states. Again, Lydia wondered at the presence of the two men.

"I've not been here for years," Mrs. Hathaway said, her gaze sweeping the scene. "My memories of the house and gardens were not exaggerated in the least. Simply breathtaking."

Lydia glanced at Mr. Steele, but he was not looking at the garden. He squinted in the direction of the river, then looked toward the stables and the outbuildings, then finally at the house. She scowled at his interest in the very dullest parts of the property.

"Miss Prescott."

Lydia turned at the voice and saw Jefferson Caraway striding across the lawn.

She waved. "Mr. Caraway. I didn't realize you'd arrived." When he reached them, she curtsied formally, knowing how important propriety was to Jefferson.

Jefferson bowed to Mrs. Hathaway, but his brow lifted and his lip curled as he studied the two men.

"If I may," Lydia said. "This is Mrs. Hathaway of Washington City. And Mrs. Hathaway, this is Mr. Jefferson Caraway of Elmswood Manor."

Jefferson took the lady's fingers and gave another elegant bow. "A pleasure, Mrs. Hathaway."

She lowered into a graceful curtsy. "The pleasure is mine, sir. And my deepest condolences on the passing of your uncle."

"Thank you." Jefferson's brow rose again as he glanced at Lydia and then to the men.

Lydia hurried to introduce them. "Mr. Steele of Annapolis, and Mr. Thatcher of . . . Oh, Mr. Thatcher, I do not believe you told me where you are from."

"Most recently, New Orleans," Alden said, inclining his head. "Mr. Caraway."

Mr. Steele did the same. "How do you do, sir?"

"Ah," Jefferson said, looking more interested and less affronted by their appearance. "A pleasure."

His voice sounded shockingly high-pitched to Lydia's ears after Mr. Steele's low tone, and she hadn't realized before how slender his shoulders were.

"I am so glad to have found you," Jefferson said. "I'd hoped for a few moments of your time, if you don't mind. We could go somewhere a bit more private."

Lydia smiled. She opened her fan and looked down demurely. "Of course, Mr. Caraway. I—"

But Mr. Steele spoke at the very same moment. "First we should pay our respects to the host."

Mr. Steele and Lydia stopped and looked first to one another then to Jefferson. Lydia's stomach grew hot when she saw that Jefferson's invitation had been extended not to her but to the men.

The heat spread to her cheeks. "Oh yes. You . . ." She turned her gaze, looking for anything that would rescue her from further embarrassment. The woman beside her was fanning herself, watching the interaction closely.

Lydia motioned toward the garden. "Mrs. Hathaway, I would love some lemonade, wouldn't you?"

"That sounds wonderful, dear."

Lydia took her arm, not lifting her gaze to meet any of the men's. "Please excuse us, gentlemen."

Mrs. Hathaway leaned close as they started away. "Once we reach a suitable distance, I'll retie your ribbon." She glanced down at Lydia's elbow and shook her head. "Bless him. Jacob meant well, but he certainly made a mess, didn't he?"

Lydia glanced back at the trio walking toward the house. Jefferson was speaking, and Mr. Thatcher seemed to be listening, but Mr. Steele's gaze was on Lydia. She looked away quickly, not liking how nervous the man made her. In the twenty minutes since they'd met, Mr. Jacob Steele, with his lack of manners and refinement had made a mess indeed.

# CHAPTER 2

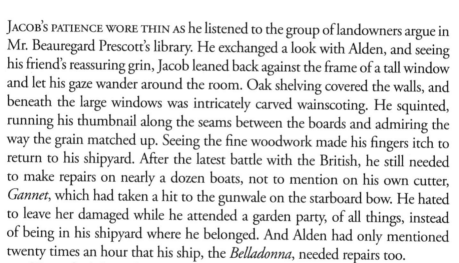

JACOB'S PATIENCE WORE THIN AS he listened to the group of landowners argue in Mr. Beauregard Prescott's library. He exchanged a look with Alden, and seeing his friend's reassuring grin, Jacob leaned back against the frame of a tall window and let his gaze wander around the room. Oak shelving covered the walls, and beneath the large windows was intricately carved wainscoting. He squinted, running his thumbnail along the seams between the boards and admiring the way the grain matched up. Seeing the fine woodwork made his fingers itch to return to his shipyard. After the latest battle with the British, he still needed to make repairs on nearly a dozen boats, not to mention on his own cutter, *Gannet*, which had taken a hit to the gunwale on the starboard bow. He hated to leave her damaged while he attended a garden party, of all things, instead of being in his shipyard where he belonged. And Alden had only mentioned twenty times an hour that his ship, the *Belladonna*, needed repairs too.

He studied the gathered men. Some leaned against shelves or sat in leather chairs. Others stood together in small groups, their animated body language typical for men's discussions during wartime. By their fancy clothing and the very fact that they were here, attending the Prescotts' rose-garden party, Jacob knew they were all wealthy. Some were young, probably here at the request of their fathers, a few were quite elderly and may have attended a similar meeting thirty-five years earlier during the Revolutionary War, and one was the undercover agent Jacob had worked with for more than a year but had not met in person. He studied each face, wondering who the spy was and what message he brought today.

"If not for Joshua Barney and his cursed flotilla, our plantations would be safe!"

Jacob turned his focus on the red-faced man whose exclamation had silenced the rest of the room.

"Steady, Jake. He's just frightened," Alden muttered in a quiet tone meant for Jacob's ears alone. His friend knew him well enough to recognize an insult to Joshua Barney was the surest way to set off Jacob's temper.

"And how so, sir?" Alden then asked the red-faced man in a calm voice, which Jacob knew was concealing his contempt for the man's ill-informed words. "How is Commodore Barney to blame?" Alden clasped his hands behind his back and waited politely, though his eyes held a spark of anger.

"He and his flotilla have provoked the British, haven't they?" The man planted a fist on his waist and waved his other hand in the air as he spoke. "And now they're taking out their anger on innocent citizens."

It was true the British were raiding up and down the coast. Most attacks so far had centered on the Chesapeake Bay and its tributaries. Cities had been burned and pillaged, people killed, women harassed, plantations looted. Jacob could understand the concerns, but to blame Commodore Barney was unacceptable. The man was a genius. A veteran of the Revolutionary War and a captain in both the American and French navies, the commodore was one of the most remarkable men Jacob knew. His plan of forming a flotilla from smaller boats to slip past the British blockades was not only shrewd but very brave. Through Steele Shipyard and his time as an apprentice and journeyman, Jacob had known Joshua Barney for close to twenty years and considered him nothing short of a national hero.

"Be assured, sir." Alden spoke in the calm voice Jacob couldn't emulate if he'd wanted to. "Vice Admiral Cochrane is one of England's most experienced naval officers. His attacks are not brash reactions but calculated strategies. He seeks, of course, to gain supplies but also to affect the overall morale of the country. If Americans no longer believe in the cause of the war . . ." He shrugged. "Then all is lost."

"But we've nobody to defend us," the red-faced man spoke again. "The militia has called up so many men, and even our slaves are deserting for the other side."

Jacob couldn't blame them. The English had made a smart move, offering freedom and a chance for escaped slaves to take up arms against their former owners. The offer had been accepted in droves as slaves fled and made their way to Tangier Island.

"We should come to an understanding with them," Jefferson Caraway said. "Give the English what they ask for if they pledge to spare our property." The sound of the man's nasally voice made Jacob's skin crawl.

Jefferson was slender with no chin and a pointy rat-like face, pale skin, and a pouf of blond hair held back in a velvet ribbon. Jacob had disliked him immediately, and these cowardly words only served to confirm his initial reaction. Was this whom Miss Lydia Prescott was waiting for behind the hedge? Because she was most assuredly waiting for someone.

Jacob smirked, remembering her surprised expression when he'd come upon her. Had the expression also contained disappointment at Jacob's arrival? And fear? He reluctantly acknowledged that it had. He'd been surprised himself when he happened upon her, but not unpleasantly so. Miss Prescott was the prettiest young lady he'd ever seen. And he could not think of any close contenders. Her large eyes were an unearthly shade of blue, her blonde curls silken. The dark-black lashes and the shine of her lips were undoubtedly the result of some cosmetic concoction, but the confident way she'd carried herself—that could not be imitated. He'd felt his own disappointment at her reaction to his appearance.

"Out of the question," Beauregard Prescott said, slamming the glass he held on to a table and recapturing Jacob's attention. "We should never negotiate with our enemies. And to support them? Intolerable. Such talk borders on treason."

"Exactly." Beau Prescott nodded his agreement. The younger man was the exact image of his father. Tall and slender, with well-defined cheekbones and an imperious expression. The moment the two had entered the room, Jacob had sensed the other man's deference. The Prescotts were most assuredly in control.

"You're suggesting we just allow them to seize all we've worked for? Our very livelihoods?" Jefferson said.

Jacob studied Jefferson Caraway. He knew from Elnora Hathaway that Jefferson had inherited his plantation merely months ago. His property was not a result of any effort of his own but was given to him at the death of a wealthy uncle. Jefferson was arrogant and cowardly and possessed every attribute Jacob despised in a person, but he supposed the refined, genteel man was exactly right for Miss Prescott. He undoubtedly had a grand manor very much like this one. He would provide for her a life and a home like the one she knew now. And she would be comfortable with that.

He looked through the windows at the picturesque landscape. The Potomac flowed along one border of the property, though it wasn't visible from the house. Why a person would build without a view of the water, Jacob would never understand. And the nearest neighbors were more than a mile away in either direction. Plantation life was charming, but Jacob preferred his home in the city. Annapolis was its own type of picturesque. Beautiful houses, good neighbors, tall trees, and the smell of the sea.

"We are suggesting nothing of the sort, Mr. Caraway," Alden said. "The flotilla patrols the rivers to protect—"

"The flotilla." The man with the red-face snorted. "How can we trust this cluster of mismatched ships? Especially when it's manned by pirates?"

The men in the room muttered to themselves, obviously uncomfortable with the idea of pirates traveling up and down their rivers. Jacob nearly rolled his eyes. The flotilla was a motley crew made up of navy sailors, merchant seamen, escaped slaves and free Negroes, watermen, and privateers. All were experienced, extremely skilled at watercraft, and willing to fight, which was more than Jacob could say for the men in this room.

"We prefer the term privateers," Alden said. Now Jacob could hear more of an edge to his friend's voice. An edge he'd only noticed over the past weeks since his friend had returned from sea. Alden was running out of patience. Many of the men who'd joined the flotilla with their captain were Alden's own crewmembers. "I assure you, no matter their origin or their history, the men in the flotilla are loyal to Commodore Barney and to the United States of America."

"And what of the navy?" Jefferson said. "Where are they when we need them?"

How could this fool have so little idea of what was happening in his own country? Jacob couldn't remain silent any longer. "In case you haven't noticed, English warships have blockaded port cities for months. The navy is trapped. And Commodore Barney has devised a solution." His anger gave his voice more volume than he intended.

The men in fancy stockings and embroidered waistcoats stared at him uneasily. Jacob often had that effect on people. Especially these sorts of people. A byproduct of his size and deep voice, he knew, which is why he'd elected to have Alden do the speaking today.

"The flotilla protects the rivers," Alden said, his tone placating. He widened his eyes at Jacob in a look that clearly said to keep quiet. "We not only attack the English ships but thwart their plantation raids."

"When you arrive in time," the red-faced man said. "And when you can escape to shallow waters."

"There are quite a few waterways, sir," Alden said. "It is impossible to defend every creek and inlet at every moment."

Jacob narrowed his eyes at the man. The reminder of the flotilla's failed attack on Tangier Island still stung. The attack had been the cause of damage to the *Gannet*. Just the memory of the crunching sound a cannonball had made smashing through the carefully varnished boards had him clenching his fists. Especially since the enemy had been warned ahead of time. Luckily there had been no casualties. The attack had done little but anger the English, and the flotilla had retreated into the shallower creeks where the battleships could not follow.

"True," Beauregard Prescott said. "And therefore, you should guard the waterways that are most likely to be threatened. As a citizen of the United States of America, I charge you to patrol the Potomac." He folded his arms and watched them steadily as if daring them to argue.

Jacob blinked at the man's boldness. Mr. Beauregard Prescott was definitely intimidating.

Beau mimicked his father's stance, though his imitation fell short of its intent.

Alden held up his hands and stepped toward Mr. Prescott. "Sir, I understand your concern. But we, of course, take orders from the commodore."

The other men grumbled among themselves, but none spoke loud enough to be heard clearly.

"The Potomac is the surest route to Washington City and the capitol." He motioned with a wave of his hand in the direction of the river. "This creek, my plantation, is in the most danger, so the flotilla should be here." He poked his finger downward as he said the last word. Jacob noticed the man's eyes were the same bright blue as his daughter's. He also noticed the color wasn't as attractive on the tall haughty man.

The grumbling grew louder.

Jacob scratched his chin, noting how Beauregard Prescott's concern was at odds with what he'd told his daughter. Lydia had been reassured that her home was in no danger. Jacob wondered whether it was wiser to keep the young lady free from worry or to tell her the truth.

"Our intent is to protect everyone," Alden said.

Beauregard Prescott stepped close. "I will pay." He spoke in a quiet voice that only his son, Jacob, and Alden could hear. "What is the cost of the flotilla protecting my land?" His chin lifted, and Jacob's opinion of the man dropped even lower.

Jacob and Alden had come to the Prescotts' gathering to reassure the river plantation owners, encourage confidence in the flotilla, and in truth, they'd hoped, to gather donations. The flotilla was funded by the secretary of the navy, but the military supplies were never enough, and the sailors weren't risking their lives out of generosity. But the way Mr. Prescott spoke to them in secret, as if unconcerned what happened to his neighbors as long as his plantation was protected, turned Jacob's stomach.

"Mr. Prescott," Jacob said, noticing how the room quieted when he spoke. "As representatives of the United States Navy, all Americans are entitled to our protection."

He looked at the various men in the room. "However, the flotilla requires repairs, food, and weapons to operate . . ."

***

An hour later, Jacob stood on the porch while Alden remained in the library to answer questions, collect donations, and reassure the gentlemen that the flotilla would do everything in its power to keep their property safe. He leaned his shoulder against a pillar, listening to the orchestra as his gaze traveled over the guests and watched for subtle things—out of place conversations, tension, anything that might give information. Because in his line of work, information was fundamental.

Even before the war began, he'd been an operative commissioned by the United States government to gather intelligence, and he realized the responsibility had hardened him. He trusted few people. British spies were everywhere, in every level of society. Very likely there were spies at this very party, listening to conversations, asking innocent-sounding questions. Whereas before it had been a thrilling game, once war had been declared, a small slip of the tongue could mean life or death, divulging a battalion's position, or revealing a secret strategy. Something he knew all too well after the attack on Tangier Island.

Jacob trusted Alden, of course. The man was like a brother to him. Raised by the Hathaways, they'd grown up together until they'd chosen different vocations, and their paths hadn't crossed for years. One good thing had come from this war: his brother had returned.

And Jacob trusted Elnora Hathaway. The two were as close to family as he knew. He and Alden were orphans, taken in as apprentices at the shipyard in Washington City by Mr. Thomas Hathaway and as sons by his wife. Jacob's gaze found Mrs. Hathaway near the pond, and his heart softened. He couldn't have asked for a more loving foster mother.

He looked again toward Miss Lydia Prescott. Not for the first time. And as Jacob had observed over the past hour, his wasn't the only gaze drawn to her. He noticed nearly every eye on the young lady as she moved smoothly between groups of guests. As he'd considered what it was about her, aside from her beauty, that caused people to take notice, he again determined it to be her confidence. Lydia moved with purpose. She knew precisely how to behave with each person she encountered and adapted effortlessly. With some she flirted or giggled, while with others she took on a more thoughtful approach. She was a master of social interaction.

Jacob found it fascinating, since he'd spent most of his adult life staying back, hiding in shadows, listening, evaluating. Were Miss Prescott's words and actions calculated? Or did the ease come naturally? He envied that ability to move among people so effortlessly. A pity she was a flirt without a sensible thought in her head. She most likely worried only about ribbons and dresses and which men had the fattest pocketbooks.

Alden stepped up beside him. "Well, I didn't particularly enjoy that, did you?"

Jacob grunted.

"But I see you've found something much more pleasant to think about." He gestured with his chin toward Miss Prescott.

Jacob faced him, folding his arms across his chest. "I'm thinking about the state of national security, the future of our country, and our obligation to the safety of our citizens. Not that my thoughts are any of your business."

Alden fixed him with a flat stare that quickly turned into a grin. "I'm certain you are."

Jacob turned back to watch the guests. "Where is our contact?" he muttered. "I'm ready to leave."

"Oh, you know we won't go anywhere until Elnora is ready. And by the looks of it, she'll remain for the duration."

Jacob grunted again, knowing Alden's words were very likely true.

"She has an unfortunate father—demanding and used to getting his own way," Alden said, rubbing a finger over his chin. "And the brother as well. But the mother is pleasant enough. Flippant, I think, but pleasant."

Jacob hadn't realized he was watching Miss Prescott again. He turned purposely toward another part of the garden. "As usual, I have no idea what you're talking about."

"I don't blame you. She is extremely beautiful."

"And she knows it," Jacob said. "Alden, I have neither time nor patience for—"

"Pardon me, gentlemen."

Jacob spun, grateful for the interruption, but he tensed, ready for a confrontation once he saw the speaker.

The blustering man with the red face stood before them. "I don't believe I had the chance to introduce myself earlier." He took Jacob's hand. "David Burlington of Richmond."

"How do you do, sir?" Jacob said. He watched the man warily.

Mr. Burlington took a step closer. "Two weeks ago, troop transport ships left Portsmouth for Bermuda." The man's face remained friendly, as if they were simply exchanging pleasantries, but his voice had lowered, barely discernable beneath the sound of the orchestra. "Thirty-five hundred regulars and one thousand marines under the command of General Ross."

Jacob's heart jolted. Weathered veterans fresh from fighting Napoleon were on their way to join the English troops. Such a thing would be devastating for the exhausted and untrained American militia to contend with. With the additional soldiers would come weapons and supplies and . . . A sense of urgency dampened Jacob's brow. He tipped his hat, maintaining a calm expression while his mind raced through the implications of the man's message.

"A pleasure to meet you as well." Mr. Burlington shook Alden's hand then gave a small bow and strode toward the garden.

"Well, that was unexpected," Alden said. "Thought he was coming to yell at us some more."

"He's our contact." Jacob spoke under his breath. "With intelligence from England." This news couldn't wait. He must inform John Armstrong, the secretary of war, as soon as possible.

Alden nodded. "Anything to be concerned about?"

"We must leave for Washington City immediately." Jacob started down the porch stairs. "And *concerned* doesn't even come close."

# CHAPTER 3

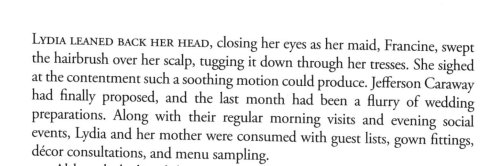

LYDIA LEANED BACK HER HEAD, closing her eyes as her maid, Francine, swept the hairbrush over her scalp, tugging it down through her tresses. She sighed at the contentment such a soothing motion could produce. Jefferson Caraway had finally proposed, and the last month had been a flurry of wedding preparations. Along with their regular morning visits and evening social events, Lydia and her mother were consumed with guest lists, gown fittings, décor consultations, and menu sampling.

Although she loved the attention of being a bride, Lydia was exhausted, and with her parents and Beau gone to a reception in Richmond, this was the first night in nearly a month that she didn't have an engagement of any sort. "Once I'm married, you'll come with me to live at Elmswood Manor, won't you?" She cracked her eyes just enough to see Francine's face in the mirror.

The dark skin around the maid's eyes tightened, but she smiled. "If that is what you want, Miss Lydia."

"I'm glad." Of course, as a slave, Francine would go wherever she was told, but Lydia liked to think that her maid would remain with her because she wished to. A tinge of discomfort pulled in Lydia's chest. When she left Rosefield Park, Francine would also leave behind her sister, Henrietta, and her nephew, Ezra. The discomfort grew as Lydia wondered if her own parents would miss her as badly as Francine would miss her family.

One family member, she knew, missed her. Lydia's brother Emmett was a major in the U.S. Army, fighting the English on the Canadian border. Though ten years separated them, she loved her brother more than anyone on earth. How she hoped he'd be at the wedding. She'd still not met Emmett's new wife, Abigail.

A wedding was exciting and beautiful, with flowers and well wishes, and Lydia knew her mother's party and her bridal gown would be talked about for months. But in the end, she would be with a man she hardly knew, living in a place she'd only visited once, years earlier. She didn't like the feeling in her stomach when she thought past the wedding. And where was he? Jefferson hadn't even visited in the weeks since their engagement. Was he simply busy? Or had he gone to be among high society in Baltimore or Washington City? Lydia sat up and gave herself a mental shake. Where had these doubts come from? She loved Jefferson Caraway. He was handsome and sophisticated and . . . her mind searched for other attributes that would make Jefferson a good husband. He was good and kind. At least she thought he was. And he was very wealthy. If nothing else, she would be comfortably situated in a fine house. And she'd have Francine.

She shifted as Francine separated a section of Lydia's hair and wound it around a rag, tying it in a knot at her scalp. She started on another section, rolling with practiced movements as she'd done every night for as long as Lydia could remember.

Francine had first been Lydia's nursemaid, then nanny, and now lady's maid, and as difficult as it was for Lydia to think of leaving her home and family, the thought of not having Francine with her made it difficult to breathe. Of course, they would visit Rosefield often, she tried to reassure herself, and Francine could see her family then. But the reminder didn't make her feel any better.

Francine brought a candle closer and scrutinized Lydia's face. Thoughtfully, she selected bottles from a box on the dressing table. She opened a jar of face cream and poured in a few drops of oil then stirred with a wooden spoon.

When Francine held it toward her, Lydia dipped her fingers into the jar and then spread the cool mixture over her cheeks and forehead. Francine's various skin concoctions could erase blemishes, stop the pain of a sunburn, and according to Lydia's mother, soften wrinkles. A few times a week, Francine rubbed the women's faces with a cream mixed with sand that left their skin radiant, and when the weather grew cold, she made a waxy salve that kept their lips from becoming dry and cracked. Ladies envied the Prescott women's glowing skin and inquired often about their beauty regimens, not knowing a very talented slave woman's skill deserved the credit.

As Lydia massaged the cream into her face, Francine turned down the bed and picked up Lydia's discarded clothing. "Will there be anything else tonight, Miss Lydia?"

"No, thank you."

Francine curtsied and left.

Lydia rose, pulling tight the belt on her nightclothes wrap. She thought she saw lights moving outside, but when she squinted through the dark window, she couldn't detect anything out of the ordinary. She must have just caught a glimpse of slaves returning to their quarters for the night. Or perhaps fireflies were playing tricks on her eyes.

Lydia took the holder of a lit taper and made her way down the darkened staircase. She hoped Henrietta was still awake to prepare another slice of lemon cake. With Lydia's parents gone, nobody would scold her for eating a second dessert and spoiling her waistline.

The kitchen was empty, which meant Henrietta had likely gone to her cabin for the night. Lydia crossed the room, her night slippers tapping on the wooden floor. She opened the pantry door and found the cake. Lifting the domed lid off the cake stand, she inhaled the sweet aroma.

Men's yells came from outside. Lydia froze. One voice sounded like the foreman's. Were workers being reprimanded? She'd never heard something like that so close to the house, and it was dark. The sound gave her a sick feeling.

She crept toward the pantry door, and the shouts grew louder. Loud bangs made her start. Gunshots? Her mind scrambled for an explanation. Hunters? Or perhaps target practice? But she knew it was neither. Something dreadful was happening. Her skin went cold.

The kitchen door opened, and quick footsteps came toward the pantry. Lydia pressed back against the shelves, wishing she'd extinguished the candles.

"Miss Lydia." Francine's familiar figure stepped into the doorway. She took the glass dome lid from Lydia, blew out the flame, and then pressed a finger to her lips.

Relief made tears swell in Lydia's eyes. "What's happening?" she whispered.

A crash of breaking glass came from the front of the house. More shouts and bangs, this time from the parlor.

"English soldiers." Francine set the cake lid down quietly. She peeked into the kitchen then pulled Lydia across the room. She eased open the outside door, and the sounds grew louder. Shots, yells, thuds; the sounds of chaos.

Tremors shook Lydia's body, and she pressed a hand over her mouth. The foreman and his assistants must be fighting back, trying to defend the plantation.

A crash from behind made them both jump, and Francine jerked Lydia through the doorway. "Run!"

Lydia needed no encouragement. In a panic she bolted toward the nearest building, the storehouse.

"Not there." Francine yanked on her arm, changing their direction. "They'll be searching for food." The pair ran instead to a storage building and hurried inside.

Francine shut the door behind them. "Hide, miss." She pointed to the far corner.

By the moonlight shining through the one window, Lydia found her way through the dusty room, stepping silently past the irregular shapes: a sofa with a broken leg, extra tables and chairs for parties, a ladder. She crouched down against the wall behind an old baby cradle.

Francine joined her, pressing into the small space.

Lydia held herself tightly. Her breath came in rasps, and she was shaking even though the night was warm. "Will they come inside?" she asked.

"Nothin' in here worth steal—" Francine's words were cut off when the door swung open, slamming into the wall beside it.

Lydia closed her eyes and scrunched down, trying to make herself small, and covered her face with her hands.

"It's just old furniture," a voice said.

Lydia peeked through her fingers and saw the flicker of firelight on the walls as the men moved through the room, holding torches aloft and shoving objects out of their way as they went. She pressed her hand against her mouth, hoping not to make a sound, though she was certain they could hear her heart pummeling her ribs.

Something heavy slid over the floor and a man grunted. "We're wasting our time in here." His voice sounded angry. "Keep moving." A moment later, they were gone, slamming the door behind them and leaving the room once again in moonlight.

Lydia sagged in relief, but the two women remained where they were, huddled in the corner in silence as the noises outside continued.

More gunshots sounded, and the light through the window grew brighter. Francine crept toward the door, pulling it open, and peeked through the crack.

Lydia stood as well, creeping quietly through the room but staying near the wall. She reached the window and peered outside. The light was coming from the other direction and she couldn't tell—

"Move away from the window!"

Lydia spun, startled by Francine's scream. "What—" The window beside her exploded in a blast of glass and flames. Lydia flew backwards crashing into a pile of furniture. She lay stunned. The fishy smell of oil stung her nose, and the room was bright. Beyond the heat, Francine was screaming her name. Lydia was in danger but couldn't remember why. She felt sleepy and . . . pain. She tried to call out, but something was wrong. She touched her face, and pain lanced through her cheek. Then, she slipped into darkness.

***

Lydia felt soft. Like her bones were gone. She didn't want to open her eyes, ever. Not when lying here felt so nice and warm. Far away, she heard voices but didn't want to expend the energy to understand what they said. They did sound familiar though.

She drifted, and a vague feeling tickled her mind. There was something she was supposed to do. Or remember. The feeling grew stronger, and blurry bits of memory came with it. The cake dome. A dusty old cradle. A flash of heat. Glass sparkling in the air. Fear. Pain.

Lydia pushed herself to wake, but her eyes were heavy. And her mouth tasted bitter. Laudanum. She remembered the flavor from long ago when the doctor had bandaged her wrist.

Unable to wake fully, Lydia concentrated on the voices. She recognized them now. Mother and Papá. Had they returned from Baltimore early?

"He can't do this. What of her reputation?" Mother was crying.

"Can you blame him?" Papá said. "Just look . . ."

Who were they talking about? He? Who was *he*? Another memory floated into her mind. She was being carried. Fire was all around. Who held her? She tried to picture the person, but all she could remember were strong arms holding her tight, taking her away from danger, and a feeling of safety.

She forced open her eyes.

"Miss Lydia." Francine's face moved into view, looking blurry. "How do you feel?"

Lydia blinked. She opened her mouth to respond, but something felt wrong. One side of her face was tight, and it hurt. She reached up.

Francine caught her arm. "No, don't touch that."

Lydia looked into her maid's face and remembered Francine screaming her name.

"Are you hurt?" Lydia asked.

"No, Sweet Pea." Francine set her arm down gently. "I'm not."

Something in her voice sounded strange. Tight. And Francine hadn't called Lydia Sweet Pea since she was a child.

"Your parents are here." Francine patted Lydia's hand.

Lydia looked past her, remembering she'd heard her parents earlier. "Mother, Papá, you've returned." Again, her face moved wrong. She reached up, but Francine caught her hand again.

"Yes, Dearest." Mother smiled, but her eyes looked sad. Papá's gaze was on something over Lydia's head, and his expression was serious. With a jolt, Lydia remembered the attack. That was why her parents had returned early. And why they looked upset.

"The English were here." Lydia tried to sit up, but her head was still heavy from the effects of the opiate. She blinked, trying to focus. Trying to remember. "Is everything all right? There was a fire. Was anyone injured?"

Mother put a hand over her mouth.

"We lost a few outbuildings," Papá said. "A storehouse of tobacco burned, windows broken, pillows slashed, furniture broken. But the invaders were stopped eventually."

"I'm sorry, Papá."

Tears fell from Mother's eyes as Father described the damage done to their home.

"Don't cry, Mother," Lydia said. "We can postpone the wedding until the house is repaired."

Mother put her other hand to her mouth and sobbed.

"Mother?"

"There won't be a wedding, Lydia," Papá said.

"I don't understand. Did something happen to Jefferson?" Her mind ached as she tried to figure out what was happening.

"Lydia . . ." Papá breathed out a heavy sigh. His brows were drawn. Was he angry? Tired?

A heavy feeling came over her. "What aren't you telling me?" Lydia looked between the three of them, and her mind cleared. She remembered the explosion. The heat. The flying glass. The . . . pain.

"Francine, fetch my mirror." Lydia ordered in a voice that was much calmer than she felt.

"Oh no, Miss Lydia. You lie back down and I'll bring some more medicine."

"Francine," she snapped. "Do it now."

The maid looked to Lydia's parents, and seeing Papá's nod, she retrieved the hand mirror and gave it to Lydia.

Lydia lifted it.

The sight was worse than she could have imagined. A wound stretched across her cheek, to her jaw. The cut had been stitched, but it was red, the skin around it swollen and shiny with ointment.

She stared, unbelieving.

Nobody spoke, and the silence in the room confirmed the truth of the damage more than the view in the mirror ever could.

Lydia didn't scream. She didn't break down or cry out. She lowered the mirror and closed her eyes, feeling numb and hollow, and knowing nothing in her life would ever be the same.

*I am ruined.*

# CHAPTER 4

ONE WEEK AFTER THE ATTACK, Jacob stood in the Prescotts' library, his gaze moving over the woodwork. But unlike before, he wasn't admiring the fine craftsmanship; he was studying the cruel damage the English soldiers had wrought. The windows were covered with oiled paper, awaiting replacement of their panes. The carpets, drapes, and most of the furniture had been removed. The pieces that remained showed signs of damage where axes and bayonets had marred their fine exteriors. *A pity,* Jacob thought. Yet, thanks to the flotilla, the Prescotts at least still had a home. And a daughter.

The door opened, and Beauregard Prescott stormed into the room. "Where were you?" the man barked by way of greeting. His jaw was set and his hands clenched.

Taken aback by the man's behavior, Jacob couldn't form a response. When he had received Mr. Prescott's summons, he'd imagined a much pleasanter reception. Jacob had saved his daughter's life, after all. Rushing into a fire-engulfed building at the frantic request of a servant wasn't exactly the sort of thing one did for pleasure.

Beauregard Prescott remained still, his eyes boring into Jacob, waiting for a reply.

"I'm not certain I understand, sir," Jacob said. "If you're referring to the night your plantation was attacked, I was here with my company, fighting the English."

"But you were late." He jabbed a finger at Jacob. "I lost a warehouse full of curing leaves. The entire first cutting. Over five hundred pounds' worth of tobacco. Not to mention the damage to my home and other buildings."

*He can't be serious.* Jacob's emotions swung from disbelief to anger. "Sir, men died protecting your house and family."

Mr. Prescott didn't flinch. "You gave your word." He motioned with a sweep of his hand. "Look around. My house is destroyed. My valuable possessions ruined. And . . . Five. Hundred. Pounds." He pronounced each of the words slowly, as if Jacob hadn't grasped the exceptional value of his loss.

Jacob fisted his hands behind his back, reminding himself to be patient. Each person dealt with trauma differently, he supposed. "I understand, sir. A terrible loss. But many have lost much more."

"The entire first cutting," Mr. Prescott repeated.

"I told you I understand." Jacob no longer felt patient.

"Apparently you don't." Mr. Prescott moved around to the other side of his desk and leaned forward, resting his palms flat on the top. "I paid you. You gave your word. And I charge you with breach of contract."

Jacob wanted to laugh at the absurdity of the claim. "Mr. Prescott, the United States of America is at war. You very generously donated to the war effort, with no guarantee. Luckily the flotilla was near enough to hear the invaders' gunshots and arrived in time to protect your family and property." He stood still, not wanting to appear as if he were threatening the man; another unfortunate misinterpretation of a large man's stance when he is angry. "You are owed nothing."

"I intend to take up a suit against you and Joshua Barney," Mr. Prescott said.

Jacob no longer cared if he appeared frightening. He stepped forward, placing his own hands on the desk and leaning toward his host. "And how is your daughter, sir? I imagine she is happy not to have been burned alive."

Mr. Prescott winced. Then his face went hard. "My daughter is damaged beyond repair. And it is your fault. You should have arrived earlier."

Jacob's stomach turned at the memory of the poor young woman's injury. But "damaged beyond repair"? This man was ridiculous. She would bear a scar, but she'd heal, which is more than he could say for the three friends he'd lost that night.

"I was there, sir, and you were not, and because of this, I will forgive your ignorance. Men fought for your property and saved your daughter." He held the man's startled gaze. "Others in this war have fared much worse, losing everything they hold dear. You are one of the lucky ones, Mr. Prescott. And it is you who owe an unpayable debt to Commodore Joshua Barney and the families of the good men buried in your field." He spun and strode from the room, taking his hat from the table in the entry hall and cramming it onto his head.

He almost felt sorry for that fool, Jefferson Caraway. He couldn't imagine Beauregard Prescott as a father-in-law. As he crossed through the gardens toward the carriageway and the stables beyond, his gaze fell on the burned-out storage shed.

The smell of smoke still hung in the humid air, bringing with it the memory of that night.

He had been patrolling the river in a rowing barge with a small band when they'd heard shots. It was a miracle they'd been close enough.

Skirmishes and fires had surrounded him as he and the others chased away the invaders. Jacob was crouched behind a hogshead barrel, reloading his musket when a Negro servant woman had rushed up to him in a panic. "Miss Lydia!" was all she said as she pointed to the burning storehouse. Jacob had thrust his weapon at her and took off at a run, barging through the doors and into the fire. Luckily, Lydia had been easy to find. She lay beneath a broken window, surrounded by wooden furniture and flames. He didn't pause but had scooped her up and rushed outside.

Lydia had clung to him, small and fragile in his arms, and he held her tightly against him, some primal instinct urging him to protect this woman.

Once they were free from the flames, he'd laid her on the ground, and the servant had knelt beside her.

"Francine," Lydia had muttered.

"I'm here now, Sweet Pea," the woman—Francine—had said. "Just rest."

Lydia's clothes had been singed but not burned, and her damp hair was tied up in little rolls. Francine had turned her face to the side as the two of them gasped.

Jacob didn't think he would ever erase the image that seared into his mind; a young woman's beautiful face lit by firelight and marred by a jagged chunk of glass wedged into her cheek.

Now he glanced once more at the break in the hedge where he'd first come upon the young woman, feeling another wave of pity. Then Jacob climbed onto his horse and turned his back to Rosefield Park, glad to leave this place for the last time.

*\*\*\**

Three days later, Jacob stood in an alley speaking in a low voice to a man—Jacob assumed it was a man—he trusted but whose face he could not see.

The messenger had given the password in a whisper but kept his face hidden as Jacob reported on his meeting on Joshua Barney's behalf with the secretary of war. The man nodded his head and, once Jacob finished speaking, slipped away to deliver the message to the flotilla captain in St. Lawrence Creek. Jacob walked in the other direction, along the familiar roads of Washington City, and stepped through the door of a public house. He inhaled, and his stomach growled. He realized he'd not eaten all day. His gaze moved through the noisy, dim room until he found Alden, sitting at a table in a far corner. He made his way through the crowd, squeezing between tables and other patrons, and then slid into a chair across from his friend.

"You made it," Alden said. He motioned toward a serving woman. "Full supper?"

"Sounds perfect," Jacob said.

Alden held up two fingers.

The woman nodded.

Jacob had purposely chosen this particular location because it was notoriously crowded, and the noise gave privacy. The delicious food was an added benefit.

The woman brought drinks and left to fetch their meals.

"And how was the meeting with Mr. A.?"

Alden wouldn't say John Armstrong's name aloud. Though the room was crowded, it was impossible to be certain a conversation wasn't overheard. The British spy network was a growing source of concern as more Americans became irritated with the war effort and sided with the enemy. There was nothing Jacob despised more than a turncoat.

Jacob took a long drink. "He's agreed to help with the party preparations." Having the secretary of war's assistance with Joshua Barney's planned assault would make all the difference in the outcome.

"And he'll bring tea cakes and petit fours to the soiree?" Alden puckered his lips and spoke in a falsely high voice, raising his little finger as he took a drink.

Jacob fixed his friend with a flat stare. "He will." Mr. Armstrong had pledged ammunition and weaponry for the attack.

"Oh goody. Won't we have a grand time?" Alden clapped his hands.

"You need food," Jacob said but couldn't resist a smile at his friend's silliness.

The server set their plates in front of them, and while Alden chatted with the woman, Jacob studied his old friend. His face was leaner, the wrinkles around his eyes deeper. Not surprising for a man who'd spent years at sea. But there was something more. Alden possessed a hardness Jacob hadn't seen in him before. And he wondered what had happened to cause it.

The pair ate in silence. Jacob listened with half an ear to the conversations around him. He chewed on beef, potatoes, and gravy, and his mind moved between work at the shipyard, the planned attack, and wondering when the fresh English troops would arrive. It must be soon.

"Dessert at Elnora's?" Alden asked, pushing back from the table and patting his belly.

Jacob nodded. Elnora would be disappointed if they didn't pay a visit while they were in town.

They left the public house near the dockyard and walked up the hill toward the exclusive neighborhood where they'd been raised, passing expensive shops and restaurants.

"A quick visit," Alden said. "Then we need to return to your shipyard and take care of my lady."

"I didn't forget," Jacob said. He didn't need another reminder that Alden's ship was still in dry dock.

"It seems like it. What has it been? A month? My poor darling." Alden spoke in the falsetto voice again.

"We're fighting a war, you know."

"And neglecting the love of my life."

"We'll repair your ship," Jacob said. "And we also need to get the flotilla's gunboat and barge in shape for . . . the soiree." He was a bit disappointed that Commodore Barney had taken him and Alden off patrol duty, but their time would be much better utilized preparing boats for the attack and then finding ways to smuggle them out of Annapolis—smuggling was Alden's specialty.

As they crossed the street, Jacob heard his name called. He spun, not recognizing the voice, then grimaced once he saw the speaker.

Jefferson Caraway stepped through the doorway of an expensive eating establishment and strode across the street toward them, waving his handkerchief to catch their attention.

Alden groaned. "Not the fop," he said under his breath. "I thought we were finished with—Mr. Caraway! A pleasure to see you again, sir."

"Gentlemen." Jefferson swept off his hat and gave a deep bow.

"Mr. Caraway." Jacob inclined his head.

"I am so glad to have found you," Jefferson said. "I mean to lodge a complaint about the patrols."

"A complaint?" Jacob asked, curiosity overriding his annoyance. "What have they done?"

"Yes, well, it's what they *haven't* done, you see. They aren't there."

"They aren't on the river?" Alden asked. He sounded as baffled as Jacob.

"Precisely." Jefferson folded his arms over his pink-embroidered powder-blue waistcoat. "I've seen no sign of the flotilla on the *James*."

Jacob knew for certain the patrols were doing their job. He and Alden shared a confused look.

"Has your plantation been attacked?" Alden asked.

"Goodness, no." Jefferson touched his forehead. "Nothing like that. I just like to know the flotilla is doing what it's supposed to."

*You know the flotilla is not in your employ,* Jacob wanted to say. But using a colossal amount of self-control, he remained silent.

"So, your complaint is you haven't actually seen the clandestine patrols with your own eyes," Alden said.

"That is it exactly." Jefferson nodded smartly.

Alden motioned for Jefferson to move closer and put his hand to the side of his mouth as if he had a secret. "If you can't see the flotilla, neither can the English."

"Yes, well . . . I'd like to know—"

"Trust me, Mr. Caraway. The flotilla is there." He winked as if he'd let the man in on the answer to a riddle.

Jefferson straightened and brushed at his sleeves. "Very good." He nodded.

Jacob was again amazed at his friend's silver tongue. It was his own preference to remain silent; to listen and observe. Which was probably why he and Alden got on so well.

Alden patted Jefferson on the shoulder. "By the way, sir. I hear congratulations are in order."

"Congratulations?" Jefferson said.

"I was under the impression that you were to be married."

"Oh, no. Not anymore." He waved his hand. "I cried off."

"You cancelled your engagement to Miss Prescott?" Jacob asked.

Jefferson glanced up at him, perhaps only now remembering his presence. "I certainly did. Couldn't go through with it. Not after seeing her face." He pointed at his cheek and gave an exaggerated grimace and shiver as if he'd just tasted something sour. "Could you imagine being married to—well, I spoke to her father. Rescinded the offer."

Bile rose in Jacob's throat and red tinged the edges of his vision. "Did you care at all about the lady's reputation?" He could snap this little man in half, and he just might do it. He clenched his fists until his knuckles cracked.

"Easy, Jake," Alden murmured.

But Jefferson didn't appear to have noticed the men's reactions.

"Her reputation? She has no need for it now, not looking like a monst—"

To save the man's life, Jake spun and walked away as quickly as he could. He didn't think a person had ever made him so angry. How could he do such a thing to Miss Prescott? Reject her so coldly? Her reputation would be permanently damaged from such a blow. She already had her injury to come to terms with, not to mention the trauma associated with it. The supper he'd eaten churned around in his stomach. And Beauregard Prescott's words came into his head. *She is damaged beyond repair.*

Jacob remembered how it had felt to hold her in his arms. She'd been so helpless and small, and the need to protect her returned so powerfully that he couldn't ignore it.

He heard footsteps running behind him and stopped.

Alden caught up to him panting. "Can you believe that arrogant—"

"I need to return to Rosefield," Jacob said.

"What? Why? No. These people's lives are not our concern. Are you forgetting you said you never wanted to go back there?"

"I didn't forget."

Beauregard Prescott was the last person he wanted to talk to, but he knew what he had to do. And what her father would ask for in return. Five hundred English pounds was an enormous amount of money. Mr. Prescott would think his action was a result of guilt. Alden would think it was a result of pity. But he didn't care what either of them thought. In his work as an intelligence operative, he'd learned to trust his gut, and this is what it told him. Besides, he knew, as Mr. Prescott did not, that a young woman was more valuable than a cutting of tobacco.

# CHAPTER 5

LYDIA'S BEDCHAMBER WAS A MESS of confusion as her mother and Francine packed away her things into trunks. Gowns were laid across her bed. Bonnets, gloves, and slippers covered every flat surface.

"Oh!" Mother lifted a rose-colored ball gown and held it up. "You love this one. Remember how beautiful you were at the Hamiltons' ball last year?"

Lydia shrugged and looked back out the window. She didn't know how long she'd sat on the window seat as stockings and ribbons were piled around her, and she didn't care. She didn't want to think about the Hamiltons' ball or gowns. Or be reminded that she was once beautiful. And she especially didn't want to think about her wedding tomorrow.

Her insides knotted. Mr. Jacob Steele. The large frightening man from the rose garden picnic. Was he the only man her father could convince to take her? And what must he have paid to convince Mr. Steele to accept a disfigured bride?

"Lydia?" Mother held a cloak with a furry trim at arm's length, looking it up and down. "You wore this last winter in Baltimore, didn't you? Or was it the year before? Perhaps it needs to be altered; you may have grown too tall."

"I'm sure it is fine, Mother."

Francine took the cloak and folded it carefully then laid it in a trunk.

Mother lifted another dress. "Oh, you love this one. Remember . . ." She put a hand over her mouth as tears filled her eyes. "You were just so beautiful," Mother whispered. She thrust the gown at Francine and hurried from the room.

Lydia rested her forehead against the cool glass of the window and closed her eyes. She would never have believed a three-inch cut could change her life so completely.

Her mother's tears had been a regular occurrence over the past weeks. She couldn't manage to be in Lydia's presence for longer than a half hour before her loss became too much to bear.

Father couldn't even look at her. And Beau unsuccessfully tried to hide his revulsion at her appearance. Lydia knew her family would be relieved once she was gone.

And, as frightening as marriage sounded, Lydia wondered if she'd be relieved as well.

***

The next morning, Lydia stood before her mirror as Francine fastened the rows of buttons up her back. Her dress was breathtaking. Sky-blue satin matched her eye color perfectly. Ribbons and lace adorned the sleeves, waist, and neckline. Francine had arranged her hair with small roses tucked among the curls. Ringlets spilled over her shoulders and framed her face.

Lydia deliberately did not look at her face. Although the swelling was gone and the sutures removed, the red line stood out boldly against her fair skin. She focused on the gown and how delighted she'd been when she tried it on for the first time. Mother and the modiste had clapped their hands, and Lydia had spun around, looking at her reflection from all sides. But try as she might, she couldn't recapture the feeling.

Anxiety skittered over her skin like water bugs on a pond.

Mother entered the room, a forced smile on her face. "The gentlemen are here."

Lydia nodded.

Her mother inspected the dress and her hair, and finally looked at Lydia's face. "Francine, perhaps a cream or powder would conceal it."

Francine shook her head. "The wound is too fresh."

"You could arrange her hair to cover . . ." She fussed with the curls on the side of Lydia's face for a moment then wrinkled her nose, clearly disappointed that the cut was still visible. "Well then. I will see you downstairs, my dear."

Once her mother left, Lydia let out a heavy breath. She straightened her shoulders and then turned to follow her from the room.

"Miss Lydia," Francine said. "Wait a moment, please." She stepped into the dressing room and returned with a bouquet of roses bound with ribbon. "A beautiful bride needs flowers."

"Thank you, Francine." Lydia took the bouquet, admiring the different colors. Francine must have asked her nephew, Ezra, an assistant gardener, to cut the roses. She breathed in the fragrance she'd always associated with home, and her eyes prickled.

"You *are* a beautiful bride," Francine said. "Remember that."

Lydia studied her maid's face, seeing no trace of pity or disgust as the woman looked back. "Thank you," she whispered, and then she turned to face her future.

Lydia peeked through the parlor door. Her eyes immediately went to Jacob Steele. How could they not? He was the largest man in the room. He'd be the largest man in almost any room. Mr. Steele was wearing a black coat and cravat and was speaking with the minister, Mr. Graves. On the other side of the room, Papá listened as his solicitor spoke and pointed at items on a document. Mother and Beau were on a sofa speaking to Mr. Alden Thatcher, who sat on a chair facing them.

The room was noticeably bare. The window coverings were gone, furniture and ornaments were missing, and holes in the walls had been patched but not yet painted. The entire scenario was a far cry from the elaborate wedding plans of only a month earlier.

She looked back to Jacob Steele and wondered how he'd imagined his wedding day. Had he envisioned cakes and flowers and rooms full of guests? Or did men even think about things like that? Whether or not the setting was a disappointment for him, she thought for certain his bride would be.

Taking a deep breath to steady herself, Lydia stepped forward. When she entered the parlor, the room went quiet, and every gaze turned to her. Mr. Thatcher and Beau stood.

She tucked down her chin and turned her face to the side, feeling fully aware of her wound. This was the first time anyone aside from her family and servants had seen her injury.

Mr. Steele stepped toward her and offered his hand.

Lydia took it but kept her face averted. She didn't want to see the look on his face when he saw her disfigurement.

He led her forward, and Lydia kept her gaze downward as the minister began to speak. She studied Mr. Steele's boots. They were worn but had been polished to a shine. Glancing to the side, she saw his face was thoughtful as he listened to the words of the marriage ceremony. What she wouldn't give to know what he was thinking.

Lydia answered in the proper places, and Mr. Steele did as well. When prompted, they signed the marriage document. Beau and Mr. Thatcher signed as witnesses, and the whole thing was finished.

Mother and Papá walked with the minister and solicitor toward the door, thanking them for coming. Beau and Mr. Thatcher followed.

Lydia was left alone with her new husband.

Mr. Steele cleared his throat.

Nervous, she lifted her gaze, but kept her cheek tucked against her shoulder.

"I like the flowers." He looked pointedly at the bouquet in her hand.

Lydia had forgotten how deep his voice was. "Roses are my favorite." She looked down at the bouquet. "My maid, Francine, gave them to me."

"I should have thought to bring you flowers. I apologize. I've never done this before."

His lips twitched, and she smiled at his attempt at humor. "Neither have I."

Mr. Steele's face became serious as he studied her. He lifted her chin, turning her face to the side.

Lydia braced herself for his reaction. Would he wince? Pull back in disgust? Tip his head and look at her with pity?

Mr. Steele's gaze took in her entire face, lingering for a moment on the wound, but returning to hold her eyes. "You do not need to hide your face from me, Lydia."

Resisting the impulse to turn away, she looked back steadily at Mr. Steele's chocolate-brown eyes. "All right."

"Or from anyone else." He nodded once as if they now had an understanding.

"Oh, there you are." Mother swept into the room. "Your father is showing Mr. Thatcher the roses while we wait for Cook to finish preparing luncheon. Perhaps you'd like to join them?" She fussed with Lydia's curls, brushing them forward to cover the cut. She took the bouquet from Lydia and studied it then handed it back. "The flowers were a good idea, don't you agree, dear?" She brushed forward the curls again. "Just the thing to draw attention away from . . ." She motioned toward Lydia's cheek.

"Would you like to see the roses, Mr. Steele?" Lydia said as her skin heated. She wished her mother would just stop.

"Jacob," he said. He took Lydia's hand, turning his shoulders to insert himself between the women. His eyes took on a darker shade.

"If it isn't too much bother, perhaps the cook might prepare luncheon to eat aboard the boat," Jacob said. "We'll need to leave soon to reach Annapolis by nightfall."

"Oh, I'm certain that will be fine." Mother looked relieved.

Jacob intimidated her, Lydia realized. She looked down at the man's large hand holding hers and realized with equal surprise that her own impression of the man was changing. Jacob may not be the fearful giant she'd assumed.

"I should put on a different dress." Lydia pulled her hand from Jacob's. "If you'll excuse me." She didn't think her wedding gown would suit for water travel. She hurried from the room and held the thick skirts as she climbed the stairs.

"Miss Lydia." Francine closed the bedchamber door when Lydia entered. "I have something to tell you." Her maid's eyes were wide.

"What is it?"

"That man. Mr. Steele. He is the man who rescued you."

Lydia furrowed her brows. "Jacob?"

"Yes. I did not know his name before. He carried you from the fire."

Lydia thought back to that night. She remembered being held in strong arms, feeling safe and protected. And now the protector had a face.

Jacob Steele, her husband. Warmth filled her from head to toe as she thought of Jacob. The way he'd looked into her eyes and hadn't flinched away from her injury. But the feeling dissipated just as quickly, replaced by a cold burst of shame. Her father had convinced Jacob to marry her. She did not know by what means, but knowing Jacob had done it against his will hurt.

An hour later, she and Francine stood on the deck of Jacob's boat. "A cutter," he'd called it, his face shining with pride as he showed her the belowdecks quarters and small galley. Deep in their own thoughts, the two women watched the thick trees on the river's edge, occasionally glimpsing fields through gaps. Once in a while they saw a dock or a slender creek, but the majority of the coastline was a constant blur of green.

Francine excused herself to see to Lydia's berth, but Lydia suspected her maid needed a moment alone after leaving her family behind. She turned back to watching the coastline. The sounds of the creaking ropes and splashing on the hull soothed her nerves. She'd never been away from home without her parents, she realized. Did she even know how to be a wife? What lay ahead for her in Annapolis?

"Hungry?"

Lydia started. She hadn't noticed Jacob approach.

"Come, join me." He motioned with a tip of his head.

She followed him belowdecks and sat on a bench across from him at a small table attached to the wall of the boat. A simple meal of bread, cheese, and turkey was arranged on tin plates.

Lydia and Jacob both caught their plates at the edge of the table as the boat's movement made them slide.

He poured sweet tea into tin mugs.

Lydia broke off a piece of bread and bit into it.

Jacob took a drink and cut a slice of turkey.

The quiet stretched uncomfortably.

"Francine told me you saved me from the fire." Lydia's voice sounded loud in the small space.

Jacob looked up. He nodded.

"That night has been all confused in my mind. I didn't remember before. But now I do." She ran her finger along the edge of her plate. "I owe you my thanks."

"I was just doing my duty." He leaned back on his bench, watching her.

"Not just for saving me from the building but also, thank you for marrying me." She spoke quietly, her eyes on the table. "I know you must not have wished to."

Jacob was quiet for a long moment, and Lydia didn't dare look up, afraid she'd see confirmation of her words in his face.

"And I thank you for marrying me, as well," Jacob said. "I don't think you wished to either."

The silence felt as heavy as the humidity in the stuffy dining room. Lydia couldn't remember a more uncomfortable conversation, and without warning, her nervousness took control and she burst out in a giggle.

She slapped a hand over her mouth and looked up, horrified.

Jacob's eyes widened.

"I'm sorry." She giggled again and shook her head, willing herself to calm down. "It's just . . . This must be the worst wedding luncheon conversation in history."

Jacob laughed, a low rumble. His face relaxed into a smile. Lydia hadn't seen his smile before, and she was pleasantly surprised. When he wasn't looking fearsome, he was rather handsome.

"I think you're right," he said.

She laughed again, the tension she'd built up over the past weeks making her silly.

Jacob joined her, his low chuckle sounding like distant thunder.

Footsteps sounded on the stairs, and Alden entered the room. He raised his brows, looking between the pair. "Thought I should come check on the happy couple." He grinned. "I didn't think to find you quite so happy."

"Join us, Mr. Thatcher," Lydia said. "You must be hungry."

"This party is too rowdy for me, Mrs. Steele. *I* am a gentleman." Alden grabbed a slice of bread and gave a wink before he left.

Lydia froze. *Mrs. Steele.* She hadn't even thought of it, but that was her name now. She glanced across the table and saw Jacob watching her with the alert gaze that made her feel utterly exposed. That man was her husband. She was aboard a stranger's ship, sailing to her new home. For a moment, she'd been caught up in the laughter and teasing and forgotten about her cheek, her disgrace, and the humiliation of a forced marriage.

She stood abruptly. "Excuse me, please, Jacob. I'd like to rest now." She started down the narrow hallway to her berth.

He rose as well, hunched over in the small space. "Lydia?"

She turned.

"I *did* wish to."

If only she could believe him.

# CHAPTER 6

JACOB LEFT THE HARBOR, STRODE past the shops on Main Street through Church Circle, and came to Bloomsbury Square. He noticed more shops closed and more houses empty with each passing day. The English ships in the harbor and word of British raids in coastal towns had the city in a state of alarm, and many, fearing attack, had fled. Including the governor. In spite of the sense of worry, Jacob enjoyed the daily walks to and from the shipyard. The exercise was refreshing, and he liked the time to ponder. Alden had stayed behind today, probably to pine over his ship, and Jacob was glad for the time alone with his thoughts.

In the three days since he'd returned from Virginia, he'd worked long hours, staying at the shipyard past supper. The detour to Rosefield had put him behind schedule. He'd promised Joshua Barney the boats would be repaired and in fighting shape in time for the attack, and he had only a week to make that happen.

Along with long hours at the shipyard, Jacob was spending late nights with Alden laying plans for how they'd smuggle the newly repaired boats past the blockade and organizing intelligence missions. The English transport ships would arrive any day. Invasion was imminent, and the government needed information. With his consuming schedule, he'd only seen his new wife in passing, but Jacob didn't think his being at home for longer hours would have made a difference in that regard.

According to his housekeeper, Mrs. Pembroke, Lydia kept to her rooms. She did not take callers, nor did she go out walking. "She's very polite," Mrs. Pembroke had told him, peering over her spectacles. "An efficient household manager. I've nothing to complain about in that regard. But she moves in the shadows, avoiding all the staff. Excepting myself and her maid, of course."

Mrs. Pembroke liked to think herself very perceptive, Jacob knew. "Poor dear. Sensitive about . . ." She'd tapped her cheek.

With his hand on the front gate, Jacob paused outside his house, glancing up at Lydia's window. Mrs. Pembroke's words made him sad. And he didn't know how to help his new wife. He'd never seen a person so transformed by a tragedy as Lydia was. She'd gone in an instant from a confident, flirting socialite to a shadow in her own house. Her parents hadn't helped in that regard. He'd been furious at the way her mother had treated her and the way her father had spoken about her, as if her very value as a person was diminished by her injury. Jacob could not get her away from Rosefield fast enough.

But now that she was safely away, what could he do? Of course he hadn't believed that marrying her would solve all her problems. He was not that presumptuous. But he'd hoped it would help. Maybe she would like to attend the theater. Young ladies seemed to enjoy that sort of thing.

If only she had something she cared about. A cause or a project. Accomplishing a goal would give her a feeling of self-worth. And perhaps he'd see her smile again and hear her laughter as he had on their wedding day.

Maggs, the butler, took Jacob's hat upon his entry. "I will inform the cook that you are home in time for supper, sir." He gave a stiff bow, showing the shiny pate among the thinning white hair atop his head.

"Thank you." Jacob didn't miss the disapproval in the older man's sniff. He also didn't particularly enjoy being made to feel guilty for not keeping the staff apprised of his schedule.

Seeing movement on the upstairs balcony, he stepped back. "Francine," he called up to the maid.

She peered over the railing. "Yes, Mr. Steele?"

"If you please, would you ask Mrs. Steele to join me for supper tonight?"

"Yes, I will, sir." She curtsied and hurried toward Lydia's rooms.

Remembering what Mrs. Pembroke had said, Jacob moved back toward the door and fished through the bowl on the entryway table, looking at the calling cards and invitations. Quite a few ladies had stopped to visit with the new Mrs. Steele. And if the housekeeper was to be believed, she'd received none of them.

He pulled out some of the larger invitation cards. Even though the city was losing residents, society still managed to keep itself entertained. Garden parties, luncheons, a musical exhibition . . . One invitation caught his eye.

The Holts were giving a ball next week. His lip curled as he thought of Gerald and Miriam Holt. Young and attractive, the couple was the center of society in Annapolis. But Jacob was convinced there was more to the pair than people saw.

Gerald's mannerisms didn't sit well with Jacob, though he could not say exactly why. The man seemed to be . . . artificial somehow. His actions and words too perfect, as if he'd practiced his responses beforehand. Even his opinions on manners of politics or business were safely moderate. And Miriam . . . Jacob grimaced. As a young man, he'd courted her for a short while but ceased his attention when he realized she had her eye set on the owner of the local textile mill.

Alden and Jacob had warned the other members of their network to watch the Holts carefully. Though they'd no evidence, Jacob suspected they might be British spies. Their cover was excellent, with access to all manner of information. Being wealthy didn't necessarily make a person wise, and Jacob had occasionally heard information shared at society parties that should have been kept confidential. If they were indeed spies, the Holts needed to be exposed. But of course, this was all speculation.

He tapped the invitation against his palm then set it back into the bowl. The ball might be just the thing to bring Lydia out of her shell. While the gathering wouldn't be the crush she was used to, quite a few attendees would be there; Lydia was sure to make new friends. If only she could muster the courage to allow herself to be seen.

*** 

Lydia entered the drawing room in a cream-colored gown. Her blue eyes were bright, and her hair shone golden in the candlelight. Jacob's wife truly was beautiful.

He stood when he saw her. "Good evening."

She inclined her head and gave a very small smile.

He wondered if her cheek pained her when she smiled. "Thank you for joining me. I apologize that my schedule has prevented us from spending more time together."

"I understand. Ships must be built."

Again the small smile. She seemed timid. Was she still frightened of him? He motioned to a chair, waited for her to be seated, then sat across from her, hoping he looked less intimidating in this position.

"How do you like Annapolis?" he asked then immediately regretted the dull question.

"I've not seen much of the city, but your house is splendid."

"*Our* house." He corrected her.

She blushed. "*Our* house has gorgeous views of the harbor, and I love the woodwork throughout. Did you choose the designs?"

A swell of pride nearly popped Jacob's chest. "I did choose the designs." He scratched the back of his head. "And . . ."

She blinked. "Oh. You built them. I should have realized. You must have carved the flowers on my bedchamber mantel as well."

"I did."

"Roses . . ." She looked down, and her blush deepened.

"I remember." Jake was pleased, not only that she'd noticed and admired his work but at the fortunate happenstance. He'd had no way of knowing years earlier when he carved the mantel that his future wife would come from a home surrounded by roses. But he was very gratified that the carvings were, without his knowing, created for the right person. Like she belonged in the room. His ears heated, and he looked for something else to talk about.

"The ivy border on the shelves is from an old pattern I found in a book."

Lydia stood and crossed the room to study the carvings on the shelves. "Beautiful." She ran her finger over the woodwork.

Jacob joined her. Seeing her appreciate the details he'd invested so much time and effort into was very satisfying. When he'd purchased the grand old house, he'd found the structure to be sound, but water damage and neglect had taken its toll on the plaster and wood. A single man with a talent for woodcraft, he'd replanked the floors and seen to the immediate repairs, and then he'd spent years on the decorative features. He was particularly proud of the staircase balustrade.

But he needed to change the subject before the conversation turned to him boasting of all the improvements he'd made to his home.

He leaned his shoulder against the wall, hoping to look casual. "I saw a pile of calling cards in the hallway. You must have had a great deal of visitors. How do you find the ladies of Annapolis?"

She looked up at him then back to the ivy carving. "I haven't . . . received any visitors."

"Why not?"

She turned her face to the side, tucking down her chin. "You know why."

He took her shoulders, turning her toward him and lifting her face. "Lydia, remember what I said? You don't need to hide away."

She pulled away. "You don't understand. You're different, Jacob. You and Francine are the only ones. You don't look at me with pity or horror. Even Mrs. Pembroke and Alden sometimes . . ." She folded her arms and shook her head. Her lip quivered.

"You can't worry about other people's reactions. Once they spend time with you, they won't even notice. Do you honestly intend to hide away forever?"

She shrugged and looked back at the bookshelves.

"Next week, there is to be a ball. The Holts always host a fine event. Come with me. All of Annapolis society will be there. You can make friends, meet people . . ."

Lydia backed away, her eyes wide. She put her hand over her cheek. "Jacob, I can't. I can't attend a ball."

"A ball!" Alden said from the doorway. "Are we going to a ball?"

Jacob closed his eyes and gave a longsuffering sigh. "We are not."

Alden came into the room and sat on the sofa. "Pity. I thought I'd enjoy dancing with Mrs. Steele."

"Lydia," she said. She took her hand from her cheek and pushed down her shoulders. She mustered a smile then crossed the room to join Alden. "You should call me Lydia."

"Well, then, Lydia." Alden grinned. "When shall we dance together? I am very good, you know. Light on my feet."

Jacob rolled his eyes.

Dinner was announced, and the trio made their way into the dining room.

Jacob saw the table had been prepared with three settings close together. Much better than the more formal arrangement with the mistress of the household at the far end.

He held out a chair, and Lydia sat, facing Alden, while Jacob's seat at the head of the table was between the two of them.

A servant brought bowls of creamy crab soup, and they began to eat.

"How was business today?" Lydia asked. She sat tall, holding her spoon delicately.

Jacob straightened, remembering the lessons in table manners Elnora had taught. From the corner of his eye, he saw Alden do the same.

"Business was good," Jacob said. He didn't like discussing the shipyard's operation, especially since one misplaced word could lead to a British attack.

Lydia took a dainty sip of soup. "And what are you doing now? What type of construction are you working on? A battleship? Riverboats?"

Jacob's guard went up. Of course her question was innocent, but one could never be too careful with classified government operations. "A little of this and a little of that."

"I'll tell you what he's *not* doing," Alden said, giving Jacob a glare. "He's not fixing my ship." Alden sighed as if he were in pain and rubbed his eyes. "My poor darling."

"I told you I'd get to it." Jacob said.

"Your ship is damaged?" Lydia asked.

"A tragedy," Alden replied. "The magnificent *Belladonna*, all alone, wounded . . ."

"I'm sorry," Lydia said. "What happened?"

Jacob cleared his throat, reminding Alden to remain quiet about his involvement in the battle.

"Oh, just typical wear." Alden shrugged. "All of this is very boring talk." He set down his spoon. "Lydia, why don't you tell us about yourself."

She blinked. "I . . . I don't know . . ."

"Did you ever have a pet?" Alden said.

Jacob shot his friend a quizzical glance. *A pet? What type of question is that?*

Lydia smiled. A real smile that made Jacob both grateful for his friend and jealous that he'd not been the one to elicit the expression. "I did. A kitten named Princess Whiskers."

"Now, *that* is an excellent moniker," Alden said. "I once knew a man with a parrot called Euripides."

"A natural name for a parrot." Lydia nodded. "Though I myself would have chosen Yellow Feet or Green Feathers. I am not a creative animal-namer, you see."

Alden leaned back so the server could replace his soup bowl with a plate of beef and potatoes. "And Jake had a dog, if I remember right."

Jacob couldn't believe the idiocy of the conversation. "The dog wasn't mine. Just a mangy thing that slunk around the shipyard." He cut a slice of beef and took a bite.

"Slunk around because you fed it." Alden pointed his fork at Jacob. "He hid breakfast sausage in his pockets," he told Lydia. "Elnora was furious about the grease stains."

Lydia seemed to be enjoying the silly dialogue. Jacob didn't know how Alden always managed to set people at ease, but he envied the skill. A dinner alone with his wife would likely be very uncomfortable as they searched for conversation topics.

"What was the dog's name, Jacob?" Lydia asked.

"Dog."

The other two laughed.

"That is a terrible name," Lydia pointed out. "Worse than Princess Whiskers."

"She's right." Alden nodded sagely as if giving weighty thought to the matter. "A very terrible name indeed."

"And what did you do today, Lydia?" Jacob asked. He'd had quite enough criticism over his animal-naming skills.

"I . . . well." She pursed her lips. "I wrote a letter to my brother Emmett. And planned the week's meals with Mrs. Pembroke."

"This one is fantastic." Jacob motioned at his plate with his fork.

"I'm glad you like it. She told me you're very hungry when you return home in the evening."

"Show me a man who isn't," Alden said.

Lydia set her utensils down and placed her hands in her lap. "Jacob, if you don't mind, I have something to ask."

He turned more completely toward her, giving her his full attention. "Certainly."

"I wondered if I might plant a rose garden. There is a nice spot in the front of the house—"

"Lydia, you don't need my permission for such a trivial matter. Of course you can plant roses. Tear up the entire yard if it makes you happy." Jacob was elated. Perhaps this was just the thing to bring her out of her melancholy. A project. Something she loved. Why hadn't he thought of a garden himself?

"There is more." Her brows pulled together, making a wrinkle above her nose. "Ezra is one of my father's under-gardeners. He has excellent skill with roses . . . I wondered . . . perhaps we could send for him since you only employ a gardener a few times a year." She spoke quickly, her words tumbling out as if she worried he'd stop her before she finished. "And Mrs. Pembroke told me your cook is thinking to leave the city. I thought perhaps my mother's cook,

Henrietta—you remember her lemon cake?—she could come as well." The wrinkle between her brows deepened as she waited for him to reply.

"I'm sure you could find servants here in Annapolis," Jacob said.

"Ezra and Henrietta are especially hard workers."

"Lydia, you know I don't keep slaves," Jacob said.

"I know."

"You're asking me to purchase these workers from your father, grant their freedom, then hire them?" He had done the same for Francine, but of course, she was specifically Lydia's maid. And he'd seen the woman's loyalty and the care she took of her mistress.

Lydia's face fell. "You are right, of course. It is very expensive. I should not have asked. It's just that . . ." She folded her napkin and set it on the table. "Henrietta is Francine's sister and Ezra her nephew. I just thought . . ." She stood. "I'm sorry to have bothered you with it. Shall I wait for the two of you in the drawing room?"

Jacob was surprised Lydia would go to so much effort for her maid. It was refreshingly compassionate for a southern debutante to care so much about a slave. And her fears about approaching him with the matter made him realize there was still trust to be built in this relationship.

"Don't wait," he said, remembering her question. "I'm afraid Alden and I have work to do tonight."

"Oh yes, of course."

She left, and the instant the door closed behind her, Alden kicked Jake's shin. Hard.

"What was that?"

Alden's face was serious. An unusual look for him. "Honestly? We have work to do tonight?"

Jake was confused. "We do. I have reports to write, and we still need to figure out how to get these boats past the blockade to the Patuxent River by next week."

"You have time to spare for your wife."

"Alden—"

"Listen to me, Jake. I know your marriage began under unusual circumstances. But you can't just leave it alone and expect it to flourish on its own."

"I'm not leaving it alone." He scowled. He was here, wasn't he? He'd left tasks unfinished to come home early.

"You haven't been home for supper in three days. You're working late into the night. I don't know much about marriage, but I think a man usually wants to be with his wife at night."

Jacob's ears grew warm at the insinuation. "Lydia—"

Alden pressed his palm on the table. "Lydia is special. And you don't know pain until you lose someone and realize it was because you were a coward."

Jacob didn't like the accusation in Alden's voice. A coward? He'd married the woman when nobody else would. He'd pulled her from a burning building. He'd protected her. His defiance lost its strength when he saw the pain in his friend's eyes.

"Alden . . . I'm sorry." This was the first hint of what Alden had been through, and he ached for his friend.

"Open up to her, Jake. Involve her. She's clever. You can trust her to keep a secret."

*That* he couldn't do. If she even breathed a word of the attack or his network of spies, even innocently, people would die. "I can't." He rubbed his eyes. "Not with this."

# CHAPTER 7

A GENTLE HARBOR BREEZE BLEW Lydia's hair. She shook the curls from her eyes. Even though the morning was still early, the day was already warm.

"Just there," she said to the hired man, pointing to a patch of earth where the rosebush should go. "But not too close to the others."

He cut the shovel into the soil with a grunt then looked to where she stood on the porch. Seeing her nod, he continued digging until he had a size-able hole and dragged the potted bush toward it.

She surveyed the new garden, and a sense of pride grew like a bubble in her chest. The white roses would look striking against the brick of the house, and the fragrance would give a lovely first impression to visitors. Stepping down the porch stairs, she walked along the front path and turned, studying the view of her new home. Based on the other buildings she could see, Lydia decided the house was built in the style characteristic of the neighborhood: A charming city design that seemed neat and elegant, built of red brick with white window frames and thin chimneys. Tall columns supported a rounded balcony above the entryway. The yard around the house spread down a gentle slope on either side, giving space between neighbors, and a long brick walkway led in a straight line from the gate at the road up to the front door.

The garden had been small and neglected, but Lydia had determined to change that. She was thrilled with the prospect of designing and choosing the plants herself. She tipped her head, trying to picture the finished product. *Perhaps some dark-green hedges surrounding the rose beds,* she thought. *And trees on the sides, to add height.*

She'd been pleasantly surprised by Jacob's home. The rooms were large and well-lit, the layout was welcoming, and the woodwork was finer than any she'd seen. The other décor was dated and, in some cases, shabby. She suspected Jacob had spent the majority of his effort on the wood trim, fireplaces, and staircases. But she could see that once the entirety was refurbished, it would be a grand home indeed.

She stood on the walkway, enjoying the sun on her skin, and watched the hired gardener work. As she contemplated whether pine trees would add or detract from the roses, a voice called out.

"Hello, there! You must be the new Mrs. Steele."

Lydia spun, her hand flying to her cheek. A fashionably dressed couple with a baby pram stood at the garden gate. The woman's arm was tucked into the man's, and as she waved, her beautiful face lit up in a smile.

Lydia waved back.

"I apologize for startling you," the woman called. "My name is Miriam Holt." She inclined her head gracefully, dark curls escaping her head covering to brush over her forehead.

"Lydia Steele." Lydia removed her hand but turned her face, hoping her bonnet would shadow her cheek. She inclined her head as well. "Pleased to meet you." Miriam's eyes were a deep brown that matched her hair, her skin was smooth and creamy, and she had high cheekbones and small pink lips.

"Lovely to meet you, Mrs. Steele. Might I introduce my husband?" When Lydia nodded, Miriam placed her free hand on the man's chest, gazing up at him with a soft smile. "Gerald Holt."

Gerald gave a smart bow, tugging at the brim of his hat. He wore his fair hair tied back in a queue. Intelligent gray eyes looked out from beneath arched brows. He was handsome, Lydia thought, but perhaps too elegant for her taste. The thought surprised her. When had her taste changed?

Lydia dipped in a curtsy. "How do you do, sir?"

"A pleasure, madam."

"And of course, this is little Alexander." Miriam released her husband's arm and turned the pram to give a better view.

Lydia moved toward the gate, opening it and peeking beneath the shade cover of the pram. She'd planned to give a polite smile and comment, but once she saw the baby, she didn't need to pretend. Little Alexander was adorable. When his gaze found Lydia, he grinned a toothless smile that lifted his round cheeks.

"Oh, he is a dear," Lydia said. "Hello, Alexander."

The baby grinned again, and Lydia smiled in return. She'd had only a very few encounters with children and wasn't entirely certain how to act. But one would have to be made of stone not to fawn over this lovable cherub.

"I'm so glad we finally get to meet you," Miriam said. She took the baby's hand, allowing him to grip her finger. "There are so few of us in the city now, and we're always pleased for the opportunity to make new friends."

Miriam released her baby's hand and patted his head. "It was quite a surprise when we heard Jacob Steele had returned to Annapolis with a new bride."

"Yes," Lydia said. "We did marry rather quickly."

"When one meets the right person, why wait?" Miriam looked up at her husband with adoring eyes. He returned the gaze, looking every bit as infatuated with her.

"Where are you from, Mrs. Steele?" Gerald asked.

"Virginia. A plantation on the Potomac. Rosefield Park."

He widened his eyes and nodded. "I know it. You must be Beauregard Prescott's daughter."

"I am, sir."

"I've made your father's acquaintance on a few occasions. And your mother's as well. Fine people." He patted his wife's hand. "You remember the Prescotts, don't you, dearest?"

"Yes, of course," Miriam said. "We made their acquaintance at the governor's ball a few years ago, if I remember correctly."

"That's right." He studied Lydia. "Yes, I can see the likeness. You certainly have your father's blue eyes."

Lydia fought against the urge to cover her cheek as the pair scrutinized her face. But surprisingly, though they could obviously see it, neither reacted at all to her scar.

"And are you going out for a stroll yourself?" Miriam asked. "Gerald and I prefer to walk in the morning before the heat of the day becomes unbearable. And of course, little Alexander enjoys it as well."

"No," Lydia said. "I was just supervising the planting." She motioned to where the gardener was working. "I'm installing a rose garden."

"Oh, roses." Miriam nodded her approval. "Won't that be beautiful?"

Alexander made unhappy baby noises, and Gerald pushed the pram back and forth, trying to soothe him.

"Excuse us, Mrs. Steele, but we should keep moving," Gerald said.

"Oh yes, our little darling becomes much less pleasant when his morning constitutional is interrupted." Miriam smiled fondly at the baby. She turned back to Lydia, holding out a hand. "Why don't you join us?"

"Oh," Lydia said. "I wouldn't want to impose."

"I insist." Miriam closed the gate and linked her arm with Lydia's. "We'll just take a turn around the park here and deliver you back quick as can be." Her smile lit up her brown eyes.

Lydia smiled in return. "Very well, then. I should be happy to join you." She hadn't spoken with another woman besides Francine, Mrs. Pembroke, or her mother for so long, she'd forgotten how much she enjoyed it. She quite liked Miriam Holt and her amiable family.

The women followed along behind Gerald and the baby, walking at a comfortable pace beneath the trees that lined the street. The feel of the city reminded Lydia of walking near her parents' second home, in Baltimore, but without the carriages and crowds.

"How do you like Annapolis?" Miriam asked.

"I've only been here a week, but I've found it to be very nice. The trees are beautiful, and the houses." She grimaced. "I'm afraid I've not seen much else."

"You will like the people here," Miriam assured her. "Our society is very good-natured."

"Where is your house?" Lydia asked.

Miriam turned and pointed behind them. "You can just see the tops of the chimneys through the trees."

Lydia squinted. The Holts lived close, on the other side of the park. She liked the idea of having neighbors that were near enough to visit regularly.

"The homes on either side of you are empty," Miriam said. "Unfortunately, much of the city is abandoned right now. But those of us who remain manage to entertain ourselves."

Lydia studied the empty houses and wondered if the streets were typically this quiet in the morning or whether it was a result of so many residents leaving their homes.

"I would love to hear about your home in Virginia." Miriam put a hand on her chest and gave a sigh. "Plantation life sounds so delightful."

"It is," Lydia said. "Wide spaces with rolling fields, and we are very close to the river. But friends don't walk past my door." She smiled at Miriam. "One must travel quite a ways to meet another person."

"And so you journey to Baltimore or Washington for society," Miriam said.

"Yes. My parents have a home in Baltimore."

Miriam tipped her head and studied Lydia. "How is it that we've never met? Gerald and I travel regularly to Baltimore. I do enjoy attending theatrical performances."

"We usually visit the city in winter," Lydia said. "After the tobacco harvest."

They crossed a street and turned, following along another side of the park.

Miriam released Lydia's arm and moved ahead to peek into the baby's pram. "He's sleeping," she whispered when she returned to walk beside Lydia.

The three walked in silence around the park and at last turned back onto the street with the Steele residence.

"You know, we are to have a ball next week," Miriam said. "I do hope you received the invitation I sent."

"I did," Lydia said carefully, thinking of the words to decline.

"Please say you'll come." Miriam squeezed her arm tighter. "I should be so happy to have a new friend there."

Lydia opened her mouth to give her regrets, but she stopped. A ball sounded enchanting. She'd not been out in society for weeks. But her hands felt clammy and her stomach turned as she imagined walking into a crowded room and having the entire company turn to gawk at her injury.

"I hope to attend," Lydia said at last.

"Do try." Miriam gave another smile.

Lydia opened the gate and stepped through.

Gerald remained on the walkway, moving the pram back and forth to keep the baby sleeping, but Miriam stepped up beside Lydia.

"I love this house," Miriam said, motioning toward Lydia's home. "You are no doubt making changes to the interior as well as the garden?"

"Eventually, that is my plan," Lydia said.

"If you'd like advice on textiles or furniture, I do know the very best shops."

"Thank you," Lydia said. "I'm certain I'll need help. And another woman's opinion is invaluable." She smiled at her new friend. "And once everything is finished, you and Mr. Holt should come for supper."

Miriam's eyes tightened, and she chewed on her lip. "I'm not certain that is a good idea."

Lydia blinked. "Oh." Perhaps she'd assumed too much. Her face got hot.

"Mr. Steele was a suitor of mine," Miriam said. "Years ago." She glanced at the house. "I worry my company may be uncomfortable for him—in an intimate gathering."

"Oh, I see." The explanation didn't ease the heat but rather spread it down Lydia's neck to her chest. She studied Miriam Holt. She'd never considered that Jacob must have courted women. He obviously had known others besides her. Of course, it shouldn't come as a surprise that he'd liked Miriam. She was pleasant and lovely and very elegant.

"Thank you for the walk," Lydia said, not quite certain how to end the conversation after Miriam's revelation. In spite of the turmoil inside her head, she gave a smile and a curtsy. "And it was a pleasure to meet you, Mrs. Holt, Mr. Holt."

Lydia hurried inside and closed the door behind her, feeling unsettled. She handed her bonnet to Maggs and ordered tea to be delivered to her rooms, where she paced as she waited, trying to understand what had happened. It took a while to realize the strange emotion turning her throat bitter was envy. She didn't think she'd ever been jealous of anyone before, and she didn't like the feeling one bit.

*** 

"Supper was delicious as usual," Jacob said. He set down his utensils and leaned back in his chair. "Thank you, Lydia."

Lydia was pleased she'd found another meal he'd enjoyed and that she'd convinced the cook to attempt to replicate the recipe. She'd loved the stuffed ham when she first tasted it at a luncheon at Miriam's house two days earlier.

Not knowing whether it would hurt him to be reminded of her, Lydia still hadn't mentioned to Jacob that she and Miriam had become friends. The entire idea of Jacob caring for Miriam made Lydia feel sick, and she pushed away the thoughts whenever they arose.

Alden patted his stomach. "With the way you're spoiling me, I'll need to loosen my trousers before I return to sea." He darted a look at Jacob. "If I ever have a ship to return with."

Lydia stood before Alden could launch into his typical tirade about the *Belladonna*'s damage. "Gentlemen, come along to the parlor."

The men rose as well, their expressions surprised as they shared a glance.

Jacob squinted at Lydia and tipped his head. "Come along?"

"To the parlor?" Alden asked.

"We've an appointment." She turned without waiting for a reply and left the room, pleased that she'd caught them off guard.

When they entered, Jacob's valet and another man stood from their seats on the sofa.

"Owens," Jacob said. He looked at Lydia then back at his valet. "What's going on here?"

"Sir, this is Mr. Casey." Owens motioned to the other man.

"He comes highly recommended," Lydia said, but she didn't mention that it was Gerald Holt who'd recommended him. She didn't know how Jacob felt about Gerald, since he was the man who'd married Miriam.

"Recommended?" Jacob looked between Lydia and the men. He turned to Mr. Casey. "I'm sorry. Who are you?"

"A tailor," Lydia said. "The best in Annapolis." She shrugged. "I thought you might want something new to wear to the Holts' ball."

Jacob's brows rose. "The ball? I thought we weren't attending."

"I've already accepted the invitation." Seeing the confusion still on his face, she gave a playful smile. "I changed my mind. I do tend to do that." Since she and Miriam had met the week before, the women had paid one another regular visits and had become fast friends. She couldn't miss the ball now.

Alden rubbed his palms together and smirked. "Now, Lydia Steele, you shall see I wasn't exaggerating about my dancing skills. I'll try not to put you to shame, Jake."

"I don't need a tailor," Jacob said.

Lydia fetched the pile of silk squares Mr. Casey had brought and spread them on a table. "Owens and I searched through your wardrobe. It seems you have only black waistcoats."

"Entirely appropriate for a ball," Jacob said.

"Yes, typically." Lydia held up a square to look at it in the light. "But one does not need to be overly formal in the summer. And black is so harsh." She studied another square. "Besides, a lighter color will soften your presentation, make you more . . . approachable." She set aside her favorite squares and glanced at her husband. "You tend to loom."

"I *loom*?" Jacob lifted his arms as the tailor measured around his waist with a tape.

"She's right," Alden said, smirking. "You do loom."

Jacob shot him a glare.

"Perhaps something like this?" Lydia showed a gold and green pattern to the men.

"Black will suit just fine," Jacob said.

Mr. Casey measured Jacob's shoulders, jotting down notes on a pad. "I know for a fact, sir, that Mr. Townsend just purchased a pink and gray paisley waistcoat for the ball."

"I will not wear pink." He folded his arms. "Or paisley."

"Maybe a soft lavender brocade." Alden spoke in a silly high voice, tapping his chin and pouting his lip. "With butterflies and posies and lovely lace trim." He waved his hands in the air.

Jacob gave his friend a flat look then turned to Lydia. "Black is just fine. I don't want to look—"

"You will look handsome no matter what you wear." She cut off his protests. "But a different color would be nice." She chose a square. "Gray and black stripes? It's mostly black with just a bit of . . . lighter black."

Jacob studied her for a moment as if she'd caught him off guard. Then he sighed. "Very well."

"Excellent, sir," Mr. Casey said. "I will have it delivered before Friday."

"And a lavender brocade with butterflies and posies for Mr. Thatcher." Lydia mimicked Alden's silly voice and then laughed.

Alden guffawed, slapping his knee, but Lydia did not look at him. She was captivated by Jacob's smile and the way it grew when their gazes met. A shiver moved through her middle and made her heart light and hot. She looked back down at the fabric squares, trying to calm away the flustered feeling.

A shadow fell over the table and she looked up to find that Jacob had joined her, which only served to unsettle her further.

"You're certain about the ball?" he said in a quiet voice.

"I think so."

He nodded.

"Are *you* certain?" she asked. "People might stare." She concentrated on stacking the fabric squares.

"Oh, I'm certain they will." His lips pulled into a smirk. "They'll stare at my new waistcoat and wonder why I appear so approachable."

Lydia tried to smile, but her heart was still flustered and her insecurities about her scar resurfaced. "You know what I mean."

Jacob lifted her hand, kissing it and sending a jolt through her. "I'll be with you," he said. And the simple phrase was more comforting than all the assurances in the world.

# CHAPTER 8

JACOB COULD FEEL LYDIA SHAKING as she took his arm to enter the ballroom. She hesitated, and he put his hand over hers where it rested on the bend of his elbow.

He turned to catch her eyes and gave a smile meant to be encouraging, but her face was pale and her lips quivered. A surge of emotion welled up inside him. Lydia was brave, and he wished she knew how beautiful she was. Her dress was airy and feminine, with lace at the neckline. The gown was white with pink and blue flowers embroidered into the fabric, and matching buds were woven through her curls. She looked stunning. And he prayed others would see past the scar to the woman beneath.

"Are you ready?" he asked.

She nodded, lifting her chin, but fear still tightened her blue eyes.

The pair entered the room, and Jacob was surprised to see the sparse crowd. It saddened him that the city he'd come to think of as home had lost so many families. But with warships anchored in the harbor aiming their cannons at the city, he could not blame the residents for fleeing.

The Holts had evidently planned for a diminished assemblage, arranging the ballroom to feel smaller. Tables with floral arrangements were set in the center, dividing the dance floor in half, and leaving the other side of the room in darkness. The gathering felt intimate, and Jacob wondered whether Lydia would be relieved by the smaller company, or would she wish for more people to divert attention?

Alden joined them, straightening his new waistcoat which was *not* lavender with butterflies and posies, but a very classic blue pattern, and Jacob had no idea whether it was brocade or not.

He glanced down at his own new waistcoat and couldn't help the warmth that filled him when he thought of Lydia fussing over his clothing.

As he'd considered what had felt so significant that evening, he'd come to the conclusion that it was the first time he'd felt like a husband. He loved watching her laugh and tease Alden, and he had enjoyed her concern for him and his clothing. And Lydia may not have realized it, but that evening she'd told him he was handsome. He'd been surprised by her words and the straightforward way she'd said them, as if it were a truth and she was just stating a fact. Did she truly consider him handsome? He was nothing like the soft-fingered southern gentlemen she'd flirted with at Rosefield. Was it just something a wife said to a husband? And why did he continue to think of it? He wasn't the type of man to care about flattery. But her words hadn't felt empty or manipulative, but affectionate, and each remembering of them made his heart skip. That reaction alone surprised him more than anything.

The Holts stood near the doorway, greeting their guests. Jacob led Lydia toward them and bowed.

"Mr. Steele," Gerald said. "I am so glad to see you, sir." He glanced at Lydia and opened his mouth.

"Allow me to introduce my wife, Mrs. Lydia Steele. Lydia, these are our hosts, Mr. Gerald Holt and Mrs. Miriam Holt."

Lydia looked between the couple, her brows pulling together in a strange expression. She dipped in a hasty curtsy. "A pleasure to make your acquaintance, Mr. Holt, Mrs. Holt."

Her awkward reaction must be a result of her worry about her cheek. Jacob hurried to defer attention from her. He motioned to his friend. "And please let me introduce Alden Thatcher, whom you so graciously extended the invitation to include."

"How do you do, Mr. Thatcher," Miriam said. "Welcome, all of you."

"Thank you," Alden said.

"Please, enjoy yourselves." Gerald motioned his hand toward the room.

Lydia smiled but did not meet the gaze of either host. Seeing her nervousness, Jacob squeezed her hand.

The music changed, indicating the dancing would begin. "If you'll excuse us," Jacob said. "I promised my wife the first dance."

He led Lydia to the floor, and they took their places for the cotillion. Seven other couples joined them, occupying the reduced dance floor. The Holts had planned well; the room appeared to be filled.

Lydia was, of course, a graceful dancer. Jacob could tell the very moment when she stopped worrying about her scar. She smiled, making comments as they came together. He wondered if she'd have acted the same if they hadn't known one another and he'd asked her to dance. Would she have teased and flirted? Or pouted and wished the dance would end? Based on his impression of her at their first meeting, it was unlikely he would have sought her as a partner in the first place. And if he had, it was even more unlikely that she'd have accepted.

Jacob still didn't know his wife well, and if their relationship hadn't developed in its very peculiar way, he didn't think their paths would have crossed socially.

"Why do you look so thoughtful?" Lydia asked, taking his hand as they skipped up the line.

He shrugged.

"You should be enjoying yourself," she reprimanded him with a falsely stern look. "This is a ball, Mr. Steele, not a prison."

They released hands and joined with other partners, moving through the line until they met again.

"If it were a prison, I'd at least be able to remove these shoes," he grumbled. Breeches and stockings were much less comfortable than his usual attire of practical trousers and boots.

"But not the waistcoat." Lydia pretended to look horrified by the thought.

"True," he said. "I'd want to impress the guards."

"And the rats," she said. "They do appreciate a finely dressed man." She winked as she turned away with her next partner.

And Jacob decided that as much as he disliked dancing, he would do it every evening if it meant seeing Lydia so carefree.

The dance ended, and before Jacob had even returned Lydia to the side of the room, Alden came from the other direction and snatched her hand, twirling her around and leading her back toward the dance floor.

Jacob stopped midstep. He turned, annoyed as his wife was taken away. Lydia laughed.

"Prepare yourself, Lydia Steele." Alden waved his hand with a flourish. "You shall now be a witness to unrivaled dancing skills the likes of which inspire poetry."

She rolled her eyes and grinned, her right cheek wrinkling in its peculiar way.

The pair took their place, and the music began.

Jacob watched the dancers, particularly those who drew near to Lydia. He wasn't sure whether it was unconsciously or deliberately that she turned her face to the side when a new gentleman partnered with her. He noticed she relaxed when Alden or Gerald Holt stood opposite her. Strange that she should feel so at ease with Gerald when they'd only met moments earlier.

As Lydia danced, Jacob moved along the edge of the room, instinctually listening to snippets of conversation as he kept his eyes on the dance floor.

He heard men discussing the attack at St. Leonard's Creek and couldn't help but feel proud that he'd had a hand in helping the flotilla move the repaired boats into place. With Alden's excellent planning, the two of them and a few other members of the flotilla had been able to smuggle the barge and gunboat from Annapolis Harbor under cover of darkness. For the past three days, Jacob and Alden had been moving boats from the shipyard, past the blockades, to the safety of the side creeks off the Potomac to wait for the commodore's signal. A land and sea attack had given the flotilla the cover they'd needed to escape from the creek and flee up the Patuxent to Benedict.

His only frustration was that Commodore Barney still considered him of more value as a shipbuilder than a soldier. He'd been ordered back home to the shipyard before the attack had even begun. Jacob wanted to fight the cursed redcoats—send them back to England where they belonged.

". . . a true beauty if it wasn't for that terrible scar."

The words stopped him short. Jacob looked at the gossiping women from the corner of his eye.

"A pity," another woman replied. "How do you think her father convinced Jacob Steele to—" Jacob turned fully around, and she cut off her words abruptly.

He glared at the women, taking no pleasure in seeing their faces redden as they recognized him and moved away. Jacob seethed, every bit of him heating as he scrutinized the other guests. Were they all gossiping about Lydia? If she overheard just one insensitive word, it would devastate her.

His heart ached, and his hackles raised. The impulse to protect her was so strong he fisted his hands to keep from stomping onto the dance floor, hauling her over his shoulder, and spiriting her away from everyone. He was strangely torn between wanting her to confront her fear, to overcome it, to be strong, not caring what others thought; and wanting to hide her, far from anyone who might hurt her.

He was still wound tightly when the dance ended and Alden returned Lydia to the side of the room.

"I know you shall forevermore compare all other dancers to me. It is unavoidable, I suppose . . ." Alden winked at Jacob, bowed to Lydia, and then excused himself, heading toward a dessert table.

"That man," Jacob said, letting out an exasperated breath. "He is . . ."

"Entertaining?" Lydia offered. "Amusing?"

"I was going to say annoying."

She shrugged, watching Alden take a bite of a small cake. "Perhaps. But he makes people happy." She pointed at Jacob. "He makes *you* smile." Her expression turned pensive. "And I think he acts the way he does to hide from something. Some heartbreak he does not want to remember, or . . ." She wrinkled her nose thoughtfully. "I don't quite know. But sometimes I see pain in his eyes."

"I agree," Jacob said, surprised by her insight. She'd only known Alden for a few weeks, and they'd rarely spent more than an hour or so together at a time. "I do not know what happened to Alden, but he is different from when I knew him before."

The music changed, and excited whispers started around the room. The Holts were playing a waltz. And so early in the evening. Jacob thought now would be a nice time to join Alden for a dessert, but if he left Lydia, another man could ask her to waltz, and that was simply unacceptable. He stepped back, turning to face his wife. "Would you care to dance, Mrs. Steele?"

She took his hand, inclining her head. Her bright blue eyes held a teasing sparkle that both frustrated and captivated him. He imagined this enticement was what drew the gentlemen of Virginia to follow her around like ducklings. "I would love to, Mr. Steele."

He led her to the floor, placing a hand at her waist. Her palm rested comfortably in his, small and soft. She had to step closer to reach up to his shoulder.

Jacob realized, aside from carrying her from the burning barn, this was the closest he'd been, physically, with his wife. Everything about Lydia was soft and petite. She appeared delicate, but she could be determined, stubborn even. One would never call his wife weak-minded. He counted the beat of the music and stepped forward, pulling her even closer as he led her in the dance.

Lydia followed his lead splendidly; he thought how pleasant it felt to hold her close. They settled into the rhythm of the dance, moving together over the floor, and after a moment, he could feel her relax, her hand resting more heavily on his shoulder, her muscles less tense where he touched her waist.

"Are you glad we came tonight?" he asked, hoping her worries about being out in the public eye were easing.

Lydia looked up, tilting back her head to see him. "Yes. Are you?"

"I am." Bending his neck so far forward was uncomfortable, but he didn't want to loosen his hold and draw back to see her better. "Often, the fear about a thing is worse than the thing itself, don't you think?"

She smiled, lowering her lashes. "You sound just like my brother."

He hadn't expected that. "Beau?"

She shook her head. "Emmett. Surely I've told you about him."

"I believe you've mentioned his name, but you've not said much."

"Emmett is a major in the United States Army, stationed right now in Canada." She sighed. "He's the brother I'm close to. He loves me." She looked up then back to his waistcoat. "Em used to comfort me when I was afraid. He'd talk to me about my fears and show me that the things I was frightened of were never as bad as I thought."

Her hand moved over his shoulder, settling lower onto his chest. Her arm must be tired. "It's funny how things change," Lydia continued, the same faraway look in her expression. "Things you fear will happen don't, and things you never imagined do. And some are so much worse than you pictured, and others aren't as bad . . ." She shook her head. "I'm rambling." Her forehead creased as she looked back up at him.

He pulled her closer, moving his hand around to the small of her back. "What is it you fear?" He dreaded her answer. Of course she was afraid of ridicule, of people looking at her scar with disgust, avoiding her. But he liked her brother's wise approach of discussing her fears, confronting them, instead of pretending they didn't exist.

Her expression grew solemn, and her fingers tightened on his lapel. "I have a dream. A nightmare. I always have, since I can remember. In the dream, I'm all alone. Not the type of alone where everyone else is just in another room or gone for the day, but truly alone. Somehow, I know *everyone* is gone. Really gone." She pursed her lips together. "They're all dead." She whispered the word and shivered, her brows furrowed. "And when I wake, I still feel it, that sense of being utterly alone, and it terrifies me."

Her voice had gotten so soft that he'd leaned forward to hear.

"Em or Francine would hear me crying at night and come to reassure me. But, even when they talked to me and I could see them and knew the dream wasn't real, I still felt it. Sometimes the feeling doesn't leave. Even though the truth is right before me." She kept her gaze on his waistcoat. "Em would press my ear to his chest and tell me to listen to his heartbeat. And for some reason that convinced me that he was there and alive, and I could calm down."

She shrugged, looking up at him shyly. "Rather childish, don't you think?"

Jacob didn't think it was childish at all. Not when he saw her face pale at the memory and felt her hand trembling in his. "Do you still have this dream?"

"Not often," she said.

He thought of how her family had treated her when her face was cut. *Deserted* her. Her friends, her fiancé. All had left her. He'd have guessed her worst fear was not being the prettiest woman in the room or perhaps something trivial like wearing the wrong gown, but that wasn't it at all. Her true fear went much deeper, and Jacob's throat felt tight when he thought of her alone in Annapolis, in a strange house with no friends or family. He glanced around the room, willing the other guests to see the kind, insightful woman he'd married. Hoping with all his heart they'd accept her into their society.

Movement from Alden caught Jacob's gaze. His face was serious, and he motioned with a tilt of his head toward a darkened corner of the room.

Jacob glanced toward it but saw nothing. He looked back at Alden, who repeated the same gesture. Something had happened, and Alden needed to speak with him privately. But nothing on this earth could force him to leave Lydia alone among strangers after what she'd just shared.

"But we should talk about something else, don't you think?" Lydia said, recapturing his attention.

"Such as?" He bent his neck back down.

"You." She squinted, studying his face. "You're different than I thought you would be, Jacob."

"And how am I different?"

She shrugged. "You are quiet and . . ."

"Looming?"

Lydia smiled. "Sometimes. But you are not fearsome. Rather the opposite, I think."

In the candlelight, he could see a blush color her cheeks.

"I still feel as if you're a bit of a stranger. You have an entire life I know nothing of."

Jacob jolted. Had he given himself away? What did she suspect?

"I know nothing of shipbuilding, of course," she continued, not noticing his alarm. "And you spend so many hours at the shipyard. And there's Elnora and Alden; I have heard only the smallest bit about your childhood . . ."

Realizing her comment was innocent, he relaxed. He touched beneath her chin, lifting her face and letting his thumb brush her lower lip. "Then, we should spend some time becoming better acquainted, don't you think?"

He felt an immense satisfaction seeing Lydia's blush deepen.

She looked down. "I do."

The music ended, and Jacob reluctantly released his wife.

Alden walked toward the dark corner, and Jacob knew he was expected to follow. But he couldn't bring Lydia with him. If she were to overhear something, it could put the other operatives in jeopardy. He walked with her toward the edge of the dance floor, trying to think of a solution. Perhaps she needed to step into the ladies' withdrawing room for a moment.

As if in answer to his quandary, Gerald Holt approached. "I hoped for an opportunity to dance with you, Mrs. Steele." He looked to Jacob for permission then to Lydia.

"I would like that very much," Lydia said.

Jacob watched her face for a sign of discomfort but saw none. She appeared pleased with the idea. And it would give him a moment alone to speak with Alden. But Jacob's gut feeling about Gerald Holt was one of distrust.

"Are you certain?" Jacob asked her, not caring if he insulted Gerald. Lydia was much more important.

"Yes. Thank you. Go find Alden. Surely he needs saving before he embarrasses himself." She gave him a little shove and an encouraging smile.

He studied her face once more before releasing her hand and nodding to Gerald. He watched the two join the other dancers, his senses on high alert, but seeing Lydia's contented smile, he chastised himself. His overprotectiveness of her and dislike of her companion were making him paranoid.

Giving one last glance at the dancers, he walked casually around the room, picking up a glass of brandy as he headed toward the darkened corner. A pleasant glow filled his chest, and he couldn't help but smile like a fool. In spite of everything, he was growing fond of his wife, and he suspected Lydia might feel a similar affection for him. If he'd been told on the day of the rose-garden picnic that he'd find himself enamored with Lydia Prescott, he'd never have believed it.

"Jake, we have a problem," Alden said in a low voice.

Jacob squinted into the darkness where only his friend's outline was visible. But he didn't need to see his face to recognize the worry in Alden's voice.

"What's happened?"

"Brian Gallagher was ambushed."

"Ambushed?" Jacob asked. Brian was one of America's best spies. If he'd been captured . . .

"While you were flouncing around the dance floor making moon eyes at your wife, I spoke with Mr. Townsend. Brian Gallagher and John Rumson were dispatched from Richmond ten days ago with crucial information. John went to Washington, and Brian was supposed to bring his message to Annapolis. But he didn't arrive when expected."

Jacob's stomach was heavy. Brian wasn't careless. If he was expected somewhere, nothing would keep him away. And if he carried vital information . . . Jacob rubbed his eyes.

"Yesterday, Brian arrived in town," Alden said. "He was injured, bleeding from a bullet wound to the shoulder. Claimed he'd narrowly escaped after being attacked on South River Bridge." Alden's voice tightened.

"They knew he was coming." Jacob said.

"Not only that—they knew who he was," Alden replied.

"But how?" Jacob stared back toward the lit area of the room. Mr. Townsend, an affluent member of the community, and a loyal agent chatted with Mrs. Miriam Holt. The man gave no indication that he was worried, not that Jacob expected him to. He was one of the best at maintaining his cover.

"How could they have known?" Jacob muttered. The dance ended, and Gerald Holt and Lydia walked toward Mr. Townsend and Mrs. Holt. "Only you, Townsend, and I knew the identity of those two operatives." The brandy tasted sour in his mouth. Jacob trusted Alden and Townsend implicitly. Neither of them would betray the spies. He searched his mind for an answer.

Lydia took Miriam Holt's arm and smiled at something the woman said. She tapped Gerald on the chest then turned back, leaning close to Miriam as the two shared a laugh.

The hairs on the back of Jacob's neck prickled. Lydia and Miriam weren't acting like women who had just met. His instincts flared with doubt. Was his wife deceiving him?

Jacob watched Gerald Holt. He'd never trusted that man. And he knew Townsend was keeping a close eye on him as well. What were they devising?

And how was Lydia involved? Had she been feeding information to the British? Suspicion and anger mixed in his gut. He'd been so easily charmed with a pair of blue eyes.

"Jake?"

Jacob realized Alden had been speaking. "What?"

"I said, 'Don't you want to hear the message?'"

"Tell me."

"Two weeks ago the transport ships landed in Bermuda. America must prepare for invasion."

# CHAPTER 9

LYDIA TURNED HER FACE TO the side, opening and closing her mouth and watching in the mirror how her scar bunched with the movements of her cheek. The cut had healed, but it was still uneven and red, thicker in some places than in others. Lydia grimaced, rubbing it with her fingers.

"That's enough, Miss Lydia," Francine said.

She was glad her maid continued to call her by the name she'd used since she was a child. Hearing the woman she was closest to refer to her as Mrs. Steele would have felt uncomfortably formal.

Francine brushed through a section of Lydia's hair and wound it around a strip of fabric, rolling it for the night. "It is what it is, and there's no changing it." She tied off the rag and started on another.

"It's grotesque." Lydia was feeling sorry for herself. The ball had been two nights earlier, and she hadn't seen Jacob since. What had happened that night? The evening had started so well. Jacob had been so handsome, their conversations easy, and at times, even romantic. When he'd held her in the waltz, she'd felt airy, as if a breeze could have blown her away. Her heart had fluttered when his gaze held hers, and a delicious warmth had filled her all the way to her toes. For a short while, she'd contemplated her arranged marriage wouldn't lack affection. Perhaps she was even falling in love.

But whatever had happened between them, it was felt by her alone. Jacob had said hardly a word to her after the dance with Gerald Holt. Not only had he been quiet, his manner had changed completely. Once he joined the group, his behavior had been cold, nothing like the teasing banter of only moments earlier. She couldn't help but think her scar was to blame. When Lydia stood beside the beautiful Miriam Holt, Jacob had surely seen a stark contrast between the two. "I am so ugly, Francine."

Francine ceased her hair brushing. She moved around to look at Lydia, lifting up her face and staring hard into her eyes. "Stop that right now." She wagged a finger. "Such words are ingratitude to God."

A wave of shame flowed over Lydia's heart. She knew the injury could have been much worse. A bit higher, and she'd have lost her eye. And if the glass had struck lower, it could have sliced her neck. "I don't mean to be ungrateful. But . . ." Her shoulders slumped, and her eyes prickled. "Everyone stares at it."

Francine released her chin, and Lydia turned back to the mirror. "Can't you make a face paint to cover it? Or we could arrange my curls—"

"No matter how you try, you'll not hide it completely. It will be seen. There's no helping it." Her dark eyes were soft, and she spoke in the practical way she'd done since Lydia was a child. Her manner was not to flatter or give false praise. She spoke plainly, truthfully, and Lydia knew it was her way of showing love. "People will look. They will wonder, but if they sense shame or embarrassment, they'll feel uncomfortable too. If they see it doesn't bother you, they will look past it. And there is much more to Lydia Steele than just her pretty face." She moved behind Lydia, putting her hands on her shoulders and looking at her in the mirror. "The scar is part of you, and you cannot get away from it. But it is only a small part." Francine held up her fingers three inches apart. "And it will get smaller."

Lydia gave a halfhearted smile. Of course Francine was right.

The maid nodded with a *hmph* and returned to rolling Lydia's hair.

Lydia opened the jar Francine had mixed specifically for her scar. She applied the shiny ointment faithfully morning and night, exactly as her maid had instructed. Francine had promised it would keep the skin smooth and soft and shrink the scar over time to a thin pink line. Lydia wished it would work faster. She touched her fingers to the cream, wrinkling her nose at the fragrance, and smoothed it over her cheek.

From the corner of her eye, Lydia saw movement. She snapped her head around just as a mouse darted across the floor and into her dressing room.

Lydia screamed and pulled up her feet.

Francine let out a yelp.

The women's gazes met in the mirror.

The door flew open.

A footman—Hawkins—rushed into the room. "Mrs. Steele?" He looked wildly around. "What happened?"

"A mouse!" Lydia and Francine said at the same time, pointing toward the dressing room.

Hawkins scowled, his typically cheerful expression looking determined. "Not to worry, ma'am." He snatched up a candleholder and stalked across the floor to the dressing room. "I'll find the little beast."

Maggs, the butler, poked his head into the room, his thick brows lifted. "Is everything all right?" he asked in his formal voice.

"A mouse," the three said. The two women pointed at the dressing room as Hawkins peeked through the doorway then stepped inside.

"Oh dear." Maggs wiped his forehead with a handkerchief.

Lydia and Francine moved to the dressing room door.

Hawkins surveyed the floor, shining the candlelight into the corners. "Don't see 'im, Mrs. Steele."

"We can't just leave him in there," Lydia said. "What if he crawls on me when I'm asleep?"

To his credit, Hawkins nodded, taking his duty very seriously. "Right, then." He handed the candleholder to Francine. "We'll search."

"I'll fetch a lantern." Maggs hurried away.

Hawkins peered around the dressing room, looking on shelves, under shoes and hatboxes, and poking between gowns. He opened drawers, nudging aside stockings and underclothing.

Lydia stood behind Francine, bracing herself in case the rodent leapt out and startled them.

Maggs joined Hawkins in the dressing room, holding the lantern high and pointing out different mouse-sized places for the footman to investigate.

Finally, Hawkins poked his head back into the bedchamber. "Could be anywhere," he said. "Only thing to do's take everything out, piece by piece." He looked at Lydia. "If that's all right with you, ma'am."

"Yes, I think that's a good plan," Lydia said.

Hawkins set the candle on the dressing room table and picked up a shoe, turning it over and shaking it. He did the same with the other shoe then handed the pair to Francine.

She set them in the bedchamber.

Maggs shook a gown, patting it to make certain nothing had climbed inside, then handed it out.

Lydia took it and laid it on the bed.

Before long, piles of gowns, stockings, bonnets, coats, underclothing, shoes, and hair ribbons covered every surface of the bedchamber. For an instant, Lydia's mind returned to the day before her wedding as her mother and Francine packed away her clothes. That day she'd felt nothing but despair at a future that loomed ahead, uncertain. But now, though the situation was similar, the feel of the room was very different as the four cooperated happily with a common goal.

Maggs opened a hatbox and looked through it carefully before returning the lid and handing it to Francine. Hawkins held out a handful of silk stockings.

Lydia accepted the stockings. The sound of a throat clearing made her turn.

The others stopped their activity as well.

Jacob stood in the doorway, his brows pulled together as he studied the mess. He looked from person to person. "What is happening?"

"A mouse," the four spoke in unison, pointing toward the dressing room.

Jacob pushed his fingers through his hair and yawned. "The hour is past midnight. All of you should sleep. The mouse can be found in the morning."

Lydia piled the stockings onto a chair with the others. "I can't sleep with a mouse in my room."

"It could crawl on her while she sleeps," Hawkins added helpfully.

Jacob fixed a look on his footman then closed his eyes, letting out a tired-sounding breath. "Let's find the mouse, then." He started for the dressing room.

His reaction nettled Lydia. She didn't like feeling as if her worries were a bother. They hadn't been to the others. "Please don't concern yourself, Jacob." She put a hand on her hip. "We can do this ourselves. And we will be quiet so you can sleep."

She hadn't meant her words to sound so rude, but the fact that her husband was only now returning home for the night, the memory of his coolness to her at the ball, his absence at supper the past two evening, and the grudging way he'd offered assistance vexed her.

Jacob paused his steps, studying her. The irritation in his expression lessened. "It is not an imposition. Not if it's upsetting to you."

Lydia shrugged. "Have at it, then, if you'd like."

His eyes tightened in what appeared to be a wince as he entered the dressing room.

Lydia felt sorry for acting so spitefully, but she wasn't ready to forget his offenses. She didn't like the niggling feeling that Jacob was keeping secrets from her. And she didn't want to admit, not even to herself, what those secrets might be, especially now that she'd allowed herself to feel affection for the very person who was deceiving her. Letting down her guard would only result in her being hurt.

Hawkins explained the procedure to an irritated-looking Jacob—the plan of action that had included shaking and patting each item before handing it to the ladies.

Francine stood with her arms folded, waiting for the process to start again, and Lydia felt another wave of guilt. While she could sleep in the morning, the servants would need to rise early. They should hurry.

She moved to the dressing room doorway.

"You have a lot of clothes." Jacob handed her a gown.

Lydia took it and shrugged. "I suppose I do." She laid the gown on the bed and returned to the dressing room doorway. The room was nearly emptied. Lydia wondered if the mouse may have slipped past them in the confusion.

Jacob held out a bonnet, and as she reached to take it, the mouse darted from beneath its cluster of flowers and ran onto his hand.

Lydia screamed, and Jacob jumped back, crashing into a shelf. Hats fell down around him.

He cursed and rubbed the back of his head, looking around the floor. "Did anyone see where the little devil went?"

"In there, sir." Hawkins pointed to a vase of parasols.

Francine knelt to pick up the hats, and Maggs lifted the lantern.

Jacob snatched up a boot and held it high as he stalked toward the parasol vase.

Lydia grabbed onto his arm. "Wait! Don't kill him!"

He stopped, his brows drawing together as he studied her face. "What?"

"Just catch him." Her throat was tight as she thought of the panicked animal hiding inside the vase, with its heart pounding. "We can release him into the garden."

He closed his eyes and let out a breath. "Lydia . . ."

"Please? You saw him, Jacob. He's so little and helpless. He must be frightened out of his wits." She retrieved a box from her dressing table, dumping out the hairpins and combs. "Catch him in this." She took the boot from Jacob.

He accepted the box. "In another hour, you'll have given it a name and made it a pet," he grumbled.

Hawkins helped remove the parasols, shaking each one before laying it aside.

Once it was empty, Jacob motioned for Maggs to bring the light closer. He peered into the vase. "It's in there," he whispered.

Lydia cringed away, not wanting it to startle her again.

"The vase is too smooth." Jacob still spoke in a whisper. "It can't climb out."

Hawkins lifted the vase, tipping it slowly, and Jacob held the box, catching the mouse inside and clapping on the lid.

The entire group breathed a sigh of relief.

Lydia clapped her hands. "We did it! Thank you, all of you."

Jacob held the box tightly and motioned with his head. "Shall we release it?"

"Yes," Lydia said. "I'll . . ." She looked around her bedchamber, then to the mirror over her dressing table. Her hair was only partly wrapped in rags, she wore her dressing gown, and the room was utter chaos. "Oh dear." Lydia didn't know which was worse: her own appearance or the disaster surrounding her.

Francine pushed her toward the doorway. "Off you go. We'll put everything back together quick as you please."

She squeezed her maid's hand. "Thank you, Francine." Then she turned to the other servants, giving a smile. "And thank you as well, Hawkins, Maggs. It is very late, and you both must be tired from such a harrowing night of mouse-hunting."

Hawkins grinned, his eyes lighting up at the praise. "Not a worry, Mrs. Steele."

Maggs tipped his head forward, maintaining his formal demeanor. "You are quite welcome, madam."

Lydia took a candleholder and followed Jacob down the darkened staircase and through the front door, shielding the flame with her hand. She stepped outside and the sound of cicadas, katydids, and crickets, and the smell of her rose garden struck her with such a rush of homesickness that she gasped and stopped on the front steps.

Jacob turned. "Cold?"

She shook her head, unexpected tears filling her eyes. "No. I'm . . ." Emotion stopped her words. Being tired gave her tears extra fuel. Clearing her throat, she wiped her eyes. "Excuse me."

Jacob stepped back onto the porch. "I won't hurt the mouse."

She nodded. He must think she was addled, the way her emotions bounced around so unpredictably tonight. "I know." She tried to smile but could tell it wasn't convincing. "I'm just tired."

He considered her a moment longer then nodded. "Wait here, then. I'll release it away from the house so it doesn't find its way back." Following the path, he walked down toward the gate. Shoulders broad, he made an impressively large shadow as he moved away into the darkness.

The breeze moved through Lydia's hair, reminding her it was still only partly arranged. A mad woman with wild hair, angry, afraid, laughing, and crying, all within an hour. Frightening indeed.

Jacob's shadow crouched down, and Lydia imagined she saw the mouse run out of the box, but of course, it was too dark.

He stood and returned, holding the empty box for her to see. "Well, that's done."

"Thank you."

He stepped onto the porch and motioned for her to precede him into the house.

"I think I'll remain out here a bit longer. The night is so lovely, and I'm certain my bedchamber is still in uproar."

Jacob seemed to hesitate.

"Go on, you're tired," she said, moving to the edge of the steps. "No need to remain with me."

He entered the house, and she stepped down and sat on the porch step, watching the fireflies and letting the fragrance of the roses fill her. In the day, the smell had been a comfort, reminding her of home, but tonight she felt lonely. What had her parents been doing this evening? They'd probably visited a neighbor, playing cards and chatting. Or perhaps they'd attended a musical performance or even a dinner party. Did Beau miss her? When would she receive a letter from Emmett?

The tears returned, and, indulging in a great bout of self-pity, Lydia rested her forehead on her arms and wept.

Hearing a noise, she raised her head, wiping her eyes and cheeks. She sniffled and swallowed away her blubbering.

Jacob sat on the step next to her, holding two plates. "I found cake in the kitchen."

Taking one of the plates, Lydia made an embarrassing noise somewhere between a laugh and a sob. "Cake sounds divine." She took the offered fork and cut into the slice. The raisin cake was delicious, but she still missed Henrietta's cooking, and she knew Francine missed her family. She wondered briefly if she should again mention bringing the cook from Virginia, but not wanting to upset her husband, decided against mentioning it.

Jacob watched her. "I'm sorry about the mouse," he said hesitantly. "I didn't think it would upset you."

She shook her head. "I'm not upset about the mouse." She looked at the roses. "Just a bit homesick."

"Ah." He took a large bite of cake, and Lydia wondered if he'd eaten supper. "I apologize for my absence lately. Work at the shipyard has consumed more of my time than I'd expected."

Lydia poked at a raisin with her fork, not for the first time wondering what could keep a shipyard in a blockaded harbor so busy.

"Mrs. Pembroke tells me you've been paying visits and attending luncheons," Jacob said. "I hope you're pleased with Annapolis society—what little there is."

Lydia glanced at him but didn't sense anything in his question but polite curiosity. "I am. The ladies I've come to know have been very pleasant."

"I'm glad you're finding friends." He set down his plate on the step and leaned back on his hands, crossing his ankles. "You seemed to get along well at the Holts' ball."

"I enjoyed it immensely." She glanced at him. "I don't think you did, however."

Jacob was quiet, and Lydia wondered if she'd offended him. Perhaps he didn't intend to answer.

She set down her plate and prepared to stand.

"I'm afraid I had a great deal on my mind that night," he said. "I do hope I didn't make your evening less enjoyable."

She turned fully toward him, trying to distinguish his expression in the moonlight. His tone was strange, and again she knew he was keeping secrets from her. "Mr. Townsend seemed occupied as well," she said, hoping Jacob might expound on his previous statement.

"Was he?" He tipped his head, and though Lydia still couldn't fully see his face, she sensed her observation had surprised him.

"Agitated, I think. He seemed tense, glancing at the doorway and tapping his fingers against his leg."

"I didn't notice," Jacob said, but something in his tone made her think he wished to change the topic. "Who else did you meet?"

"Mr. Leonard Blackwell." She grasped at the first name that came to mind.

"Oh? And how did you find him?"

"Polite, but I believe he is ill, isn't he?" In fact, that had been the reason Mr. Blackwell had attracted her attention in the first place.

"What makes you say that?"

Perhaps it wasn't common knowledge after all. "His coat was quite loose, and his waistcoat, as if he'd lost a great deal of weight in a short amount of time. It was not an old coat and was very stylish. I imagine he'd have had it tailored if the weight loss hadn't come on so quickly." When Jacob didn't answer, she continued talking. "However, I know nothing about the man's circumstance. Perhaps he borrowed the clothing."

Jacob didn't say anything, and Lydia worried she'd said something wrong.

"I apologize if I've caused offense. I do not mean to gossip."

"I'm not offended," he said, sitting up and turning toward her. "Your observations are fascinating. What other scandalous tidbits did you pick up?"

"Jacob!" She opened her eyes wide, pretending to be offended.

He chuckled. "Or non-scandalous."

She liked that he was impressed or at least surprised by her commentary. The easy conversation was much better than their earlier stilted dialogueue.

"It's all speculation, of course." She smiled.

"Of course," Jacob said.

"I wonder if Mr. Duelmeier and Mrs. Avery have a history. Or perhaps a disagreement. The two went to great lengths to avoid looking at one another. She even stepped around him, utterly avoiding his gaze, to greet Mr. Blackwell."

"That *is* scandalous."

Lydia shrugged. "Or it is nothing."

"And what about the Holts?" Jacob asked. "How do you find them?"

Lydia's throat went dry. She'd avoided discussing the Holts, pretended not to even know them at the ball, for fear of Jacob's reaction. She couldn't bear to see in his expression or actions confirmation that he still cared for Miriam. "They seem very nice. I'm afraid I don't know them well."

Jacob went quiet. He took her plate with stiff movements. "Your room should be put in order by now." He rose and went inside.

Lydia watched him go, his reaction verifying the exact thing she feared. He was still in love with Miriam Holt. And knowing it for certain wrenched her heart, hurting more than she'd believed possible.

# CHAPTER 10

THE MORNING AFTER THE MOUSE hunt, Jacob rose late, head throbbing. He sent for coffee and sat on the edge of his bed, rubbing his neck as he drank the hot liquid.

Not only had he stayed up into the early hours of the morning, he'd worked late into the night the day before. With Alden's help, one of the flotilla's damaged boats, a twenty-ton sloop, had been smuggled past the harbor blockades two nights ago with a damaged gun deck and fractured mast. Jacob had set a full crew to work on the vessel, hoping to finish it quickly and send it off. If the English discovered he was aiding the flotilla, they'd have no qualms about destroying his entire shipyard.

Owens brought hot water for a shave, but Jacob waved it off, heaving himself up with a grunt.

"You look ill, sir," Owens said. "Perhaps you should return to bed."

Jacob glanced into the looking glass, noting that he did indeed look ill. Dark bags looked like smudges under his eyes, and he'd not shaved in days. The strain of wartime ship repair and maintaining a spy operation were taking a toll. "I'm not ill," he said. "Just fatigued."

Owens brought a clean shirt and trousers. "Aye, heard there was some excitement last night." He grinned. "Hawkins has been going on about it all morning."

"Mrs. Steele discovered a mouse in her bedchamber," Jacob said, pulling on the clothes.

"Quite a fuss, from what I hear." Owens pursed his lips as he tied a careful knot in Jacob's neckcloth.

Jacob smirked. "You can imagine."

The valet laughed. "If you don't mind me sayin', sir, we're all right fond of Mrs. Steele." He held up Jacob's coat. "Always pleasant, she is, now that she's gotten past her shyness. And the household operates more efficiently than ever before."

Jacob slipped his arms into the coat. "Glad to hear it, Owens." Jacob had noticed how smoothly the household was managed, and in truth, he was fond of Mrs. Steele himself. His thoughts returned continually to the Holts' ball, the feeling of holding her in his arms . . . but inevitably, the memories turned, and a hot stone settled in his belly. Lydia was lying to him.

He'd given her the opportunity again last night to tell the truth. And she'd failed. He knew from Mrs. Pembroke that Lydia had developed a friendship with Miriam. The two spent quite a lot of time together. So why maintain the charade? What did she hope to gain by pretending not to know the Holts?

His instinct had warned him from the start not to trust Gerald, and now his own wife was untruthful about her relationship with the couple. Could Lydia possibly be working with Gerald against the American army? The idea was preposterous, especially when one considered that Lydia's injury was caused by a British raid. But the fact was that somebody was giving information to the enemy. He and Alden were increasingly convinced the spy was someone close to them. The two messengers were most definitely betrayed. The South River Bridge was well traveled, yet those two alone were targeted. But for the life of him, Jacob could find nothing to indicate who else knew their identities.

Jacob bid Owens farewell, took his hat from Maggs, and departed for the shipyard. His late arrival would surprise the crew. Tardiness was not usual for Jacob Steele. But his workers were well trained. They would have been hard at work since the first light of dawn. The repairs on the sloop were surely well underway, and perhaps Alden had arrived with new information about the turncoat.

Hoping to save a few moments, Jacob walked through the park instead of taking the longer path around. He used to come on this path often, strolling leisurely to admire the tall trees during the various seasons and sometimes pause to watch the squirrels darting overhead, but over the past years he'd not taken the opportunity. His duties had consumed far too much time.

His connections in Washington City, location on Chesapeake Bay, and friendship with Joshua Barney had thrust Jacob unexpectedly into the business of espionage. At first he'd delivered the occasional message, and then as his skill at uncovering intelligence became more apparent to the country's military leaders, he'd become part of a larger network, sending men on missions and reconnoitering, gathering, and passing on information. The responsibility was surprisingly exhausting.

He stepped out of the trees on the far side of the park but then pulled back, staying in the shadows as he saw Gerald Holt pushing a baby pram farther up the road. But for once, the sight of the man wasn't what captured Jacob's attention. Lydia and Miriam walked behind Gerald, arms linked, laughing and chatting together.

Jacob closed his eyes and blew out a breath through his nose. He forced his jaw and fists to unclench. For a moment he was tempted to storm up the road and confront them. But what good would it do? What would he accuse her of? Secretly being friends with people she had every right to be friends with? People he himself had encouraged her to know socially?

Once the party turned at the corner, Jacob left the shadow of the park and walked in the other direction.

Knowing he was being made a fool of, being deceived, burned sour in his throat. But there was a bigger picture than his pride.

Was she a spy, betraying Jacob's messengers to the English? He couldn't believe it. Why would she do it? Was she somehow being deceived?

He thought of her last night, laughing with the servants and worrying for the mouse. He remembered her tears. The night of the fire, she'd been helpless, and he'd held her . . . He shook his head. It couldn't be. Her actions must have some other explanation.

He came in sight of the harbor, taking in a deep breath of the sea air. The beautiful view of Chesapeake Bay was marred by the English man-o'-war in the harbor. Jacob glared at the ship, even as he admired the magnificent vessel and the technology required to create something so extraordinary. A smaller vessel, a sleek-looking brig, was anchored alongside, most likely delivering provisions and possibly orders. What he wouldn't give to overhear the messages being delivered. If only he could disguise himself convincingly . . .

Something tickled at the back of his mind. Lydia had noticed things that even he, with his experienced eye, hadn't seen. Things a spy would notice. If he were to be honest, the woman would make a superb agent. She knew what to say to people, and they trusted her. She noticed things and interpreted them, and in the business of espionage, knowledge was everything.

Jacob didn't share her ability to move easily among company, nor did he possess Alden's skill of blending into the background. He lacked social skills for one approach and was far too large for the other. But Lydia was a natural. His stomach turned over, not liking the path his mind had taken.

He continued down the hill toward the sheltered cove on the far side of the harbor, the familiar smell of sawdust and sea filling his nostrils as he entered the shipyard. He appraised the area, noting the young boys with buckets and tools rushing about on errands, laborers hauling planks, and the more experienced journeymen directing them.

Pride expanded his chest as he listened to the noises of hammering, sawing, and men calling to one another and observed the vessels in various stages of construction held on the shore in stocks and floating at the dock.

His foreman, David Brown, strode toward him, wearing his usual glower. David was a free black man from Boston. It had taken quite a bit of work to convince him to come south and work in Annapolis, but Jacob had known from the moment he'd met him that this man had the experience and calm demeanor he wanted for his shipyard.

"Sloop needs a new aft mast," David said, jerking his head toward the pond then started walking in that direction. Not one for small talk, David didn't bother with greetings or inquire as to why Jacob was late. His ability to focus solely on his duty was one of the things Jacob admired about him. That and his unwavering work ethic and attentiveness to detail. Besides, it didn't hurt that the man's scowl and gruff manner kept the apprentices a little afraid.

Jacob fell into step beside him, appreciating the man's consideration—David could have competently chosen a mast, but out of respect, had left the task for the master shipwright.

"And how do you find her?"

"Very little structural damage. Keel's solid. Two ribs cracked. Sawyers are fitting and soaking planks today."

Jacob nodded. The repairs would only take a day, maybe two, as long as the weather held. He looked up at the clear sky. The day was warm and dry, and hopefully tomorrow would be the same. The mast would be set, and he could send the sloop away within a week.

Jacob looked up as they walked past a large ship, a brigantine commissioned by the navy. He'd hoped to complete it months earlier, but the blockade had made urgency unnecessary. The surrounding scaffolding that should have been busy with activity stood empty. Seeing it half-complete, sitting in stocks, with no progress being made was discouraging. He'd designed the ship for speed and strength with a sturdy, graceful shape and had anticipated seeing it completed. Now, it just appeared like an abandoned skeleton on the beach. *Soon,* he thought. *The war must end soon.* He could finish the brigantine, repair his own *Gannet,* and return to the regular business of designing and building ships.

They arrived at the mast pond, and Jacob stood with his hands on his hips, looking down at the long straight pine trunks soaking in the water to keep their pitch from drying out. He'd chosen the trees himself, from the very center of a forest in Massachusetts where they grew the straightest and tallest.

"Any you recommend?" he asked David, knowing the foreman would have already measured and determined which would fit.

David pointed to a trunk that was on the slender side, and laborers with long hooks and ropes pulled it out, rolling it onto the dry ground for Jacob's approval.

The mast trunks had been inspected for cracks and irregularities, so he knew it was sturdy. He walked the length of it, envisioning how it would be shaped and set into the deck, then the boom attached, and then the sails. He gave a nod to the laborers. "Get it to the saw pits."

Jacob returned to David Brown. "Have you seen Alden today?"

"Yep." David looked toward the dry-docked *Belladonna.* "Moped around his ship for an hour or so. Think he's in your office now."

Jacob bid the foreman farewell and crossed the yard to the buildings. He was pleased to hear the echoes of blacksmiths, carpenters, and wood carvers performing their skilled work. He glanced at the partially completed brigantine figurehead as he passed, an American eagle that would be placed beneath the bowsprit. The carver had taken particular care, doing quality work with painstaking detail. A pity the skilled craftsman was needed to do menial work at present, cutting trunnels, the wooden pegs that would affix the boards to the sloop.

When Jacob stepped into his office, he found Alden slouched in a chair, his head resting on Jacob's desk, fast asleep. Alden hadn't returned to Jacob's house the night before, choosing instead to spend the evening with his crewmembers in some public house or another. Or perhaps he'd decided to don fisherman's clothing and do what he did best—listen. Alden could assimilate in any circumstance, from a fancy ball to the most squalid tavern. Jacob had watched with fascination as his friend changed his speech, his posture, his appearance, and became a person that fit in so perfectly that others didn't give him a second thought. People of all walks of life trusted him without question, confided in him, believing him to be one of them. He often wondered what his friend had been doing the past years to develop such a skill, but Alden dodged the questions whenever Jacob brought up the subject.

Jacob cleared his throat.

Alden lifted his head and pulled off the piece of paper that stuck to his cheek. Lines of ink showing words in reverse were imprinted on his skin. He blinked bleary eyes then smiled. "Good morning." Alden made a show of taking out his pocket watch and looking surprised when he saw the time.

"Yes. I slept late," Jacob said. He sat in a chair facing the desk.

"I did not think you were capable of that," Alden said.

"I am unpredictable," Jacob said dryly.

Alden snorted. "I hope it means you finally spent some time with your wife. You've avoided her quite splendidly for . . . let's see now . . . your entire marriage."

Jacob rubbed his eyes. "Alden, my wife is lying to me."

Alden blinked. "Lying? Lydia? I don't believe it."

He told his friend everything, from her strange behavior at the ball to what he'd witnessed only an hour earlier.

Alden listened without comment.

"And you should have heard the interpretations she made about particular members of Annapolis society after only one evening. She saw things, small things such as the fit of a jacket or a strange expression passed between two people, and was able to deduce more about those people than I have in years of living among them." He pushed his fingers through his hair. "But when I asked about the Holts, she said she hardly knew them." Hearing it said aloud, he was even more certain that more was going on behind his back than he realized.

Alden scratched his cheek. "There must be another explanation."

"I want to believe so." He described his conversation with Lydia the night before. "She saw that Townsend was worried about something within only a moment of knowing the man."

"Of course she's insightful," Alden said. "She notices things because mingling in society and knowing how to evaluate people and behave toward them is what she's done her entire life."

Alden was right on that account. "But what about the Holts?"

"I don't know." Alden leaned back in the chair, his brows drawing together. "But what possible reason does she have to turn on you? On America? We must ask ourselves what she stands to gain. Money? She doesn't need money. Is she being blackmailed? I hardly think a nineteen-year-old woman has enough of a past for that. Revenge? That doesn't seem likely. If anything, I'd assume she has reason to want revenge on the English." Alden tapped his cheek. "They're the ones who hurt her."

Alden's words made sense, but Jacob couldn't shake the feeling of suspicion and betrayal. She had deceived him; of that he was certain.

"Can you imagine the information Lydia could provide us?" Alden said after a moment. "Knowing who is ill or unfaithful or who carries a grudge? We'd know who could be bribed, who could be bought, who could turn traitor." He pursed his lips. "We could use the advantage."

Sensing his friend was thinking about more than Jacob's worries about his wife, he asked, "What did you learn last night?"

"That the English spy network is more extensive than we imagined." Alden let out a weary sigh. "Captain Smith has ears everywhere."

Jacob was surprised to hear the familiar name. Captain Harry Smith was a well-known veteran of the war in France. He'd fought against Napoleon and must have arrived with General Ross. That the man was one of the army actively conspiring against him gave him a chill.

"A supposed English defector was discovered just days ago in Richmond where he'd ingratiated himself with the American army, pretending to give up English secrets." Alden shook his head. "And there are similar stories coming from everywhere—probably only half are true, but at this point, it doesn't matter. The English are undermining morale. People don't trust one another."

Jacob rested back his head against the wall. The English army was so much more experienced than they were. They seemed to think two moves ahead. And he was certain they had a spy close to him. He moved to the door, opening it quickly, making certain no one was listening, then closed it, returning to his seat. "This business with Brian Gallagher and John Rumson," he said. "There must be a spy in our midst. Someone knew their names, their descriptions, and that they'd be traveling that road. Someone close to me."

"And you think it could be Lydia?" Alden shook his head. "Not possible."

"Haven't you heard what I've been saying?" Jake said. "All the evidence—"

"Jake, don't do this."

Alden's voice was sharp, and Jacob stopped short.

His friend's expression was more intense than Jacob had ever seen. "Don't ruin your relationship over a misunderstanding."

"I can't trust her, Alden."

"Why not? Because you don't know what a woman like her could ever see in a regular man like you? You think there must be some kind of deception? You don't believe that just maybe you deserve to be cared for? That you're good enough for Lydia's affection?"

Jacob was taken aback by Alden's words. "What are you talking about? This has nothing to do with me."

"She likes you, Jake. Maybe even loves you—I know it's strange, since she's your wife." He gave a halfhearted smirk. "Jake, I'm telling you. Don't ruin this. You'll regret it every moment of every day. It will eat at you . . . the hurt doesn't leave. And you'll give anything to have just . . ." He stopped, swallowing hard.

Jake watched his friend, surprised by the pain in his eyes. "Alden, what happened to you?"

Alden shook his head. "Nothing I'd care to discuss right now." He leaned forward, hands on the desk. "But I'll be hanged before I let my brother make the same mistake."

Jacob didn't know what to say. He'd never heard Alden speak so adamantly before about anything that didn't involve cake or his ship.

Alden stood. "I need to sleep, and you need to think." He crossed the room and paused with his hand on the doorknob. "Just remember why you married her in the first place."

Once he left, Jacob moved to sit in his chair. He rested his elbows on his desk. Why *did* he marry Lydia Prescott? Was it out of pity? Partly. Anger? A bit. Duty? He supposed there was some of that. But he'd *married* her. Not just given Jefferson Caraway a dressing down or sent flowers to express sympathy for her injury. He'd known without a doubt that he should marry her. No decision in his life had felt so certain, so clear. He'd of course been attracted to her. Interested in her. He'd noticed her. But why had he married her? He'd better figure out the answer to that question, and soon.

# CHAPTER 11

AFTER THEIR STROLL, LYDIA ACCEPTED the Holts' invitation to stay for a visit. She was happy to have an excuse to chat longer with her friends and of course play with the baby.

Sitting on the sofa, she held little Alexander on her lap, tickling him beneath his chin to make him giggle. She loved the toothless grin and couldn't help but smile back. Miriam sat beside her, and Gerald on a chair facing the women. The sitting room was welcoming, with gauzy curtains and tall windows letting sun bathe the space. Fresh flower arrangements sat on the tables. Lydia took note as to how she could redecorate her own sitting room to achieve the same pleasant ambiance. But she supposed the company also contributed to the cheerful mood.

Lydia tucked the blanket tighter around Alexander, adjusting him so he cuddled against her. "He is such a dear. I wonder, are all babies this happy?"

"Not by a long shot," Gerald said. "We're fortunate he has such a pleasant temperament." He grinned proudly as he often did when he spoke of his son.

"He favors you, Lydia." Miriam smiled at the baby. "And of course my child is an excellent judge of character."

A sudden pang tightened Lydia's throat. She looked between Miriam and Gerald, wishing her marriage was filled with love and tenderness as theirs was. She held up the baby, cupping his head against her shoulder and turning away her face as tears burned her eyes. It seemed her tears from the night before hadn't completely dried.

"Whatever is the matter, dearest?" Miriam said.

Lydia shook her head and glanced at Gerald, not wishing to speak of personal matters with him present. "It is nothing."

Gerald cleared his throat and picked up a book, moving to a chair at the far side of the room to give the women privacy.

"Are things not improving between you and Jacob?" Miriam asked.

Lydia shook her head. Though her marriage had not begun in a conventional manner, she was determined to make the best of her situation. She wanted a happy relationship, wanted a loving home, and aside from Francine, had no one else to confide in beside Miriam. "I thought taking on some of the household duties would give him less to worry about." She thought of all the extra time she'd spent with Mrs. Pembroke, orchestrating the staff's schedules and planning the menu a week ahead to make the kitchen run smoother. "But I don't think he's even noticed."

"Of course he has, dearest." Miriam put a hand on Lydia's shoulder. "You said yourself Jacob has simply been extra busy of late."

Lydia bounced the baby, not wanting to look at her friend. "It's true, but I worry he's avoiding me. He remains at the shipyard well after suppertime, and sometimes days will pass when I don't see him at all." Her face heated at confessing such personal details. She glanced up to see Miriam's reaction. "Jacob hardly speaks to me. And when he does, I sense he's displeased."

"Surely you're mistaken."

Lydia shook her head, feeling miserable. "I don't know how to make this better."

"Perhaps we should ask Gerald?" Miriam kept her voice low, giving Lydia the opportunity to reject the idea without her husband overhearing.

Lydia opened her eyes wide. The idea of confiding her marital concerns to another man felt like a betrayal to Jacob. "No, I don't—"

"I will leave out the details," Miriam cut in. "Trust me. He's used to my strange inquiries."

Still feeling uncomfortable, Lydia grimaced. "If you think it will help."

"Gerald," Miriam spoke in a louder voice, capturing her husband's attention. She waved her fingers. "Come join us."

He set aside the book and returned to his seat across from them. "What can I do for you, ladies?"

Lydia's stomach grew tight as she wondered what her friend would say. She shifted the baby around, cradling him in her elbow as his eyes blinked sleepily.

"Lydia and I would like your opinion, my dear," Miriam said. Her voice sounded casual, as if she were inquiring about whether or not rain was likely this afternoon. "What would you consider the best way to win a man's favor?"

Gerald folded his arms and stretched his legs out in front of him. "I should wonder at the reason behind the query, since both of you are happily married."

Miriam waved her hand. "No reason. We are simply having a discussion, considering what advice we might offer to a lady of our acquaintance."

She looked at Lydia, who nodded innocently.

"For example," Miriam continued. "If Lydia had just met Jacob and wished him to fall in love with her, what advice would you give?"

Lydia's face heated, but she kept her expression friendly, as if they were simply playing a game of speculation.

"Very well, let me think." He tapped his lip with his index finger, looking thoughtful. "Men are simple creatures," he said. "We like to feel important. So, I would tell you, Lydia, to find out what interests Jacob, and learn about it. Or better yet, ask him to teach you."

"And don't forget to compliment him," Miriam said. "Men love to hear how wise or how strong they are." She gave a teasing smile to her husband.

Gerald shrugged. "Like I said, we're simple."

"I know Jacob enjoys building ships," Lydia said.

Gerald snapped his fingers. "Exactly. In Jacob's case, you would ask him about his ships. You could even visit the shipyard."

"And ask him to explain everything in detail," Miriam said.

Gerald looked excited by the prospect. "You can ask who he's building the different ships for and how many guns they hold, how long until a particular ship will be finished . . . things of that nature." He ticked the different items off on his fingers.

"Then make certain to listen as he answers." Miriam winked at Gerald. "Or at least pretend to."

Lydia nodded, her excitement growing. She'd never been to the shipyard, and of course, Jacob would be proud to show her what consumed his time. "That is exactly what I will do . . . *would* do, I mean." She hugged little Alexander close, kissing his forehead, then handed him to Miriam. She didn't want to wait another moment before setting the plan into action. She stood. "Thank you for the stroll and for the pleasant conversation. I will hopefully see you again tomorrow."

Gerald stood as well. "You are always welcome, Lydia."

"And I wish you luck . . . with whatever you do today," Miriam said, stumbling over the words.

Gerald tipped his head and gave his wife a confused look.

Lydia's cheeks heated again, and Miriam smiled. "We'll talk tomorrow."

"Yes. Until tomorrow then. Good day." Lydia curtsied and hurried away.

By the time Lydia arrived at home, her plan was fully in place. She spoke to the cook and arranged to have a luncheon packed into a basket. Then she asked Maggs to order the carriage.

With Francine's assistance, she changed from her morning dress into a light muslin gown and spencer jacket, which she thought looked particularly nice with a flower-embellished chip bonnet. Francine rearranged her hair, letting down some curls to rest on her shoulders and frame her face.

Lydia pulled on the bonnet, tying the ribbons and studying the effect. "What do you think?" she asked her maid. "Does this look suitable for an afternoon at the shipyard?"

Francine shrugged. "I assume so." She set the hairbrush and remaining pins back into their places on the dressing table. "You always look beautiful, Miss Lydia, and you know it." Her words sounded like a reprimand, but Lydia knew they were meant kindly.

Lydia grinned, feeling a thrill at actually doing something of her own initiative instead of sitting at home and wondering whether or not Jacob would return for supper. She couldn't wait to see his delighted expression and to hear everything about shipbuilding. From now on, she'd be involved in that part of his life and know what to ask when he returned home. Why hadn't she thought of it before?

She and Francine rode the short way to the shipyard in the carriage. Not knowing the harbor area of the city very well, Lydia had decided against walking. And also, she wasn't completely certain she'd be able to locate the shipyard. She'd only been there once, on the day they'd arrived from Rosefield, and it had been dark.

Watching out the window, she saw the harbor come into view and had to keep from bouncing in her seat. She twisted her fingers nervously. What would Jacob say when he saw her? Would he be delighted she'd visited, or would he be bothered she'd interrupted his work? He had to be happy, didn't he? She thought about what Gerald had said. Showing an interest in things that were important to Jacob would surely please him. Wouldn't it? This was no time to doubt herself. Lydia smoothed her skirts.

The carriage came to a stop, and the driver took Lydia's hand as she stepped out.

Francine handed her the luncheon basket. "Enjoy yourself, Mrs. Steele," she said, sitting back in the seat, situating herself to do some mending as she waited.

A simple wooden fence surrounded the shipyard, separating it from the rest of the harbor. Behind it, Lydia could see tall masts and the rooftops of buildings. Smoke billowed upward, likely from a blacksmith's forge. Following the sounds of construction, Lydia walked through the open gate and stopped, overwhelmed by the activity and noise of the place. It seemed chaotic and orderly at the same time, with people moving about quickly, but each walking with purpose and surety. Some men carried enormous loads of timber on their shoulders or heavy mallets. Young boys rushed around. People shouted back and forth. Lydia turned her head in every direction, unable to take it all in. Craning her neck, she looked at the large partially built ships surrounding her.

Shifting the basket to hang from her elbow, she glanced around, not knowing where exactly she would find Jacob, and unsure whom to ask. Finally, she started toward the buildings. Those seemed the most likely place for the shipwright's office.

A Negro man carrying a sheaf of papers hurried toward her. "May I be of assistance, madam?"

"Yes, thank you. I'm looking for Jacob Steele."

The man didn't respond but watched her patiently. He seemed to be waiting for her to state her business.

"I'm his wife," Lydia finally said.

He removed his brimmed hat and gave a bow. "David Brown at your service, madam. I'm Mr. Steele's foreman."

She nodded.

David glanced toward the buildings then back at her. "Is Mr. Steele expecting you? I don't believe he mentioned . . ."

Nervousness wiggled through her stomach. Perhaps Jacob did not like to be bothered at the shipyard. "No. I thought to surprise him." She held up the basket as if its presence justified her barging in without an appointment.

"Yes, of course," David said. "Mr. Steele is in his office." He motioned toward the centermost building. "If you'll follow me . . ."

He led her through a two-story workshop. The doors at each end were open wide to allow a breeze, but the space was still sweltering. The clamor of hammering and the grunts and voices of laboring men echoed through the space. Lydia sneezed as sawdust tickled her nose.

She slowed as they passed an incomplete carving. It was tall. At least ten feet high, she guessed. The wood was rough, but she could still identify the statue. An eagle. Perhaps a ship's figurehead. She could clearly see the beak and crudely shaped wings. Knowing this uncompleted piece of wood one day would grace the bow of a sailing ship gave her a tingle of excitement. Seeing a project of such magnitude through to completion must be very satisfying indeed. She could very well see herself developing an interest in her husband's work and couldn't wait to share in this part of his life.

David stopped outside a closed door. He knocked then pushed it open, indicating for Lydia to enter before him.

Her heart pinged nervously. She stepped into the office and hesitated.

David entered behind her.

Jacob sat at a desk in the center of the room, a quill in his hand. When his gaze met hers, his expression clouded. "Lydia?" He turned over the paper he'd been writing on and stood, dropping the quill into the inkpot. "What are you doing here?"

Lydia tried to reassure herself that he was not displeased, just surprised, by the interruption. She glanced around the room, seeing tidy rolls of paper, which she assumed were ship schematics, stacked on a shelf. Books lined another shelf, and below were various tools. "I thought we could take luncheon together." She set the basket on the corner of his desk. "I know it is early, but I thought you could show me the shipyard this morning."

Jacob looked at David, his brow lifting in question.

David shrugged and left, closing the door behind him.

Lydia ignored the interaction, determined to do what Gerald Holt had suggested. She crossed the room and studied a framed picture, a drawing of a ship with numbers and words scribbled around it. "*Gannet*," she read beneath the hull in the drawing. "This is the plan for your ship, isn't it?" She glanced at Jacob, pleased that she'd remembered, then looked back at the picture.

"Yes."

She would need to ask better questions if she was going to get more than one-word answers from him. On a table below the picture was a wooden model. The miniature ship was complete, with small sails and ropes and little cannons on the deck. There was even a tiny figurehead of an eagle on the bow. The detail was fascinating. "And this model . . . did you make it?"

"No," Jacob rounded the desk and joined her. He stood stiffly, with his hands behind his back. "It was built by one of my carpenters."

"Incredible." She pulled off a glove and touched one of the sails. "Is it a model of a ship you've completed? Or is it still under construction?"

"Under construction."

She bent down and peeked into the small portholes. "What kind of ship is it?"

"A brigantine." Jacob's voice sounded strained. "Lydia, I appreciate you bringing lunch, but I am very busy."

"Oh, but surely you have a little time to show me the shipyard." She turned back to the model, searching for another question. "This brigantine will hold twenty cannons?"

Jacob's jaw was tight as he studied her. "Come, I'll walk you out. You brought the carriage?" His eyes were hard.

She nearly shriveled beneath his stern gaze, but she wasn't ready to give up yet. She replaced her glove then took his arm and walked back through the workshop out into the sun.

Lydia cast her gaze around, determined to give another effort. On the far side of the yard, workers were crowded busily around a vessel. "What about that ship over there?" She pulled on his arm. "Is it the brigantine? Will you show it to me? And where is Alden's ship?"

Jacob looked toward the ship she'd pointed out and then back at her. His expression didn't change. "A shipyard is no place for a lady, Lydia. I'd appreciate it if you'd not come again."

Inside, Lydia wilted. She felt as if she'd been struck, and her eyes burned. "I'm sorry to have bothered you, Jacob." She released his arm, humiliation turning to pride. She wouldn't allow him to see how he'd hurt her. "I can find my way to the carriage."

She stormed away, furious. And she became all the more furious when he didn't try to stop her.

When she reached the carriage, Burnett, the driver, hurried to open the door and help her inside.

Lydia sat on the bench, not meeting Francine's gaze. She knew if she did, her anger would dissolve into tears, and she wanted to hold on to her outrage a bit longer. A woman couldn't think straight when tears were involved.

Francine knew her mistress well enough to keep silent.

Lydia lifted her chin, looking out the opposite window, avoiding the view of the shipyard. "Very well, Jacob Steele," she said under her breath as the carriage started away. "You have made your feelings very clear, and I shall not pine for your affection one instant more."

# CHAPTER 12

JACOB RUBBED HIS EYES. THE late nights of the past months were taking a toll. His shoulders ached, and he massaged his neck, bending his head from side to side. He and Alden had returned from a rendezvous with Mr. Townsend well after midnight, and the two had spent the better part of an hour in his library as Jacob confided his latest suspicions about Lydia.

"I've an absurd idea for you." Alden held up his index finger. "One you have likely never considered."

"And what is that?" Jacob asked, not liking how smug his friend looked.

"You could just *ask her*."

He puffed out a breath. "It isn't that easy."

Alden nodded and shrugged one shoulder. "Oh, I'm certain the conversation will be a bit uncomfortable, but—"

Jacob cut him off. "A *bit* uncomfortable?"

"I do realize, charging one's wife with wartime espionage is never pleasant. But Lydia should have an opportunity to defend herself. I'm certain her actions can be explained away simply." His expression turned serious, and he leaned forward in his seat, leaning his elbows on his knees. "And you must ask yourself, what is the alternative?"

Jacob scratched his cheek. He was exhausted, his responsibilities and worries pulling him in every direction until he was unable keep up with all of it. "I honestly don't know."

"Avoiding her? Finding excuses to return home well after supper for the rest of your life?"

Jacob resented how the conversation had been turned around. *He* wasn't the guilty party in this case. "I told you the questions she asked at the shipyard. She was gathering information. She's working for someone."

"You must admit, the way she went about it . . . she wasn't exactly stealthy." Alden shook his head. "Lydia is much cleverer than that."

"But—"

"I still think her behavior is innocent . . . perhaps she just wishes to know her husband better."

"She inquired directly about the brigantine." Jacob's frustration that his friend couldn't see the very obvious truth made his head throb. "And why else would she ask about Commodore Barney's sloop?"

Alden gave him a flat look. "In spite of other, more deserving vessels needing care, the sloop is the only ship being worked on at the moment. With all that activity, of course she'd notice it. And the brigantine is an enormous hulk directly in front of the entrance."

"You're forgetting her lies about the Holts."

Alden let out a tired-sounding breath. "Jake, I think you're making excuses."

"Excuses for what?" He scowled. The situation was more complex than Alden realized, and yet his friend acted as if the answers were obvious. In this circumstance, Jacob wasn't at fault.

"You're like me. We don't trust easily." Alden sat back, his forehead wrinkled. "We're orphans. We've been abandoned, unwanted, shuffled from place to place, mistreated . . . allowing anyone to be near to us is difficult."

Jacob didn't like how close to the truth Alden's words felt. Was it truly easier to believe his wife to be guilty of treason than to make himself emotionally vulnerable? He shifted uncomfortably in his chair. No, rather, he *squirmed*.

"We cope similarly," Alden continued. "By burying ourselves in work. Easier than having empty hours that fill with unwelcome introspection." He grimaced.

Jacob was certainly guilty of that. Keeping his mind and body active prevented him from looking too closely at his insecurities.

"Honestly, Jake," Alden said. "A few moments of conversation would set this entire business to rest."

"And what if she confesses? Or lies?"

"What if you're destroying your marriage because doubt is easier?" Alden held up his hands as if they were a scale, weighing the two choices. "Because the alternative is to trust her, and that frightens you. To allow her to come to know you, to get close, to discover your faults and weaknesses and hope she doesn't spurn you or run away."

Jacob's scowl deepened, crunching his eyebrows together painfully. Was Alden right? Was he blinded by his own cowardice? The thought that he was the type of man to accuse an innocent person just to avoid facing his self-doubt was despicable. His stomach soured.

"So." Alden rested back in his chair. His manner eased, and Jacob was glad he'd decided to leave the subject. "Where are those bedeviled redcoats? Why haven't we heard anything?"

Jacob relaxed, thinking it ironic that discussing an enemy invasion was easier than talking about his marriage.

The English ships had landed in Bermuda weeks earlier. Surely the troops weren't just enjoying a seaside holiday. "Townsend fears another messenger was intercepted. We should have heard something by now."

"Or the English are lying low." Alden pursed his lips. "Waiting for reinforcements?"

"They *have* reinforcements," Jacob said. "Two transports filled with them. They'd be foolish not to utilize the fresh troops." He rubbed his eyes again. "And General Robert Ross is far from foolish."

"Perhaps they've arrived and we just haven't received word," Alden said, reiterating the discussion they'd been having for weeks. "If they've prevented messengers from getting to us or Washington, who knows what havoc those troops may have wrought?"

Jacob stood. "This same conversation is getting us nowhere."

"I agree." Alden rose and stretched. "Besides, I'm late for an appointment with my pillow." He gave a theatrical yawn.

Jacob bid his friend good night and retired to his own bedchamber. His body was bone weary, but his mind was too active for sleep. Pushing aside the curtains, he looked through the window at the moonlit garden beneath. Alden's words from this morning had haunted him all day. *Just remember why you married her in the first place.* Why *had* he done it? At the time, he'd felt so certain it was the right thing to do. But had his true reasons gone deeper than chivalry? Had he married Lydia because it was safe? Because her circumstance left her with few options, and he wouldn't be rejected?

Was he really that selfish? He hoped not.

He turned from the window and sank into a chair. The first meeting with Lydia hadn't been ideal. She'd seemed silly and frivolous, but thinking back, he'd seen that she was a person who knew what she wanted and used the means at her disposal to achieve it. She'd moved about the rose garden party with purpose and confidence he'd admired. She was witty and able to carry on an intelligent conversation. He thought of how she'd teased Alden, how she'd flirted with gentlemen at the party.

Had Jacob been jealous? Had he wished her attention had been directed at him, instead of her avoidance?

His musings left him feeling off-balance. Alden's words made Jacob question what sort of man he was, and the answers made his chest burn with shame.

He was an admirable man, wasn't he? He'd saved her from the fire. He'd charged in and preserved her honor when her vapid fiancé had cried off. She'd needed him.

Hadn't she?

Or was the reality that Jacob needed to feel needed?

Hearing a crash from the adjoining bedchamber, he jerked to attention. Another crash sounded, and a thud. Had the mouse returned?

Jacob snatched up a candle and opened the door between his room and his wife's. He stepped through, feeling a wave of uncertainty as he entered her private space through the conspicuously unused opening.

The fishy smell of lamp oil assaulted his nose.

In the moonlight, he saw Lydia's hair was wrapped in little balls held by strips of fabric, and she wore only her nightdress. She knelt on the floor, her shoulders shaking as she collected shards of glass into a pile on a handkerchief she'd spread out on in front of her.

"Lydia?"

She glanced up at him, trails of tears shining on her cheeks, then turned her gaze back down. Her lips trembled in an expression that tore at his heart.

He crouched beside her. "Are you hurt?" He took her hands, looking them over for lacerations.

She shook her head, pulling away. "Go back to sleep, Jacob." Her words were clipped and sounded angry. Apparently she wasn't going to forgive his earlier rudeness easily.

He took her hands again, this time pulling her up to stand. "You'll cut your fingers. Come now, it's just a lamp. The mess can be cleaned away in the morning." He looked down at her bare feet, worried she'd cut them on the glass.

Lydia didn't resist, allowing him to lead her away from the broken lamp.

"What happened?"

She sniffed. "I woke, and the room was dark." Her voice choked, and she pressed a hand to her mouth.

Jacob realized she wasn't weeping over the broken lamp at all. "Your dream."

Lydia nodded, her sobs growing louder.

He pulled her into an embrace and let her cry against his chest.

The outer door opened, and Francine poked her head inside. Her eyes widened when she saw Jacob then winced in apology.

He smiled and gave a nod, letting her know he had the situation in hand.

The maid departed, closing the door quietly. The duty of consoling Lydia now belonged to Jacob, and he took the responsibility seriously.

He held her, letting her cry, and muttered words meant to comfort, though he didn't know whether she listened or not. It didn't matter. The important thing was that Lydia knew she wasn't alone. He patted her back, holding her close, hoping to soothe away her fears.

As time passed, her weeping slowed until all that remained was the occasional sniff. Her ear was pressed to his chest, and he wondered if she were listening to his heart.

Lydia rubbed her hand over the wet front of his shirt. "I'm sorry, Jacob," she whispered. "It really is so childish of me to fall apart like this."

"Your fears aren't childish."

"But my reaction is embarrassing." She glanced up at him with red, wet eyes. "I know it isn't real, but my mind can't make the rest of me behave rationally."

"There is no need for embarrassment." He stepped back, drawing away.

But Lydia held on to his lapels. "Wait." Her eyes looked panicked. "Will you stay until I fall asleep?"

Jacob nodded. He stepped to the bed, lying on his back and pulling her down to lie beside him.

Lydia curled up, resting her head on his chest, her knees against the side of his leg. She flattened her palm on his breastbone.

He tightened his arm around her. Everything about the moment felt soft and warm, and Jacob realized this intimacy was something he'd longed for. This sort of closeness was how a marriage was supposed to be. Comforting one another, whispered words across pillows. If only he could dispel the uncertainty regarding Lydia's intentions. Was she manipulating him? Why couldn't he simply enjoy the moment without skepticism taking over his thoughts? Was Alden right? Was Jacob creating suspicion to avoid letting her close?

Her breathing grew deeper, and her body relaxed against him, her head settling below his collarbone.

"Aren't you afraid of anything, Jacob?"

The sound of Lydia's sleepy voice startled him from his brooding. He'd thought she was asleep. Afraid of anything? He'd always assumed himself above such nonsense, but his conversation with Alden had led his mind down paths he'd avoided for more than twenty years, and he realized he wasn't immune to fears. His were just so deeply buried he'd been able to ignore them.

"Spiders," he said after a moment. *There, Alden. How's that for being vulnerable?*

Her head moved, nestling against his chest. "But you're so big . . . and spiders are so small."

"Unnatural is what they are. The way they move, all those hairy jointed legs." In spite of himself, he shivered.

Lydia shook softly.

"Are you laughing?"

"Of course not." She yawned. "But, you know, even the very largest spiders are small enough to step on."

"They're still horrible."

More of the soft shaking. She *was* laughing.

Lydia sighed and nestled closer. Her breathing deepened.

"Jacob?"

Her voice startled him again. "Yes?"

"If you will hold me when I have a frightening dream, I will smash spiders for you."

Her words were spoken in a sleepy haze, but they were genuine, with no mocking at all. The sincerity of the statement heated his heart and spread through his body in a delicious warmth.

Lydia's breathing slowed, her head grew heavier on his chest, and the conflict that had raged inside Jacob seemed to drift far away as he inhaled the flowery smell of her, kissed her head with its silly wrapped balls of hair, and sank into a contented sleep.

A banging woke Jacob with a start. He looked around, disoriented. A moment passed before he remembered he was in Lydia's bedchamber.

Through the crack in her curtains, a faint purple shone in the sky, indicating the approach of dawn. The banging echoed through the hallway, and he came fully alert, recognizing the sound. Someone was knocking on his front door, and from the sound of it, the business was urgent.

He heard the door open and a muffled exchange take place in the entry-way below. Maggs had awoken. Jacob eased his arm from beneath Lydia and rose carefully, tucking the blankets around her, avoiding the broken lamp, and creeping out into the passageway.

Maggs met him on the stairs wearing a night coat, cap, and his usual bored expression. He handed Jacob an envelope. "Express messenger, sir."

Jacob tore it open and read. The message was brief:

*HMS Albion leading squadron en route to Pig Point. —T*

The English were going after the flotilla. Jacob's gut sank. He needed to get word to Commodore Barney as quickly as possible. The flotilla was trapped in the Patuxent, and the English warship would block their escape. They were sitting ducks.

He thrust the message at Maggs. "Wake Alden. Give him this." Jacob hurried to the library.

Alden burst into the room less than a minute later. "I'll go," he said without preamble.

"It's dangerous," Jacob said. Though his nerves tingled with the same urgency Alden displayed, he knew caution was key. "Remember what happened to Brian and John. We can't risk the message not arriving." He glanced at Alden, fear for his friend's safety making his insides tight.

"I understand." Alden paced, nervous energy apparent in his movement. "But if Barney isn't warned, the warship will take the flotilla by surprise."

"The road is being watched. *We* are being watched," Jacob said. "The risk is too great. I should go."

Alden lifted a brow. "You are hardly inconspicuous."

Jacob knew Alden was right; his large stature made him instantly recognizable. "You would be identified as well."

Alden whirled and snapped his fingers. "I'll go in disguise." He grinned and rushed from the room.

Hearing a commotion outside, Jacob moved to the window. The sun had risen fully and shone on an arriving wagon. He nodded, pleased to see the servants from Rosefield had finally arrived. Negotiations with Beauregard Prescott for the two employees had dragged out much longer than he'd expected. He'd hoped to surprise Lydia sooner. Jacob smiled, thinking how agreeable it felt to wake with her in his arms. Although he hadn't particularly enjoyed being woken so abruptly.

He watched as Mrs. Pembroke greeted the new employees and wondered how long it would be before Lydia learned of their arrival.

He turned, smiling at the vase of roses on the table and the lighter, airy curtains. In just a few months, his wife had made the house feel warmer—more like a home.

The door burst open behind him. Alden hurried in again, his arms full of fabric. "I've been waiting for an opportunity to wear this." He dumped the pile onto a chair and lifted a large mustard-colored gown by the sleeves, holding it up to his shoulders. "What do you think?"

He then showed Jacob a shawl and a bonnet. "The English will never suspect a woman."

"A woman riding alone will look suspicious."

Alden scowled. "I'm fast. They won't even have time to wonder where my chaperone has gotten to." He put on the bonnet, tying it beneath his chin. "We have no other choice."

Jacob tapped his lip with his forefinger. "There is another choice."

"The gown is much too small for you, and besides, yellow really isn't your color."

Jacob motioned Alden close, not knowing if their conversation was being overheard. The messenger would have undoubtedly drawn the notice of anyone paying particular attention to the house.

"You ride—in disguise, if you like. Take the main road." He spoke in a voice so low Alden moved closer and pushed back the bonnet so he could hear.

"I'll leave at the same time, but I'll head south and cross the river at Donovan's pier."

Alden nodded. "If we're observed, I'll be a distraction."

"We'll rendezvous at Pig Point," Jacob said. "But for now, we act as if only you are going."

Alden tapped the side of his nose and winked. "Good plan. Now do be a dear and help me with all these petticoats." He removed his shirt and pulled the gown over his head, shoving his arms into the sleeves.

"Where did you get the dress, anyway?" Jacob grimaced at the sight of Alden's muscular arms straining the lacey ruffles.

Alden smirked and shrugged. "A lady never reveals her secrets." He held out the skirts. "It flatters my figure, don't you think? I wouldn't be surprised if I received quite a few offers of marriage . . ." He squatted in a clumsy curtsy.

"Stop moving while I fasten your buttons." Jacob rolled his eyes and couldn't help but think how much more pleasant his life had been only an hour earlier.

# Chapter 13

"Miss Lydia, wake up, if you please." Francine shook Lydia's shoulder as she whispered.

Lydia cracked open her eyes and saw her maid standing beside her bed wearing a wide smile. She stretched and sat up, glancing at the window. Morning had come, but it was still early. "Francine, what's happened?" She couldn't imagine a reason for the maid to shake her awake.

"I'm sorry, I just couldn't wait to thank you." Francine pulled her into a tight embrace.

Not knowing what else to do, Lydia squeezed her in return. "Thank me? Whatever for?"

Francine pulled back, holding on to Lydia's arms. Her brown eyes were wet with tears. "Henrietta and Ezra arrived this morning." She pulled Lydia into another embrace. "Thank you."

Warmth covered Lydia's heart. "I did not know. Jacob must have . . ." The heat spread, covering her cheeks as she remembered the night before. She'd slept, warm and comforted in her husband's embrace, listening to the reassuring sound of his heart. She couldn't stop a giddy smile from growing at the memory. Jacob must have risen early. But perhaps he'd not left for the shipyard just yet. She threw off the blankets.

Francine crouched down to pick up pieces of glass.

"Don't worry about the lamp, Francine. Help me to dress. I want to find Jacob." She walked on her toes, careful to avoid the glass, and sat at the dressing table. "And welcome Henrietta and Ezra, of course."

Twenty minutes later, Lydia skipped down the stairs. Her grin hadn't faded, and her heart felt light. She found Henrietta and Ezra in the kitchen with Mrs. Pembroke. The two newest additions to the household staff looked uncertain.

Henrietta curtsied when she saw Lydia, and Ezra bent forward in a bow.

"I'm so glad you're here," Lydia said. "You will love Annapolis."

"Mr. Steele has given us freedom papers," Henrietta said. Her brows pinched together, and she looked bewildered by the unexpected circumstance.

Lydia smiled, feeling proud that Jacob had done something so selfless. He really was wonderful. "We do hope you agree to remain here in our employ—you have the choice now, you know."

Ezra looked at his mother, his young eyes still harboring suspicion.

"Thank you," Henrietta said.

"Mrs. Pembroke and Francine will show you your duties," Lydia said. "And Ezra, we have no gardener on staff, and the park needs quite a lot of work. Once you've had an opportunity to look it over, we can discuss what assistance you need."

"Yes, ma'am." He watched her cautiously, as if waiting for the truth of the situation to be revealed.

He would realize soon enough that all of this was real, she decided. She bid the servants farewell and went in search of Jacob.

Maggs stood in the front hall looking out through the curtains. He turned and inclined his head when Lydia approached.

"Has Mr. Steele left for the shipyard?" she asked.

"No, madam." He lifted his hand toward the doors on the other side of the hall. "I believe he is in the library."

Lydia thanked him. Her heart flitted around inside her chest. She heard Jacob's voice on the other side of the door, and her hands felt shaky. She arranged her curls over her shoulder and smoothed her skirts. Feeling self-conscious to be caught preening, she glanced back, but fortunately Maggs had gone.

Grinning with a fresh blush on her cheeks, Lydia pushed open the door and stepped into the library. "Jacob, I—"

Jacob spun toward her, a surprised expression on his face.

She froze, trying to make sense of the scene before her.

Jacob had been interrupted in the act of fastening a woman's dress.

Lydia's ribs squeezed until she couldn't draw a breath. Spots flashed in her eyes. This couldn't be real.

The woman's bonnet shadowed her features. Lydia couldn't bear to see the face, and before the woman could fully turn, Lydia ran.

Jacob called after her, but she didn't stop. Rushing through the dining room, then the kitchen, she ignored the servants' questions and hurried out the door. She ran into the garden, then around the side of the house, not even certain where she was going. Entering back into the house through the servants' door, she closed herself into a closet, sitting on the cold floor and wrapping her arms around her knees. She fought to breathe through a constricted throat, closing her eyes and leaning back her head against a shelf. Her entire body was hot, and at the same time, she shivered.

*I am a fool.*

Her stomach turned sour as the reality of the past months came into focus. Jacob returned home late every night. He'd been secretive, evasive. When she'd surprised him at the shipyard, he'd been angry. How had she not seen the truth? It had been there all along, and she'd chosen to ignore it. She squeezed closed her eyes. She'd deluded herself into believing—an ache pierced her heart, and she pushed her fist against her mouth, not allowing herself to weep.

How could she have ever believed Jacob would love her in spite of . . . Her finger traced the scar on her cheek.

She felt naïve and foolish. Jacob hadn't wanted to marry her. He didn't care for her. Of course her father had made Jacob an offer he couldn't refuse. Why else would he have taken on a disfigured bride?

In spite of her resolve to stay strong, tears slipped down her cheeks.

Last night, she'd hoped—

She cut off the thought. It didn't matter now. Concentrating on drawing soothing breaths, she pushed away her emotions. She needed to think, to decide how to proceed. One thing was clear: she couldn't remain here in this house any longer. She wasn't the type of woman to turn a blind eye to a husband's dalliance. Even though her name would be permanently disgraced, Lydia decided her best course was to return to her parents at Rosefield.

A pang of sadness caught in her already-raw throat. She loved Annapolis, loved this house with the roses carved on her mantel, loved her friends, and had grown fond of the household staff. Returning home . . . Despair filled her like dark smoke, but she shook it away. It was what she had to do.

Lydia remained in the closet, weeping and planning, and feeling both angry and very sorry for herself as she pondered her situation, unaware of the passage of time until she heard voices in the corridor outside the closet. She'd been so caught up in her own concerns she didn't know when the voices had begun and only now paid them attention because she didn't want anyone to see her leave the closet and question what she'd been doing hiding away.

One she recognized as Maggs, and the other was a man's voice that sounded unfamiliar. She wondered how long they intended to speak in the passageway and leaned her ear to the door to listen.

"Going after the flotilla is a diversion," the stranger said. "The real goal is Washington City."

Lydia grew still.

"Surely the squadron can't carry enough troops to attack both the flotilla and the capital," Maggs said. "It would be too heavy to sail high into the river."

The stranger laughed. "Like I said, the squadron is a diversion. Ross and his men were delivered to Benedict earlier this week. They'll march to Pig Point, destroy the flotilla, and then continue on through Upper Marlboro to Washington City. The squadron is carrying supplies and weapons. And at the same time, Gordon is sailing up the Potomac to attack Fort Washington."

"When should they arrive?"

"Two days," the stranger said. "Maybe three."

Lydia's heart pounded in her ears. Was she hearing correctly? Her mind raced to understand the implications of the conversation. If what the stranger said was true, Washington City would be caught unawares. Heat flushed over her skin. Maggs was a traitor. A turncoat living in her very house. She glared through the door.

". . . departed on horseback less than an hour ago," Maggs was saying. "A very unfortunate disguise."

The stranger chuckled, and Lydia wished she could see his face. She would be delighted to be able to identify the man who bore secrets that would lead men to their deaths.

Her heart continued to pound. She held painfully still, knowing she'd be in danger if she were discovered. She must find a way to warn President Madison, and time was of the essence.

Although Jacob Steele was the last person she wanted to see, Lydia needed to speak to her husband. He needed to be informed that his butler wasn't trustworthy, and he would know how to get word of the danger to President Madison.

Lydia waited until long after the corridor was silent, not wishing to emerge from the closet and encounter the butler. When she finally mustered the courage, she opened the door slowly then hurried through the servants' quarters, emerging in the kitchen.

Francine's eyes widened when she saw Lydia. "Madam, your gown . . ."

Glancing down, Lydia saw that her dress was covered in dirt from crouching on the closet floor. "Yes, will you help me to change, Francine?" She kept her voice light in case Maggs might be listening. She glanced around the kitchen and saw Henrietta and the cook were kneading bread. Neither appeared overly concerned by Lydia's appearance.

"Of course." Francine's eyes were narrowed in confusion, but she did not ask any questions.

When they were back in Lydia's bedchamber, Lydia asked, "Has Mr. Steele left for the shipyard?"

"I believe so," Francine said. "About an hour ago."

Lydia nodded, pulling off her soiled dress. She washed her hands and face in the water basin, surprised by the amount of dust she'd accumulated in the closet.

Francine brought a cloth for Lydia to dry herself. "Are you all right, madam?"

"Yes." Lydia made her spinning mind focus on the business at hand. "I just have a lot to think about today."

Francine helped her to dress, then Lydia sent for the carriage.

Maggs met her in the front hallway, his expression bored and condescending.

Lydia could hardly force herself to look at the man, but she smiled, hoping it appeared convincing. "I thought to pay a visit to Mr. Steele this morning," she said.

"Very well, madam." Maggs sniffed as if he couldn't care less about her plans, which suited Lydia just fine.

When she arrived at the shipyard, David Brown met her at the entrance. He pulled off his hat. "Good morning, Mrs. Steele."

"Good morning. I've come to speak to my husband. Is he in his office?"

"I'm afraid Mr. Steele hasn't arrived today." David glanced at the carriage behind her as if Jacob would step out at any moment.

"Oh." The sour stomach returned. "And do you know where he might be?"

He shook his head. "I'm sorry."

Lydia didn't know where he was, but she had an idea of whom he was with, and it made her chest burn.

"And Mr. Thatcher?"

"Haven't seen him today, either, Mrs. Steele."

Lydia returned to the carriage, instructing Burnett to take her home.

She slumped back against the carriage seat. This problem felt so much bigger than Lydia knew how to handle on her own, and she couldn't count on Jacob for help. For a moment she considered going to the Holts, but something stopped her. Part of her felt wary of trusting anyone after a man in her own household had proven to be an English informant. And another part of her felt like she shouldn't involve her friends. Information such as this could put them in danger, and they had little Alexander to worry about.

Who else could she ask for help? Most of Annapolis was deserted; even the militia had gone to fight elsewhere.

She wished Emmett were here. He'd know exactly how to handle this, but he was away in Canada, defending the northern border.

Though she tried to come up with other options, Lydia realized she was on her own. Her skin tingled as dismay filled every bit of her, but she didn't allow it to linger. Fear would only lead to despair, and there was no time to wallow. Two days was all the time Washington City had. And it would take a message at least one day to get there.

Pushing back her shoulders, she sat tall. She could do this. If she failed, the results could be catastrophic. America could fall to the English. President Madison could be captured. Men would be killed. She had to warn Washington.

But a woman could hardly march up the steps of the capitol building and demand an audience with the president. She remembered the stern John Armstrong, Secretary of War. He was a close friend of her father's. Perhaps he would receive her. But would he believe her? Or think she was just a silly woman, paranoid and given to hysterics? And there was still the challenge of getting herself to Washington. The information was too sensitive to trust a messenger. Not only would she need to travel the fifty miles, she'd need to do it without the head of the household staff knowing what she was doing.

Lydia stepped out of the carriage and told Burnett not to unhitch the horses. She'd be back soon. She'd pretend she was going to the shops on Main Street and wait to tell him the true destination once they were away from the house. For an instant she wondered if she could trust Burnett, but she told herself she had no other choice.

The driver nodded his understanding and remained with the carriage.

She found Francine right away. The two hurried up the stairs, and fortunately the butler was nowhere in sight. Once they were safely in Lydia's bedchamber, she closed the door and motioned to her maid to come closer. "Francine, can you pack a bag for me? I need to go to Washington City, and I don't know how long I'll be there." Francine would have a better chance than Lydia of stashing the bag in the carriage without Maggs seeing.

Lydia wondered whether she'd send for her maid once she was back at Rosefield, but separating Francine from her sister and nephew when the three had been so recently reunited seemed cruel. And she didn't think her father would agree to hire the former slaves back as paid servants. She shook her head, deciding to focus on one problem at a time.

"We're going to Washington today?" Francine asked.

"Just me," Lydia clarified. "And it's a secret. No one can know where I've gone. Especially not Maggs."

Francine blinked. "And what about Mr. Steele?"

Lydia considered for a moment. Should she write a letter? What would she say? She couldn't risk telling him where she was going or why. Not when Maggs might discover it. And just remembering him with that . . . that *woman* made her stomach so nauseated she could hardly think. She could leave a scathing letter telling him exactly what she thought of a man who betrayed his wife, but just putting her thoughts into words made the sick feeling worse.

She sat in her dressing table chair. "I don't know what to say to him."

Francine moved behind her and set her hands on Lydia's shoulders, looking at her in the mirror as she'd done since Lydia was a young girl. "Then, you shouldn't write anything. Not when you may regret it later."

Lydia nodded, thinking how she'd miss her maid. Francine had been a steady presence in her life. The voice of reason, of practicality and love. She put her hands over her friend's fingers, giving a squeeze. "You're right, of course."

"You'll know what to say when the time is right, Miss Lydia."

Lydia squeezed her fingers again, grateful for someone who believed in her, and hoping she could find the strength to believe in herself.

# CHAPTER 14

Jacob rode harder than either he or his horse was used to. He, at least, would be feeling it tomorrow. His back was already sore. "Come on, Hildegard," he muttered to the animal. "Just a bit farther, then you can rest on the ferry." Once he crossed the river, they'd only have a few hours until they reached the Patuxent and the flotilla anchored at Pig Point near Upper Marlboro. And he prayed Alden would be there waiting for him.

His friend's path was much easier, following a well-traveled road and crossing at a bridge. He should arrive at least an hour ahead of Jacob. But . . . Jacob spurred the horse on quicker. If Alden met with any opposition, if their plan had been overheard and enemies lay in wait to intercept him . . . Jacob's mouth was dry as he imagined his closest friend—his brother—coming upon trouble.

He and Hildegard boarded the ferry, and Jacob tapped his foot nervously as the ferryman conveyed them over South River. His worry only increased as he thought about Commodore Barney's flotilla. With no warning of the English ships bearing down on them, they'd be destroyed. Men would die, and the British would confiscate vessels and cannons to use against the American army. And who knew what their plans were from there? They'd be in a good position to attack Annapolis and Baltimore, not to mention Washington City.

Once they disembarked and paid the ferryman, Jacob swung into the saddle again, wincing at his sore muscles but pushing himself and the animal onward. Hildegard was a good horse, and he really should ride more often, but as with everything else he used to enjoy, he'd been too busy of late, as his aching back testified.

He wondered if Lydia rode. Perhaps she'd enjoy an outing with him along the bay. Maybe even a picnic.

This morning, Lydia's reaction to seeing Alden's disguise had come as a surprise. She'd hurried away, leaving the two of them questioning what exactly she'd been thinking. Had she worried she was interrupting an important meeting? Or had the sight of Alden in a yellow dress so horrified her that she'd been unable to look upon the abomination any longer? That was the theory he'd proposed to Alden.

But his friend had shaken it off, claiming Lydia had been jealous of how well he carried off the look that she'd run off out of shame, knowing she would never match his elegance.

Even though his friend was not there to see, Jacob rolled his eyes.

He rode away from the river and along a path through the trees. Even though it was still morning, the day was already hot and humid, and the shade was a relief. This summer had been the hottest in recent memory, and he hoped the British soldiers, sitting in their sweltering ships, were miserable.

Jacob's senses were on alert, wearing him out more quickly than usual. Traveling alone had never worried him. He'd journeyed on horseback along most of the roads in the southern states at one time or another, but today, he was extra vigilant, listening, scrutinizing the sides of the path carefully. He knew there were enemy spies watching the roads, and the message he carried made him feel vulnerable. He tightened his hand over the musket that lay across his saddle.

Why *had* Lydia fled the library? Had she overheard their plans and hurried away to tell someone? He shook his head, not wanting his mind to travel that path again. She'd likely thought Jacob would be alone and, when she'd seen that he wasn't, had wanted to give him privacy.

Neither theory felt right. And his earlier suspicions pushed their way back into his thoughts. Her action had seemed . . . unusual. And that set his instincts on alert.

But even if Lydia was the one giving information to the English, he had to believe she wouldn't betray Alden. Lydia was kind. She loved her father's slaves and worried for their welfare. He knew she was fond of Alden. She just couldn't be capable of hurting a person she cared about. Or at least pretended to care about.

These very thoughts had been the source of discord from the beginning, and he'd not allow them to destroy his marriage. "Stop," he said aloud to himself, pushing the doubts from his mind.

Hildegard's ears poked upward.

He reached forward and patted the horse's flank. "Not you, old girl."

Once he could see the tops of the sailing masts through the trees, Jacob let himself relax. He'd made it. The cool river air blew over him, and he could hear the noise of the men's encampment.

As he approached the bend in the river where the flotilla was anchored, two militia soldiers stepped into the road ahead of him, muskets at the ready.

Jacob recognized one of them. "Good afternoon, Mr. Davis."

Michael Davis lowered his musket and squinted. Then he waved and smiled, pushing back his father's Revolutionary War tricorn hat that he wore for luck. "Well met, Mr. Steele. You've come to speak with the commodore?"

Jacob dismounted. "I have."

"Charlie'll water your horse." Michael nodded to his companion.

The man saluted and took the reins from Jacob, leading the horse away.

"Has Alden Thatcher arrived today?" Jacob asked.

Michael shook his head. "Haven't seen him."

Jacob pursed his lips and nodded.

"You look concerned," Michael said as the two started toward the waterfront.

Jacob glanced at his companion. Michael Davis had been with Jacob when they'd defended Rosefield Park. A fine fighter and waterman, Michael was in his early thirties, a few years older than Jacob. He'd been raised on a farm on the western outskirts of Washington City, where he lived now with his family. Elnora always insisted that her eggs and milk came from the Davis farm, so Jacob had known him since they were both in their teen years. He liked Michael quite a lot, respected his happy manner and his loyalty to America and Commodore Barney.

"I *am* concerned," Jacob said.

Barney's flagship, the *Scorpion*, stood out among the collection of barges and gunboats. The five-gun cutter floated beside its companion, the *Asp*. Jacob's news meant these two beautiful ships, as well as the others surrounding them, would be scuttled. Everything inside him screamed against it. He'd built some of the barges, repaired nearly all of the boats at one time or another, and the two cutters with their elegant lines and tall masts . . . the thought of destroying them was physically painful.

When Jacob and Michael boarded the *Scorpion*, they were escorted to the commodore's quarters. Jacob admired the planking on the bulwark and the deck. He ran his hand along the rail of the companionway then rubbed his eyes, knowing the ship was doomed.

Commodore Barney sat writing at a table in the captain's drawing room. The inside of the ship was sweltering, in spite of the open stern windows. Barney stood when they entered, and smiled. "Mr. Steele. A pleasure to see you, sir."

"Commodore." Jacob inclined his head.

"Mr. Davis," Barney nodded.

Michael saluted.

Barney's eyes narrowed as he studied Jacob's face. "By your expression, sir, I presume you bring unpleasant news." He motioned for the two men to be seated.

"A messenger arrived in Annapolis this morning." Jacob didn't bother with formalities. There was no time for chitchat. "*HMS Albion* is leading a squadron up the Patuxent."

Barney scowled and pulled at his lower lip. "I see."

"They're after the flotilla, sir."

"You trust the sender of the message?"

"I do."

Barney nodded then stood, releasing a heavy breath. "In that case, we've only one course." He turned to Michael. "Remove whatever cannons you're able to save, sink the rest." He squeezed his eyes shut and swallowed. When he opened them, his expression held a firm resolve. "And set explosives to scuttle the flotilla. We'll not let those redcoats take these vessels."

Michael saluted and set off to convey the commodore's orders.

Jacob was once again impressed by Joshua Barney's ability to command. He saw the situation clearly, decided on a course of action, and then implemented it without second thought. He'd been commanding ships since he was fifteen, and the confidence that radiated off him was nearly visible. A natural leader.

"You know these vessels better than anyone, Mr. Steele. If you please, would you advise the men as to where to set the charges?"

"Yes, sir." Jacob nodded, and seeing the words were meant as a dismissal, he departed.

Jacob consulted with the flotilla men responsible for the explosives, impressed at the watermen's knowledge of gunpowder, tar, and placement of the fuses. Once they'd all come to an agreement of the best methods to scuttle the flotilla, he left the men to their work and went in search of Michael Davis.

He found him directing the loading of cannons onto wagons.

"Still no sign of Alden?" Jacob asked, wiping his damp brow.

"I'm afraid not."

One of the wagons was struggling as the heavy guns sank the wheels into the mud at the edge of the river. Jacob jogged over and lent his shoulder to the cause. He joined the men, giving a grunt and shoving until the wheels came free and the horses pulled the wagon onto higher ground. It felt good to be doing something while he waited for news of his friend. Anything was better than festering and worrying.

Moving the cannons was difficult work, and in the end, the wagons were only able to save a few as well as their cannonballs. The rest of the guns were heaved overboard into the river.

Commodore Barney stood stoically on the deck of the flagship, watching the operation, and Jacob could only imagine how the man must be dreading what was to come. But if the commodore felt any hesitation about the course of action, he didn't show it—not in front of the men who would follow his orders without question. He held his head high, as he had throughout the campaign, and, Jacob imagined, throughout his years in the navy. His utter determination reassured those in his command.

Jacob boarded the *Scorpion* once again and crossed the deck to join Barney.

The commodore nodded a greeting.

"Alden Thatcher departed from Annapolis the same time as I did. He traveled the main road, hoping to divert the attention of any who might stop the message from being delivered."

"He should have arrived before you." Barney turned fully toward him, hands clasped behind his back, immediately understanding what Jacob did not say. "And you're worried he may have been . . . detained."

Jacob nodded.

"I intend to send the main body of soldiers on to Upper Marlboro, but you may assemble a band of volunteers to go in search of Mr. Thatcher."

"Thank you, sir."

"Mr. Davis will assist you."

A quarter of an hour later, Jacob, Michael, and three other flotilla men rode from the Patuxent north to the main road. They'd continue on toward Annapolis and hopefully discover Alden along the way. Jacob prayed they would find him unharmed.

"I understand you're to be congratulated on your recent marriage, Mr. Steele." Michael rode next to him, and the others behind. All the men carried muskets.

"Thank you."

"It's just been a few months, hasn't it?" Michael continued. "A happy time, to be sure. But of course, this early on, there's some adjustin' on both your parts."

Jacob glanced over at him. He had only spoken about his marriage with Alden. He hadn't even considered confiding in a person who'd actually had husband experience. "It's a bit more difficult than I'd assumed," he said tentatively.

"Don't I know it." Michael grinned. "My Martha and I had a rough patch right at the first. Sappy letters and a few turns around a dance floor don't quite prepare you for living with a person, no matter how dewy-eyed in love you may be."

Jacob watched him, hoping he'd continue without having to be prompted with embarrassing questions.

"Those first months were difficult, to be sure. Poor Martha. Missed her mum somethin' terrible. She came up from Richmond, you know. Missed her friends, her younger sisters. She had her way o' doing things, and I had mine. We were both convinced our way was right." He grimaced. "Difficult indeed."

"And what did you do?" Jacob asked.

"Well, after a while, I realized I was jes holdin' on to some things that didn't matter. And if I wanted a happy home, I had to let them go. I've never been one for having animals in the house, but Martha wanted a puppy. Wanted him to sleep at our feet at night." He wrinkled his nose. "Don't mind it so much now, but Martha—she loves that dog." He shrugged, giving a good-natured smile.

"And she won't eat cornbread, thinks it's terrible, but she knows it's my favorite. Now, don't go tellin' Martha, but her cornbread will never be as good as my mum's. That's jes a fact. But every time I eat it, I'm grateful she made it for me, wanting to make me happy. And I tell her it's the best cornbread I've ever tasted. I suppose the trick is seein' things through her eyes and tryin' to understand the reasoning behind them. Gives you an appreciation for the other person. A little give and take, that's all."

Jacob nodded, liking the man's simple words. He remembered the conversation with Lydia the night before, how she'd offered to kill spiders if he'd hold her when she was afraid. In this case, he certainly got the better end of the deal.

The party turned east on the main road toward Annapolis.

"Happy wife, happy life," Michael said. "Oh, and kiss her a lot, and tell her she's the most beautiful woman in the world. Even when she's swollen to bursting with a baby in her belly."

Jacob smiled. "Good advice."

"When things get strained, remember why you married her in the first place."

He darted a look at Michael. That was the very same advice Alden had given. Perhaps his friend wasn't so completely ignorant about marriage after all.

"How many children do you have, Michael?"

"Five," he said. "The eldest, Jem, is helpin' Martha with the farmwork while I'm gone. She has a new baby to look after." His grin looked a little less jolly as his eyes grew wistful. "That Jem . . . a fine lad he is. Thirteen years old and already managing the farm—"

His voice cut off as a carriage came into view.

The others moved to the side of the road to give it room to pass, but Jacob remained where he was.

The carriage was his.

Had Alden returned to Annapolis for the carriage? Why? What had happened?

He held up his hands to tell the driver to stop, but Burnett had already recognized him and was pulling on the reins, slowing the horses.

"I'm sorry, sir," Burnett said when Jacob rode close. "She insisted."

*Who insisted?* Had Alden's disguise managed to fool the carriage driver? Jacob dismounted and walked toward the carriage door, but as he reached for it, it opened.

Lydia leaned out. "Burnett, why have we stopped? We need to hurry if we're going to get to Washington City before—"

"Lydia? What . . . what are . . . ?" Jacob stammered, not able to even form a sentence.

Lydia's eyes rounded in surprise when she saw Jacob. They just as quickly narrowed into a glare.

Jacob's insides plummeted as the reality of the situation became clear. Lydia had been the spy all along.

# Chapter 15

Lydia couldn't believe her eyes. Nor could she believe her luck. Of all people to encounter on the road. She looked behind Jacob, wondering what on earth he could be doing so far away from the city with these militiamen.

"Pull off the road, Burnett," Jacob said. His eyes were cold as he took Lydia's arm, helping her from the carriage. "Lydia, come with me."

Jacob looked furious, which he had no right to be. If anyone should be furious, it was she. "I am in a hurry, Jacob. I've no time—"

His grip on her arm tightened, and he pulled her toward the trees. "I'd like to speak to you privately, if you please."

His voice was low and sounded as if he were barely keeping his temper in check, his polite words at odds with the tone. Was he so angry that she'd taken the carriage? Well, she had every right—

Once they were out of sight of the road, Jacob spun to face her. "For whom are you working?"

Lydia stared, not knowing what to say. What was he talking about? "I beg your pardon? Working? I have no idea what you mean." The fury in his expression only made her defensive. She crossed her arms and held his gaze.

"Enough lies, Lydia. Whom do you report to? And what have you told them?" His legs were planted wide, his arms folded across his chest. "I want the truth."

"Lies?" Lydia spoke in a carefully controlled tone. "*I* have not lied. And you, of all people, have no claim to the truth. Not when our entire marriage has been a fabrication."

Jacob's brows rose as if her declaration had surprised him. He opened his mouth but closed it again, as if he could not find the words to reply.

The sight of his discomfort was very satisfying. "I saw her, Jacob."

"Her? Whom did you see?"

His confusion was almost convincing, which only served to fuel Lydia's anger. "Do not treat me like a child. I saw you . . . the two of you . . . this morning in the library. Now, do you intend to keep up this deception, or could you do me the honor of speaking truthfully?"

"The library?" Jacob's brows knit together then smoothed suddenly. "Lydia, that was Alden."

She huffed out a breath through her nose. "I am not a fool, Jacob. But apparently I can be deluded." Inside she ached, but she maintained her firm stance, wanting to project anger instead of allowing the hurt to show. "For more than two months I've planned a fine supper, dressed, arranged my hair, and waited in the dining room each evening. And do you know how often my husband has joined me?" She paused, but not long enough for him to answer. "Eight times, Jacob."

Her cheeks heated as she admitted how she'd sought to please. "I've taken on the household duties, helping Mrs. Pembroke with the finances and planning in an attempt to relieve the strain that keeps you working late hours. I brightened the décor to make your home feel more pleasant." She ticked the items off on her fingers. "I visited the shipyard, thinking to show an interest in my husband's life, perhaps give us a common subject to discuss. I've tried everything I can think of to make you wish to be home, believing all the while your excuse that shipbuilding kept you busy late into the night—"

Lydia's voice choked, cutting off her words. She swallowed, forcing away the tears. She wouldn't let him know how hurt she'd felt, how unwanted.

Jacob sighed. He glanced over his shoulder then leaned closer. "I've been away at night working as an intelligence operative for the United States government." His voice was soft, as if he feared being overheard.

She lowered her eyes to half-mast and fixed him with a tired gaze. "Jacob. Stop." The lies were becoming exhausting.

"It's true. I've trained operatives and gathered intelligence since before the war began, but in the last few months, since the Chesapeake came under attack, Alden and I have also been helping to smuggle boats and supplies to Joshua Barney's flotilla." He held up his hands, palms forward. "This is not a falsehood, Lydia, I swear to it. You're right when you said I've kept things from you, but it wasn't for the reasons you assumed."

Lydia didn't respond. She thought about what he was saying, wondering if it could possibly be true. Could his actions be explained away so easily?

If this was real, and he was working for the government, why hadn't he confided in her?

"Today you saw Alden in disguise. A terrible disguise, I admit, but it was him." His stance relaxed a bit, and his expression grew earnest. "Lydia, I would never . . ."

She thought about the woman she'd seen and tried to recreate the image from her brief glimpse. She hadn't seen a face, and the person's shoulders were broad for a lady's, now that she thought about it. Could this all just be a misunderstanding? "Then, where is he?" Lydia asked. She was not quite ready to relinquish her anger and allow herself to trust. "Where is Alden?"

Jacob's face hardened, and a muscle in his jaw jumped. His eyes turned dark once again. "Alden left Annapolis to deliver a message, but he hasn't arrived. In the past months, at least two other messengers have been intercepted, which is why Alden wore a disguise today. Someone is communicating with the enemy. Divulging the messengers' identities. Someone from my household must have informed the English about Alden's disguise this morning. There is no other explanation."

He watched her closely as he spoke, his eyes flashing, and Lydia understood all at once what he was insinuating. "And you think it is me." She'd thought believing her husband to be unfaithful was painful, but the realization that he assumed her to be a traitor made her heart feel like it was being torn.

"You think I am spying on you?" Lydia said. "That I am delivering information to the English? That I am betraying America and putting men's lives in danger?" She channeled the pain into anger, finding it to be a perfect fuel for spiteful words. "How could you even . . . ?" She shook her head, not knowing how to continue. "Why would you?"

Jacob had believed this entire time that she was working against him. Against her country, her brother, her family. Her head spun, and heat flushed over her, making her shiver. She folded her arms, trying to keep her insides from unraveling.

"Your questions in the shipyard." Jacob spoke with clipped words. "Did you really think I couldn't see through them? And your lies about the Holts."

Lydia looked up. "Lies?"

"I saw you walking with Miriam and Gerald. You've told me again and again that you were only slightly acquainted with them, lied about visiting with Miriam. Why would you keep that friendship secret if not to hide misdoings?"

"And why should I not have a friendship with the Holts?"

He folded his arms. "Gerald Holt is on a list of suspected British spies. And your secretive relationship with the man and his wife caused suspicion."

Lydia's shoulders sagged. All these accusations and the emotions that followed left her exhausted. "You courted Miriam." She turned her eyes away, not wanting to meet his gaze. Not wanting him to see how jealous she felt when she thought of him visiting her friend. "We both decided to downplay our friendship to keep you from feeling discomfort." She looked around for somewhere to sit, and seeing a broken tree, crossed the clearing and sank down onto the rough bark of the trunk. She didn't bother sitting straight but slumped in a very unladylike fashion, resting her head in her hands.

Jacob remained where he was, and she could feel his gaze boring into her. What could be going on in his mind? Did he believe her? Did she believe him? Did she even care anymore? She hated that he distrusted her and thought back over her short marriage, trying to think of how she could have done things differently. "I shouldn't have lied to you about the Holts, Jacob," she said. "I want you to understand I did it to protect your feelings." She sighed. "And, I suppose, to protect my own."

He remained quiet.

"And at the shipyard, I asked the questions Gerald and Miriam helped me think of. I thought you might wish to share that part of your life with me and I could come to know you better." She looked up. "But I see now that it was pointless because you didn't trust me in the first place."

"Lydia . . ." Jacob rubbed his eyes. "I don't—"

"The traitor is Maggs," she said quietly.

"Maggs?" He blinked. "How do you know?"

"I overheard him this morning speaking to a stranger. The man told him the English plan to attack Washington City. I came to tell you at the shipyard, but you weren't there, so I thought to deliver the warning to the capitol myself."

Jacob studied her.

"It's the truth," she said, not bothering to try to convince him. If he didn't believe her, then so be it.

"This stranger—what did he look like?"

"I didn't see him. I just heard his voice. It wasn't one I recognized."

He continued to study her. "Where were you?"

"In the servants' quarters. I was . . ." She glanced up at him but decided there had been too many deceptions. She'd give the full truth, whether it was embarrassing or not. "I was hiding in a closet near the entrance. Maggs and the man were speaking in the passageway near the outside door."

Jacob's head tipped, but he continued to study her, probably weighing her responses. "What were you doing in the closet?"

She'd expected the question but still flushed in embarrassment as she answered. "As I said, I was hiding. I'd just seen you with . . . in the library and wished to be alone to collect myself and think of how to proceed. I don't know how long I'd been in there before I heard the men speaking. Perhaps twenty or thirty minutes."

Jacob was silent.

Lydia fidgeted, tugging at her sleeves. She wondered if the other men were beyond the trees listening. Would Jacob prevent her from carrying the message to Washington City? At this point, she didn't care either way. She was emotionally and mentally exhausted, her chest aching from the pain of discovering the man she had begun to fall in love with didn't trust her.

"Maggs," Jacob muttered after a long moment. "I should have seen it."

"You believe me?" Lydia was surprised.

"I believe you. And this news cannot wait. Now, tell me exactly what you overheard . . . every word—"

The sound of men's voices and horse's hooves came through the trees.

Jacob took Lydia's hand—she assumed so she wouldn't escape to double-cross her countrymen—and they hurried back to the road.

Inside, Lydia felt sick. He didn't care about her, didn't care that he'd crushed her heart. Jacob was only concerned with the information she could provide.

When they stepped from the trees, they saw the men gathered around. One motioned them forward. "It's Mr. Thatcher."

When they drew near, Lydia saw Alden sitting on the ground. Blood covered the front of his yellow gown. The sight was so strange she could only stare.

Alden was drinking from a flask. When he saw Jacob and Lydia, he grinned and handed the flask back to one of the men. "Ah, you were worried about me, weren't you?"

"What happened?" Jacob asked.

"Met up with a bit of trouble," Alden said. He rested an arm on his bent knee, seeming not to care that he wore a skirt.

"Are you wounded?" Lydia knelt beside him and grimaced at the blood. The dress was slashed and torn.

"Wounded?" Alden glanced down then shook his head. "I've a few scratches, but nothing to worry about." He winced as he touched his torso, making her wonder if he was downplaying his injuries. "The real tragedy is the damage to my beautiful dress. Oh, and Jake, you're going to need a new butler."

"Did you kill Maggs?" Lydia gasped and pulled back.

Alden pouted his lip, shaking his head. "Captain Westwood wouldn't allow it, though I did offer. He's to have a fair trial, along with the English spy who gave him away." He glanced at Lydia. "Now, in that, I did play a part. Didn't take much to convince him to confess the name of everyone he's ever talked to, especially after he saw what I did to his companions."

Lydia shivered. She didn't like to imagine Alden fighting or think of what he must have done to the spy to get him to name Maggs. She stood and moved a short distance away. The panicky feeling that had overcome her when Rosefield was attacked prickled over her skin. The war felt close and real. And it frightened her. Her head felt light, and she pressed her hand against a tree to steady herself.

"And that's what took you all day?" Jacob said. "Torturing a prisoner and capturing a butler?"

"I had to ride to the army encampment for the militia, didn't I?" Alden stood and brushed off his skirts.

"I hope you brought a change of clothes," Jacob said.

"In my saddlebag," Alden replied. "But in this heat . . . I wasn't ready to give up my gown just yet."

"It's time," Jacob said, pointing toward the woods.

Alden took his saddlebag and moved into the trees to change.

"Check his wounds," Jacob said to one of the men. "He'll never admit he's hurt."

The man nodded and went after Alden.

Jacob turned to Lydia, and a look of concern moved over his face. "Are you all right? You've gone pale." He took her arm, much more gently this time, and led her toward the carriage.

"I'm fine," she said, feeling a wave of nausea. She stopped and pressed her hand over her mouth, hoping she wouldn't humiliate herself by being sick. Once it passed, she held on to his arm as her head swam. She realized she hadn't eaten breakfast. "I just need to sit down."

Jacob slid an arm around her waist and lifted her into the carriage.

Lydia sat and then lay down on the bench.

"I'll fetch some water." He hurried away and returned a moment later with the water flask.

Lydia sat up and took a drink, grimacing at the stale taste. "I'm sorry," she said, lying her head back down.

Jacob climbed into the carriage, sitting across from her. "Can you tell me what the man said to Maggs? Every detail you remember? I'll send the news with Alden and the flotilla men, and you can rest as we ride to Washington City. Just stay awake a bit longer."

She nodded, closing her eyes. The world was spinning. "The squadron coming after the flotilla is just a diversion," she said. "General Ross and his troops disembarked at Benedict and are marching to Upper Marlboro. And Gordon is sailing up the Potomac to Fort Washington." She repeated the names she'd heard, not fully knowing whom she was speaking of, but she hoped Jacob knew. "They will destroy the flotilla and converge on Washington City."

"This could turn the tide of the war," Jacob said.

Did he say as *we* ride to Washington? Lydia tried to lift up her head but felt too dizzy.

Jacob brushed a curl off her forehead. "Do you know when, Lydia? When will they arrive?"

"They'll be in Washington in two days, maybe three." She repeated the words the stranger had said, feeling herself slipping away.

"Good work, Lydia," Jacob whispered.

Or at least she thought he did. The day was hot and her heart ached, but she was too weary to even hold on to the emotion. Lydia's mind was muddled, and when she heard the creak of the carriage door closing, she let go of her last bit of consciousness and slept.

# CHAPTER 16

THE CARRIAGE HIT A BUMP and Jacob put out his arm to keep Lydia from sliding off the bench. She'd been sleeping for more than an hour, and Jacob had spent the time rebuking himself, wondering how things could have gone so terribly wrong and agonizing over what to say when she awoke.

Another bump made her curls bounce, but she didn't wake. He sat back in the seat across from her and hoped she wasn't too ill. She'd gone pale hearing Alden's talk about questioning his attacker. Or perhaps it had been the blood. Either way, he should have shielded her from the ugly side of the hostilities.

In all probability, Alden's condition and his report may not have been what had upset her at all. He rubbed his eyes, wondering how he had become so mistrustful that he'd accused an innocent person—his own wife, for heaven's sake—of conspiring with the enemy. Had he become so caught up in the war he couldn't even trust a gentle young woman? Was it truly easier for him to suspect her than to admit he may be falling in love with her?

He started to feel ill himself as he thought back over their months of marriage. He'd been convinced that his actions were correct. That he was being cautious for the sake of his country. That he'd been smart. But had he been justifying hurtful behavior because he'd been more afraid of the truth? Of allowing himself to care for someone, trusting her not to hurt him, and believing he deserved to be cared for in return? Was Alden right all along?

Lydia shifted, blinked open her eyes, and pushed herself into a sitting position. She brushed back her curls. The stitching of the carriage seat left a mark on her face, and Jacob smiled at her groggy expression.

"Feeling better?"

Lydia nodded. "I am."

He offered a sack with hardtack. "It's not delicious, but it may settle your stomach."

"Thank you." She chewed on a biscuit and pulled aside the curtain, peering outside. "We're still going to Washington City?"

He nodded.

Lydia sat back. The color had returned to her face, but her eyes had lost their brightness. She looked sad. Guilt coiled bitterly inside him.

"Lydia, I am so sorry."

She turned her gaze to him but did not respond, so he continued.

"I should have come to you instead of allowing my suspicions to grow. Asked you—"

"Asked if I'm an enemy spy?" she interrupted him with a wry smile. "I don't think that would have gone well."

"The conversation wouldn't have been pleasant, but it would have been better than . . . what *did* happen. I didn't handle any of this correctly. I wanted to trust you, I just didn't know how, and every small thing just seemed to fuel my suspicions. In the end, it became easier to stay away."

"Thank you for the apology," she said.

She looked back out the window, and Jacob searched his brain for something to say that would show he'd changed, that he harbored no ill feelings toward her. That he wanted to start afresh.

The summer day was warm, and the windows were open slightly at the top to let in air, but his clothes still stuck to him. He thought how miserable the marching redcoats must be and hoped the mosquitoes were particularly thirsty.

"You did court Miriam?" Lydia asked.

"I did." Her question surprised him. "But not for long. After a few visits, it became obvious she preferred Gerald to anyone else." He shrugged. The memory didn't bring pain as it had years earlier. He thought about those days, bringing flowers, walking in the park, and wished it had been Lydia on his arm. He'd never done any of those things with his own wife, and his guilt returned. He would start. She loved roses. He could bring roses, a large vaseful of them for her bedchamber. And they could walk together in the evenings when the weather was cool. Things would be different now. He'd make an effort . . .

"Jacob, our marriage is a sham."

The bluntness of her words shocked him, and he could only stare.

"I do not know how my father convinced you to marry me, how much he paid you, but it must have been quite a lot."

An ache opened up in his chest. "What makes you think he paid me?"

She shrugged and looked back toward the window. "It is obvious you did not want to do it. You are not happy with me."

He reached to take her hand but stopped, thinking she might not welcome the touch. He knit together his fingers instead and leaned forward. "Lydia, that is not true."

One side of her lips pulled up in a sad smile, as if she didn't believe him but appreciated his attempt to reassure. "Jacob, I am leaving. Once the message is delivered to Washington, I will return to Rosefield."

She watched him, looking expectantly as if waiting for him say something, but he didn't. Suddenly he was a child again—an unloved child, desperate to belong to someone but powerless to make anyone love him. His heart screamed at him to fix this, but he couldn't. He'd expected it. Known all along that being with Lydia was too good to be true. He hadn't treated her as he should have, and that was an understatement. She deserved a better life than he could give her. Deserved a husband who didn't sabotage their relationship out of fear.

He sat back against the seat. "I understand."

Lydia winced, and the hurt in her eyes pierced him. She turned away. And inside, Jacob broke.

***

The hour was late when the carriage crossed the East Branch Bridge and arrived in Washington City. Lydia slept with her head against the side of the carriage, and Jacob had half a mind to leave her sleeping or to deliver her to Elnora's and continue on himself, but Lydia had begun the mission, and he wanted her to have the chance to complete it.

He reached over and shook her shoulder. "We've arrived."

Lydia blinked herself awake, once again looking very charming doing so. For an instant, Jacob thought how pleasant it would be to wake to the sight each morning, but he remembered with a fresh ache that they were to part.

"What is your plan, Lydia?" he said. "To whom do you intend to deliver the message?"

She looked surprised that he would ask, as if his accompanying her meant he would take charge. "I thought John Armstrong. He is a friend of my father's, and I've met him before."

Jacob nodded. The secretary of war was a good choice.

"Is that who you'd recommend?" she asked.

"I might have gone to General Winder or even to President Madison himself, but they will all hear soon enough, so in this case, John Armstrong is as good as any."

He leaned out the window and gave the address to Burnett.

Lydia smoothed her skirts and pushed her hair from her face. "I am a bit nervous," she said. "Mr. Armstrong is rather intimidating."

"I didn't think you were intimidated by anyone," Jacob said. "Your confidence is one of the first things I noticed about you."

She shrugged, giving a small smile. "I suppose I put on a convincing show."

When they arrived, Jacob alighted. He turned and assisted Lydia.

Burnett climbed down and stretched his back and then moved to the rear of the carriage to check on Hildegard. The poor horse must be tired, but her work had just begun.

Lydia took Jacob's arm, and the two ascended the stairs.

A butler answered the door, and, obviously used to visitors at all hours, he admitted them without even batting an eye. They were shown into Mr. Armstrong's office to wait.

Jacob and Lydia glanced around the room. He'd been here before, and always under similar circumstances. Maps were spread over the desk, books were piled haphazardly with papers sticking out of them. Messages, envelopes, and folded and torn papers were piled up on one side. The room had a feeling of active chaos, which seemed right during wartime.

John Armstrong entered the study wearing a night robe. His wig looked as if it had been put on hastily and sat a little off-center. He was a tall, thin man with a beak-like nose. Jacob could see why Lydia felt nervous. The secretary of war was aloof and very intimidating.

"This had better be important, Mr. Steele—" He cut off his words when he saw Lydia and assumed a more polite demeanor. "Pardon me, madam. I did not realize you were here also."

"Mr. Armstrong, this is my wife, Lydia Steele." Jacob motioned toward Lydia.

"Lydia, Mr. John Armstrong, United States Secretary of War."

Mr. Armstrong bowed and grabbed quickly at the wig that slipped, moving it back into place. "Mrs. Steele, a pleasure. You are Beauregard Prescott's daughter, am I correct?"

"Yes, sir. You remembered."

She gave a smile that had an immediate effect on Mr. Armstrong, relaxing his irritated expression. He looked almost pleased. He motioned for the two to be seated then moved to sit behind the desk. "Now, if you please, what is so important that it couldn't wait until morning?"

"I apologize for the late hour, sir," Jacob said. "But the news is urgent. My wife has discovered a plot against Washington City."

Mr. Armstrong's brows rose, crunching his forehead with wrinkles. "Indeed?" He turned to Lydia, his face polite, and gave a condescending smile, like one might give to a child who had done something sweet.

Jacob was annoyed that the man wasn't taking her seriously.

"Yes, sir," Lydia said.

Jacob glanced at her, surprised by the confidence in her voice. She somehow managed to sound both self-assured and charming.

Mr. Armstrong's expression changed, becoming serious. He looked to Jacob, but Jacob turned to Lydia. She'd overheard the message and been brave enough to cross the state to deliver it; she should be the one to tell him.

She glanced at Jacob then turned back to Mr. Armstrong. "The English plan to attack Washington. A squadron is even now sailing up the Patuxent with the intent of attacking Joshua Barney's flotilla. But the attack is only a diversion. General Ross is leading a company, marching from Benedict."

At the general's name, Mr. Armstrong's brow wrinkled. "Are you certain of this?" He turned to Jacob for verification.

Jacob nodded. "Mrs. Steele overheard a British informant who has since been captured and is awaiting trial in Annapolis."

"There is more, sir," Lydia said. "Another ship, captained by Gordon is sailing up the Potomac to attack Fort Washington."

"When?" Armstrong's brows pulled into a scowl.

"Two days," Lydia said. "Or possibly three."

Armstrong stood. He pushed aside the pile of maps until he found the one he was looking for, pulled it out, and laid it over the top. He muttered to himself as he studied it.

Jacob and Lydia shared a glance. He felt immensely proud of her. Within a moment of meeting the man, she'd known precisely how to earn his trust and give the message in the way most likely to convince him. This skill had likely served her well, as women were not always taken seriously. Especially concerning matters that were considered to be a man's domain.

With his finger, Mr. Armstrong traced the road from Upper Marlboro toward Washington City. "The flotilla will be destroyed, and an army will be in position to attack the town both by land and sea. We must pray Winder has gathered a sufficient militia."

He sat back in his chair. "The president will be appraised immediately. Washington City must be evacuated."

He rubbed his forehead then looked up as if just remembering the two were there. He rose, and they rose as well.

"I thank you, Mrs. Steele. You may have saved the lives of many Americans today, and very likely the president himself."

Lydia curtsied, and a blush colored her cheeks. "It is my pleasure, sir."

"If you'll excuse me, I've letters to write and a defense to plan." He pulled out a pile of papers and unstopped a jar of ink.

Jacob and Lydia departed.

Once they were back in the carriage, Jacob grinned at his wife.

"That wasn't so bad, I guess," she said.

"You heard what he said. You very well may have saved the president."

Lydia smiled. "I don't think he'd have believed me if you hadn't been there."

He shook his head, not allowing her to play down her accomplishment. "You have a skill with people, Lydia. Understanding them, appraising them, and knowing how to treat them."

"To manipulate them, you mean."

"To set them at ease and earn their trust."

She glanced up at him, and he could see the words in her mind as clearly as if she'd spoken them aloud. *I didn't earn your trust.*

The empty feeling returned.

The pair rode in silence, the air around them heavy with the things that had been said, as well as those that had remained unsaid.

At Elnora's, he helped Lydia from the carriage again, but this time, there was no sense of anticipation.

She glanced up at the house.

"Elnora will be pleased to have us," he said, leading her to the door. "Once you are settled, I must leave to return to the flotilla."

"You intend to fight the British?"

He scratched his neck. "I must."

She stayed silent, and he wondered if she was worried.

She started for the door, but he stopped her, laying a hand on her arm. "Lydia, I know you intend to return home, but before you do, I would ask a favor."

She turned to face him, her expression curious. "Yes?"

"Please stay with Elnora. Help her to evacuate. She'll know where to go, and Burnett will take you. But . . . she is alone."

"Of course."

He nodded his thanks. "Once this business is done, I'll find you and take you to Rosefield."

She chewed on her lip. "Will we be safe?"

"I pray that you will."

Lydia placed her hand over his. "By *we* I meant you as well. I am afraid." Her voice dropped to a whisper. "An army is coming. Here. To attack the city."

And he was leaving her.

"But you will be long gone before they arrive. Have no fear, Lydia. You are clever and brave, and I've no doubt you'll be safe."

She held his gaze for a long moment as various expressions flitted over her face. At last, she pursed her lips and gave a resolved nod. "Very well, then. But you must promise to be safe as well."

Her hand tightened on his.

He lifted it, placing a kiss on her fingers. "I promise."

# CHAPTER 17

A COMMOTION OUTSIDE WOKE LYDIA. She rose from the unfamiliar bed and crossed the bedchamber in Elnora Hathaway's house, pulling aside the curtain to look through the window. The street below was utter chaos. Horses, carriages, and people clogged the road, churning up dust as they loaded possessions into wagons. The evacuation had begun, and from the looks of it, people were not behaving in an orderly fashion.

She lifted her gaze beyond the road directly below and over the rooftops across the street to the capitol building. An impressive tree-lined road led from Pennsylvania Avenue up the hill to the classically styled structure, which was surrounded by well-maintained gardens. Though the building itself was only partially finished, the center of government was already magnificent.

Washington City was the pride of the young nation. Built on a bend in the Potomac on land chosen by George Washington himself and designed by the famed Pierre L'Enfant, the city was made up of wide avenues and beautiful parks. Elnora's home was on one of the loveliest streets, where she had a view of both the capitol building and President Madison's house.

Lydia felt a well of pride as she gazed from one grand building to the other. Below, somebody yelled, and the feeling was squelched as she remembered her reasons for being in Washington City in the first place. The English army was on its way, and she needed to get herself and Elnora to safety.

Hearing a knock at the door, she turned.

A maid entered and curtsied. "If you please, Mrs. Steele, my name's Janet. Mrs. Hathaway sent me to help you dress."

"Thank you."

Lydia glanced into the mirror, realizing her hair hung in waves instead of tight curls. Janet pulled it back and arranged it into a sensible style, which

Lydia appreciated, knowing in her rational mind that evacuating a city on the brink of attack was not the time to fret about her coiffure. But seeing it made Lydia miss Francine, and she missed her curls.

Once she was ready, Lydia followed Janet down the stairs. The house was luxurious, decorated in a style that was more ornate than either Lydia's parents' home or the house in Annapolis. The wood paneling was a deep mahogany color, and a crystal chandelier hung in the main hall, the sunlight coming in through the windows casting particles of colored light over the polished marble floors.

The house had been dark, and she'd been so tired when Jacob delivered her the night before that she'd hardly noticed her surroundings. And she gave them only a cursory glance now. She planned to gather Elnora and leave the city as quickly as possible.

When Lydia entered a sitting room, she found Elnora resting on a sofa, a blanket over her lap. Her face was pale, and when she lifted her head, she started to cough. Janet hurried to pour a cup of tea. Nearly a full thirty seconds elapsed before the fit passed.

Elnora reached an elegant hand toward Lydia, her smile looking drawn and tired. "How did you sleep, my dear?"

"Very well, thank you." Lydia crossed the room and took Elnora's hand. "Are you ill, Mrs. Hathaway?"

"Just a bit of a cough," Elnora replied. She sipped the tea and then allowed the maid to take away the cup. When she turned back to Lydia, she leaned closer, her gaze on the scar. "Oh, my dear, that must have hurt dreadfully."

Lydia's cheeks flared. She was embarrassed by the attention, but at the same time, she was glad Elnora hadn't pretended not to see it.

"I know, it is gruesome."

The corners of Elnora's mouth pulled down thoughtfully. "Scars are rarely beautiful, dear. But I'd never describe you as gruesome. It's your eyes, you know. Goodness shines from them, and that's what makes you beautiful."

"Thank you." Lydia smiled, feeling a warm glow at the words. She couldn't help but compare her mother's repulsion to Elnora's thoughtfulness.

Elnora coughed again then sipped her tea.

Lydia glanced toward the sitting room window, seeing the activity in the street outside. "Do you feel well enough to travel?"

Elnora nodded. "I will be fine. My servants are loading valuables into the carriages now." She motioned to Janet. "Bring some breakfast for Mrs. Steele."

Lydia didn't have an appetite. She twisted her fingers together nervously in her lap, feeling anxious to depart. She had no way of knowing when the English soldiers would arrive and wanted to be well gone before they did.

"And where will we go?" Lydia asked, hoping Elnora had a destination in mind. If not, Lydia would suggest they go south to Rosefield.

"My dear friend Diana lives on a plantation outside of Bethesda. She will gladly take us in. The journey won't be long, and it is well away from the main roads leading to the larger cities."

*Perfect,* Lydia thought. Soldiers would have no reason to march through that part of the countryside. Hearing raised voices, she glanced toward the window.

"I just need to rest a bit, and then we can be off." Elnora leaned her head back and closed her eyes.

Janet brought a tray. She looked at Elnora, then to Lydia, her furrowed brows indicating that the older woman was downplaying the seriousness of her illness.

Lydia's anxiety grew, as did her feeling of helplessness. She took a slice of sweet bread and chewed on it just to expend her nervous energy. Then she sipped some tea, glancing between the activity out the window and Elnora.

The voices outside became louder and sounded angry, and Lydia moved to the window. Then, seeing the argument outside involved Burnett and her carriage, she hurried through the entry hall and out the front doors.

Burnett and another man stood facing one another, both with a hand on the lead horse's harness.

"Off with you," Burnett yelled at the man. "This is private property."

The man pulled on the harness, motioning for another to climb onto the coachman's seat. "And I'm telling you again this carriage is needed for official government business."

Burnett grabbed the second man, pulling him away as he attempted to climb aboard.

The first man shoved Burnett, knocking him to the ground.

He looked surprised for a moment, probably because the man who'd pushed him wore silk stockings and ruffled cuffs. The surprise lasted only an instant. Burnett cursed and spit then jumped up, fists raised, ready to charge at the two.

"What is happening?" Lydia yelled. Her voice stopped the scuffle.

"These two think they can impound Mr. Steele's carriage, madam," Burnett said, glaring at the men.

Lydia stood between the men and put a hand on Burnett's arm, pushing down so he lowered his fists. "There has been some mistake, gentlemen. This carriage belongs to my husband."

The man who'd shoved the carriage driver gave a gracious bow, his wig tied with a deep-purple ribbon. "I apologize for the inconvenience, madam. The United States government is requisitioning this conveyance to transport government records."

His gaze lingered a moment on her scar, but she wasn't going to shy away in embarrassment. She shook her head. "I'm afraid that will simply not be possible. We need this carriage to leave the city."

"Again, I am sorry, madam." He gestured toward his partner, who climbed up into the driver's seat.

"Sir, how dare you," Lydia said.

"We have no other choice, madam." He stepped past her. "The records must be saved."

"But—"

The man ignored her and climbed inside, calling out for the carriage to drive off.

Lydia stepped back, out of the way.

"Want me to stop them, Mrs. Steele?" Burnett said.

She shook her head. "No, you could get arrested, and I need your help." She scowled at the departing carriage and then gave her driver a grateful smile. "Though I am sure those two dandies would not stand a chance against you."

Burnett grinned and puffed out his chest. "Mrs. Hathaway has a fine carriage." He nodded toward the carriage house at the side of the grand home. "Not to worry, madam. We'll get out of this city yet."

Half an hour later, the party was ready to depart. Elnora's jewelry and most precious valuables were loaded into the carriage, and she'd ordered other of her possessions to be hidden in the root cellar. Some of the staff had returned to their families; others would remain at the house; and Janet, Burnett, Elnora's carriage driver, and two footmen would accompany the two ladies to Bethesda.

As they made their way to the carriage, Elnora leaned heavily on Janet and Lydia, who exchanged worried looks. Her condition seemed to be worsening. They helped her inside, and she immediately started coughing again.

Janet unstopped a bottle of tonic and poured a small amount into a cup, and once the coughing fit eased, she helped Elnora drink. Lydia sat on the opposite bench, her concern about the older woman's health increasing. She hated the feeling of being powerless over her circumstance.

The chaos in the street had only grown as residents of the city packed up their possessions to flee the town. Noise and dust surrounded them. The weather was absurdly hot, even for late August, and Lydia fanned herself as the carriage made its way slowly along the road.

The dust seemed to make Elnora's cough even worse. They must get out of this city and allow the older woman to rest.

The conveyance drew to a halt, and Lydia peeked through the window, trying to discern what had stopped them. Angry voices came from the road ahead, and again, she heard Burnett among them.

Lydia climbed down and hurried forward, finding it nearly impossible to move between people and wagons on the busy road. A group of soldiers had halted the carriage, and despite the protests of Elnora's servants and Burnett, they were unharnessing the horses.

Some of the soldiers aimed their muskets at the servants as the others worked.

"What is the meaning of this?" Lydia didn't think she'd ever been so angry in her life. How dare they threaten these innocent people! "What do you think you are doing?" she asked the soldier who was calling out instructions to the others.

"We need these horses for artillery wagons, madam." He pointed to another conveyance, a wagon filled with furniture and children. "Get those as well."

Lydia marched forward until she stood directly in front of the man. "You may not take these horses." She crossed her arms. "I refuse to allow it."

Burnett moved to join her but backed up when one of the muskets moved to aim directly at him.

Lydia stomped her foot, knowing it was childish, but her frustration had grown past the point of restraint. "My friend is ill; we must get out of this city." She felt her eyes burning. "Please."

"Madam, please don't put up a fuss." The soldier's eyes were red and had dark smudges beneath them. He looked exhausted rather than threatening. "I'm only following orders."

"Whose orders, sir?"

"General Winder's." He let out a breath, looking as if he truly regretted what he was doing. "I'm sorry. I know it seems harsh, but the city's defense—"

An explosion shook the earth. Lydia dropped, crouching down, with her hands over her ears. Tremors shook her body, and her heart pounded in her ears.

All around, people screamed and began running. Horses whinnied, pulling on their leads. Some bolted altogether.

Lydia felt dizzy as she tried to understand. "What in the—"

"It's the bridge, Mrs. Steele." Burnett crouched next to her, his arm around her shoulders. After a moment, he helped her stand. Lydia's legs were shaking and were in real danger of giving out. She leaned on Burnett.

"They've blown the Eastern Branch Bridge," Burnett said.

"Get to safety, madam," the soldier said. He looked toward the cloud of black smoke that marked where the bridge had been. "The redcoats will be here soon."

The party had no other choice but to return to the Hathaway house. A footman carried Elnora, and the others brought her valuables and clothing.

Once they were inside, Elnora directed the servants to hide the remainder of the valuables and lock the doors tight.

"You need to rest, madam," Janet said to Elnora.

The older woman didn't argue.

Not knowing what else to do and not wishing to be alone, Lydia followed. She was still shaken, both from fear and anger that they'd been denied escape by the very people who were supposed to protect them.

Elnora rested in her bed, propped up with pillows, and Lydia sat in a chair near the window.

She watched as the streets cleared of people. Wagons and carriages whose horses had been commandeered sat abandoned, and the heat made the empty roads shimmer. Occasionally a line of soldiers or militia marched past, some carrying weapons and others dragging cannons. From her view, she could see soldiers surrounding the capitol and the president's house, but most marched northward to defend the city.

Feeling lonely and scared, she thought of Jacob, wishing he were here. His presence would calm her, make her feel safe. She wondered where he was. Had he met up with the English army? Was he even now fighting? Had he been hurt? Killed?

Her eyes burned, and she allowed tears to fall, putting her hand over her mouth to muffle the sound. What was going to happen to them? Would the English rampage through the house, looting, breaking things, and burning as they had at Rosefield? What would she do if they came? Would she flee? Where would she go? Could she protect Elnora?

# CHAPTER 18

JACOB LEANED BACK ON THE grass in the shade of a cannon. He crossed one leg over the other and closed his eyes, hoping to get some sleep before the English army arrived and the fighting began. The morning was hot, without any breeze. Around him, he heard other men settling into their own patches of shade on the slopes facing the town of Bladensburg, the spot the army commanders had designated as the battlefield. Jacob imagined weariness had made him overly sentimental as he gazed over the quiet town at the top of the Eastern Branch of the Potomac and a lump grew in his throat, thinking of the violence that would occur in this peaceful place.

Since leaving Lydia at Elnora's house the night before, Jacob had been constantly on the move. Commodore Barney's flotilla men had met him on the road to Upper Marlboro just before dawn, their wagons bearing five large naval cannons.

Alden's injuries had been tended, but even his typically lighthearted friend had been solemn as he informed Jacob that the flotilla had been scuttled. Jacob hadn't needed to be told. He'd heard the explosions and could smell the smoke, even from miles away. Once the sun rose, he'd seen the black plume rising from Pig Point. His shoulders slumped. What an enormous waste. He was glad he didn't have to see the boats he'd taken such care of burning and sinking.

Commodore had requested and was granted permission for his men to continue fighting as infantry, and General Winder had assigned the flotilla men to blow the Eastern Branch Bridge and then march north to Bladensburg. With the bridge gone, the English would have no choice but to try to cross farther upstream.

As he shifted his position against the cannon, Jacob thought how supremely easy it was to destroy something that had taken so much skill and time to construct. *There is a lesson in there somewhere, I'm sure,* he thought as he dozed.

"He looks so peaceful I almost hate to wake him."

Alden's voice sounded far away, but it only took an instant for the words to penetrate Jacob's consciousness. He squinted then sat up quickly, knowing from experience Alden's methods of rousing him wouldn't be pleasant. Lifting a hand, he shaded his eyes. The sun had moved. Though he still felt exhausted, he must have slept.

Alden and Michael Davis stood before him. Michael, ever thoughtful, stepped to the side to cast a shadow over Jacob.

"Is the enemy here?" Jacob reached for his musket.

"Nearly," Alden said. "Scouts spotted the earliest advance about two miles out."

Jacob rose and stood with the other two, looking out over the empty streets and buildings. In spite of its small size, Bladensburg was a busy harbor town with a regular stagecoach stop. It sat on the Old Post Road between Maine and Georgia. Wealthy merchants and plantation owners built spacious houses in and around the town, giving it a picturesque appeal, and it was located close enough to Washington City and Georgetown that daytrips to the bustling taverns had become popular social events.

Bladensburg had another, less pleasant, distinction. The ravine beyond the stagecoach stop was concealed by thick foliage and had become a notorious site for settling personal scores by duel. Jacob knew personally of at least seven men who'd utilized what had come to be known as the dark and bloody grounds.

But today, the fighting would take place on the sunny fields and hills on the west side of the river.

Having arrived first, the American forces commanded the high ground.

Riflemen were concealed in the shrubbery near the river, with the Fifth Regiment of Baltimore volunteers directly behind. Two other regiments covered the road to Georgetown, with the cavalry high up on the hill.

Barney's men were set up on the west side of Stoddert's Bridge, facing the town, their large naval cannons covering the road to Washington. The third and last line of defense. Should the enemy break through the others, Barney's men were all that stood between Ross and Washington.

The men had moved to their positions. Jacob, Alden, and Michael were assigned to a space between two cannons. They'd dug down, piling sod and dirt to build up a bluff for cover, and now they waited, their muskets cleaned and their packs filled with fresh ammunition. Tension made the air feel charged with energy.

Michael handed a water flask to Jacob. "We've your wife to thank for this, you know."

Jacob opened his mouth, ready to give an angry retort, but saw Michael's smile. He instead took a drink, giving the flask to Alden.

"And I mean that as a compliment, sir," Michael said.

"I'll make certain to mention my lack of sleep and aching backside next time I see Lydia," Alden said. "Honestly, I've never spent so much time in the saddle. She owes me a tremendous apology." Jacob could hear from his friend's voice that he was teasing as well.

"From what I hear, Washington would never have had the time to form a defense if Mrs. Steele had been too afraid to travel alone. Or if she'd not taken what she overheard seriously," Michael said, scratching his head beneath his father's old hat. "You must be right proud of her, Mr. Steele."

Jacob nodded his thanks, appreciating the compliment to Lydia. "I am indeed." The man's sentiment was a vast understatement for the bubble of warmth that grew when he thought of his wife's actions. She may well have saved the entire United States of America. A smile grew as the bubble expanded.

"She and Elnora got out of the city safely?" Alden took a step to the side and leaned closer as he asked the question.

His voice was no longer light, but worried. The sound set Jacob's senses on alert, and his smile dropped away. Alden didn't expect the Americans to win the battle.

"I hope so," Jacob said. He gave his friend a questioning look, which Alden of course chose to ignore.

Alden turned to Michael. "And what of your family, Mr. Davis? Do you think they evacuated?"

Michael's face darkened. He swallowed. "Martha isn't in any shape to travel, not in this heat with all the young 'uns and a newborn. And I don't know where they'd go if they did evacuate." He let out a heavy breath, his gaze turning downward as he kicked a clump of dirt. "The farm's away from the city; don't anticipate the redcoats venturing that far."

"I'm sure they're safe," Alden said. He clapped the man on the shoulder. "Women are extremely competent in times of danger." He grinned, his lighthearted manner returning in an effort to cheer the man. "Why, I'd put my life into Lydia's or Elnora's hands a hundred times over before I'd allow Jacob—"

Commodore Barney joined them, and Alden cut off his words.

The commodore nodded a greeting, hands clasped behind his back as he surveyed the land around them. His brows were furrowed, raising slightly upward in the center, and his eyes were thoughtful. He looked concerned. Jacob had never seen the commodore looking anything but completely certain. It was what gave his men their confidence.

The expression passed, and Commodore Barney lifted his chin, his gaze moving over the battlefield positions.

The commodore's moment of unease worried Jacob as much, if not more, than Alden's. Jacob himself was, of course, not pleased with the idea of fighting a losing battle against the strongest army in the world. But he realized the majority of his apprehension had to do with Lydia. Where was she? Had she run into difficulty leaving the city? Was she frightened? The last question worried him the most. He wished he could be there for her, hold her, protect her. But if he were there, would she even want him? A wave of despair darkened his thoughts. How had he let things go so wrong with Lydia? If he could go back, do everything differently . . .

". . . too far back . . . no cover . . ."

Jacob pushed away his own thoughts. Barney had been speaking to him and Alden. "I beg your pardon, Commodore. What were you saying?"

Barney squinted, pointing with his chin. "Colonel Monroe's placed the Baltimore regiments too far back to be of any support to the artillery and riflemen. Their line is within rocket range and fully exposed."

A soldier brought the commodore's horse. Barney thanked him. He continued to study the battle positions as he held on to the reins, but he didn't mount. Jacob had heard him complain often about how uncomfortable navy men are in the saddle.

A commotion made the group turn. Near the top of the hill, General Winder was speaking with the military commanders. Jacob recognized many of the leaders, and among them, he was surprised to see the diminished figure of President James Madison wearing his characteristic black coat and white wig. The president appeared to be listening, nodding his head occasionally, as the others pointed toward the various positions of the soldiers.

Before he could give much thought to the leader's presence, a shout drew their attention toward the hills on the far side of the town, and a surge of energy moved through the troops.

The first wave of redcoats marched down the hill.

Men whispered nervously and fidgeted with their weapons.

Even with his lack of military training, Jacob could see the inexperience in the volunteers' reactions.

"Too late to do anything about the positions now." Barney spun and mounted the horse then rode along the line. "Load cannons! Ready your weapons!"

His solid presence visibly raised the soldiers' morale. The flotilla men would follow their leader to the ends of the earth if he asked. It was the volunteer militia Jacob worried about.

The red uniforms of the English showed brightly against the green hills. The soldiers moved forward at a steady pace, marching in ranks, and before long, the entire hillside seemed covered with them. Jacob's heartbeat sped up as he watched the steady advance. Sweat that he didn't think could be blamed solely on the heat trickled down his spine.

"Hold this line," Barney yelled. "No matter—"

His words were drowned out by the scream then explosion of Congreve rockets. The British hadn't even paused, but individual infantrymen crouched, fired on the exposed soldiers, and then continued their forward march.

It seemed General Ross was wasting no time.

Jacob crouched down behind the hillock, as ahead of him, clumps of dirt and grass and parts of bodies blasted into the air.

The hidden riflemen on the front line let off a barrage of shots, surprising the redcoats and causing them to run for shelter in the town.

Around him, the soldiers cheered, but Jacob clenched his jaw. It wasn't going to be that easy. A moment later, the redcoats returned back into view; they moved in formation, marching double time in a rush straight for the bridge.

Overhead, the red-flamed rockets continued to shriek before smashing into the earth with a blast that shook the hill, sending debris flying.

The English crossed the bridge under heavy fire, the American riflemen sending deadly shots into their exposed ranks, but more and more redcoats joined them, replacing fallen soldiers immediately.

The first regiment fell onto the line of riflemen with ferocity that turned Jacob's stomach. Bullets and bayonets wounded indiscriminately.

Through the smoke, he could see the American volunteers scatter, unable to hold the line. As Barney had predicted, the reinforcements were too far back to provide support. The line broke, and those who could still run retreated back to the safety of the second line, and others fled the battlefield completely.

Buoyed by their success, the redcoats didn't even wait for reinforcements. They dropped their knapsacks and rushed up the slope, leaving the hill behind spotted with dead and wounded.

The English line spread thin, and General Winder took advantage of the opportunity. He ordered the infantry forward in a bayonet charge that sent the British into a retreat.

Another cheer sounded as the advance was checked, and the English regiment pushed back into the thickets by the river, but the sound was halfhearted at best. As Jacob and the rest of the third line watched, the English took up position and held it until reinforcements stormed across the bridge.

The inexperienced American militiamen and volunteers scattered, dropping their weapons as they ran. The riflemen tried to cover their retreat, but within a few moments, they too fell into disorder. With such little training and no battlefield experience, the men were utterly unprepared for the onslaught.

"Halt! Return to your positions! Hold the line!" Jacob and the others yelled at the men passing on the road beneath him, but fueled by terror, none stopped. In only a few moments, the entire first and second lines were dispersed. And the redcoats pressed forward toward the third.

Alden bumped him with his elbow. "Looks like it's up to us." He raised his musket and waited for the command.

Jacob did the same, nodding to his friend and wishing he knew something profound to say. The moment felt important, and if either of them didn't survive—

"Fire!" The cannons on either side of them discharged with a blast that sent Jacob's ears ringing.

He pushed all other thoughts from his head, focusing only on the repetitive motions of firing and reloading. Rockets continued to blast holes into the line, breaking up the militia formations into disorder. One hit close, sending a blast of dirt over Jacob and Alden.

He glanced to the side, making certain his friend was unhurt, then aimed and shot another musket ball at a red-coated enemy.

The militia on either side of the flotilla men fled. Barney maintained the position, directing his troops and refusing to let the redcoats flank the line, even after his horse was shot under him. The heavy cannons pounded the road so forcefully that the British were driven back into the ravine.

But, as before, the enemy rallied, and the onslaught was fully directed at the five hundred flotilla men.

Alden fired then spat an oath. "Where is the cursed cavalry?" Jacob could scarcely hear his friend's voice over the ringing in his ears.

Jacob shot, and as he reloaded, he glanced around the fields, and the realization that no reinforcements were coming settled on him with cold certainty. They couldn't win.

The motley band of watermen continued to fire, moving in closer to hold the line, even as their numbers grew smaller.

A massive explosion hit the middle of the line, and when the smoke cleared, Jacob's heart fell. Barney and Michael were down, and the British were closing in.

"Retreat!" The call came from behind. General Winder's orders were being passed down the line. The soldiers needed no convincing. The orderly formation disintegrated into chaos as men fled away from the British advance.

Jacob ran in the opposite direction, pushing through the retreating men and falling to his knees beside his commander.

Alden followed suit, rushing to help Michael.

Soldiers and bullets continued to fly past.

Barney's face was pale as he held his leg, a musket ball wound in his thigh. Jacob tore off his neckcloth and bound the limb. "Sir, we must retreat."

Barney shook his head. "I can't flee, Jacob."

Jacob glanced over the man's shoulder, seeing the British officers approaching on horseback. "You must, sir. Come, I'll help—"

Wincing, Barney propped himself up on one elbow. "There is no time."

"But—"

"Listen to me." His face grew paler, but his eyes were intent. "Blow the naval yard. Defend the capital."

Jacob wanted to protest, but he knew Barney was right. They couldn't allow the enemy to take the ships.

"That's an order," Barney said, his voice much softer.

"Yes, sir."

Alden tugged on Jacob's arm. "We have to move, Jake."

"Michael?"

"He's hurt. Shot in the shoulder. They'll take him as prisoner, but he'll survive. The English have good doctors."

With a heavy heart, Jacob bid Barney farewell. He grabbed his musket, then he and Alden ran through the battlefield, dodging rocket craters, enemies, and dying men. They hid in a clump of foliage at the edge of the road and watched as the English officers reached Barney. The leader, who, Jacob judged by the decorations on his regimentals to be General Ross, ordered a surgeon to attend the commodore immediately, moving him into a wagon.

"That's all we can do for him, Jake."

Jacob sighed, the horrific sounds, smells, and sights of the past two hours overwhelming his senses. Sitting behind a desk, copying orders, and assigning missions seemed like a child's game compared to fighting in an actual battle.

"We have to destroy the naval yard," he told Alden.

The two looked at one another, the reality of what they had to do hanging in the air between them. Before selling it to the navy, Thomas Hathaway had been the master of the Washington shipyard. It was where Jacob and Alden had grown into men, had become brothers, had found a family.

"Well, Thomas always said I'd end up burning the place down," Alden said with a half-smile. "Shall we?"

Jacob peeked out of the thicket. The fighting had finished, but the hillside was still alive with movement as the wounded on both sides were cared for, prisoners were taken, and the dead were counted. The English gathered in the town. They'd seemed to have lost interest in pursuing the retreating enemy. Jacob guessed they were laying plans for their attack on the capital.

Jacob and Alden had left their horses hobbled near a creek farther down the road toward Washington. Jacob hoped none of the retreating men had taken them. He reached out a hand and helped Alden to his feet. His friend's face was covered in gunpowder, dirt, and sweat, and he hadn't shaved in days. Jacob imagined he looked the same. Seeing Alden, he felt a wave of relief that he'd made it through the clash unharmed. The very thought of his closest friend lying out on the battlefield made his chest ache. "I'm glad you didn't die." He released Alden's hand and started toward the road, feeling foolish that he'd voiced the sentiment but at the same time glad he'd said it.

Alden caught up to him and put an arm around his shoulder. "Aw, Jake, I knew you cared."

Jacob rolled his eyes and shook off Alden's hold, but for once, he didn't argue.

# Chapter 19

Lydia slept poorly. Every noise in the quiet house seemed menacing, each rattle of the shutters or creak of the stairs convincing her the redcoats were on the doorstep. She was grateful once morning finally arrived and Janet helped her to dress. Elnora's health had improved marginally to the point that the older woman had moved from her bedchamber to the upstairs parlor. She coughed only occasionally this morning, obediently taking her tonic from Janet as the two took breakfast. Avoiding the topic forefront in Lydia's and Elnora's minds, they attempted small talk, but the discussion fell silent after only a few moments. Lydia had no appetite and moved instead to look through the curtains.

The household and the entire city seemed to be holding their breath, waiting either for an attack or for news that the English had been defeated and turned away from the city. But as the morning dragged on, hot and eerily silent, Lydia wondered more than once if she should try to convince Elnora to leave Washington. Perhaps Burnett could locate some horses and a wagon, or they could even walk. A glance at Elnora dismissed that idea as soon as it had formed. She wasn't certain the older woman was even strong enough to walk down the stairs.

If only there were news. Any news. The servants spoke in tense whispers, moving around the room quietly as Elnora napped.

Lydia alternated between pacing, watching the street below, and moving to the other side of the room to watch out a different window. The large parlor took up an entire side of the house, the tall windows giving views in three directions. Soldiers had gathered around the president's house and the capitol building, but there seemed to be so few. Tension made Lydia's shoulders tight, but as the morning drew on, even the threat of invasion couldn't keep away the boredom. She sat on a chair next to Elnora and turned pages in a book but couldn't concentrate on the words.

Burnett and the other servants had taken her place, moving from window to window, trying to see anything that would give them an idea of what was happening.

The hour was nearly noon when a rumble sounded. The noise wasn't loud, but it filled her with dread. Though distant, the sound was immediately recognizable: the sound of a battle. She hurried to the northern window, joining the others.

"Bladensburg," one of the servants said.

Lydia scooted to the side as Elnora joined them. The rumbling continued. They watched as the sky filled with smoke. Occasionally, the red streak of a rocket was visible, but only for an instant. It didn't matter that they couldn't actually see anything of the battle; the group stood still, their eyes fastened to the smoky horizon. Even at this distance, the ground trembled with each blast. Lydia imagined she heard voices yelling, screams of pain, calls to arms, but of course it couldn't be so. She realized she was clinging to Janet and Elnora's hands.

The battle continued for nearly two hours. Then, just as suddenly as it had begun, it ended. Even more haunting than the noise of the explosions was the silence that followed.

Janet returned Elnora to the sofa.

Lydia remained with the rest of the servants at the window long after the noise ended, squinting northward toward the smoke, hoping for answers. Who had won? Were the English turned away? The whispered speculations from earlier didn't return, as if nobody dared to put voice to their worries.

Finally she returned to her chair, sitting quietly so as to not wake Elnora.

Lydia's mind flitted from question to question. Where was Jacob? Had he found the flotilla? Were he and Alden part of the battle at Bladensburg? Were Alden's wounds tended to? What of the Annapolis house? If the army should turn east, what would become of it? Were her parents safe in Rosefield? Was Emmett, too, fighting in Canada?

Her heart hurt as she thought of the smoke and explosions and Jacob among them. Where was he? Was he hurt? She remembered the night—had it only been three nights earlier?—she'd spent listening to his heartbeat. His heart was still beating, wasn't it?

She rubbed her eyes, trying to push away the worries, but panic rose, just like in her dream. She was alone and everyone—

"There, there, my dear," Elnora said.

Lydia opened her eyes, startled by the woman's interruption into her thoughts. "I'm sorry, Mrs. Hathaway. Did I wake you?"

Elnora squeezed her hand. "I know you miss him."

Tears filled Lydia's eyes. She *did* miss him.

The older woman smiled. "That boy—that man, I should say—he's special, isn't he?"

"He is." Lydia's tears spilled over, and she wiped at them with a handkerchief. "Jacob and I didn't part well." She hadn't intended to confide in Mrs. Hathaway, but all her uncertainty and fear had grown so big that she couldn't hold it in any longer. "I should have done it differently, but . . . things have been difficult between us."

"I understand."

"You do?" It was a polite sentiment, but the woman couldn't possibly appreciate the obstacles their relationship had faced.

"I imagine being married to Jacob has its challenges." Elnora coughed and leaned back on the sofa. "Bless him. He has a difficult time trusting, doesn't he?"

Lydia nodded. Perhaps the woman understood more than Lydia had given her credit for.

"He spent most of his childhood in an orphanage, you know," Elnora continued. "Had a hard time of it."

Lydia turned toward her, wanting to know everything. Wanting to understand this man who was still such a mystery.

"You see," Elnora said. "Jacob has a tender heart, but it's all concealed in that big body. When people look to adopt a child, they are hoping for a soft-spoken, wide-eyed little boy or a gentle, pretty little girl." The older woman gave a sad sigh. "He's a protector; took the younger ones under his wing, cared for them, then watched them leave, one by one, taken away to families."

Lydia's throat was tight, thinking of the large boy alone, watching through an orphanage window as his friends went away with their new parents. She pressed her lips together and wiped her already dripping eyes as her heart broke for the hurt he'd endured.

"Jacob always blamed himself for his parents leaving. Of course, it wasn't his fault, but he couldn't understand that. His father deserted his mother shortly after he was born. The man had accrued so much debt he thought it easier to run away, probably west to find his fortune." Elnora's lip curled, her dislike for the man obvious. "Jacob's mother died a few years after that—drank herself to death. Jacob thought if only he'd been a better son or taken better care of his mother . . . He truly believed all of these adults' mistakes were his fault."

"Oh, Jacob," Lydia whispered.

Elnora wiped away a tear of her own. "Mr. Hathaway found him at the orphanage. He was looking for a strong boy to help at the shipyard." She smiled. "But Jacob was more than he'd expected. More than either of us expected. That boy was intelligent, he caught on well, he was generous and kind, and we both fell in love with him." She laid her hand on her chest, her smile soft. "Thomas and I never had children of our own. Eventually we asked Jacob to live here with us. We sent him to school, raised him like our own son, he and Alden." She frowned. "But Jacob never fully trusted any of us. He worried it would all be taken away; even after all those years, he never fully believed we wouldn't leave him. He was always polite, always kind. He loved us, but he kept a part of himself back."

Lydia remembered Ezra's similar reaction when he received his free papers. "He kept a part of himself back," she said. "That's it exactly. I feel like I don't know Jacob at all and that maybe he doesn't want me to." Was he afraid for her to know him? His story gave her quite a lot to think about.

Elnora coughed and took a sip of tea. "Do you know what I think?" she asked. "I think Jacob doesn't believe he's worthy of love. That's why he doesn't trust it when it's given."

Lydia's heart hurt. "Oh, but he is. He's a good man and—"

"I know it," Elnora said. "And you know it. Don't worry, dear. He'll come around. He needs someone to understand and to give him the chance." The woman squeezed Lydia's hand again and sat back in her chair, closing her eyes.

Lydia thought of all she'd learned from the short conversation. Did Jacob truly feel himself unworthy of love? Was he keeping part of himself back, protecting his heart from being hurt?

If that was so, she'd done exactly what he'd feared by telling him she planned to return home to Rosefield. He'd accepted the declaration, reacted indifferently, as he would have if she'd told him they were to have chicken for supper. He hadn't asked her to stay, and that had hurt more than Lydia was prepared for.

She believed the things Elnora said were true, but Lydia feared she wasn't the person to give him a chance. Jacob had been coerced to marry her; he'd avoided her, suspected her, and then accepted her intention to leave without a second thought. The truth was, she loved Jacob, but she wouldn't remain with a man who didn't love her.

The sound of voices at the window drew her from her self-pity, and she raised her head. "What is it, Burnett?"

"Soldiers, Mrs. Steele."

Terror burst over her in a wave. "Redcoats?"

"Americans." His expression looked somber.

That was good news, wasn't it? She rose and joined him at the window. The soldiers weren't marching in formation but moved through the streets of the city in groups of two or three. Sometimes they were alone. Some men limped, others helped an injured comrade.

"They're retreating," Lydia said.

"They are, Mrs. Steele."

Images from the night she was injured came to her mind. Fire, breaking glass, gunshots, yelling, and over it all, the fear that she couldn't escape. Wrapping her arms around her middle, she looked to the north but could only see smoke. Somewhere up there, an English army was gathering to invade the capital, and Lydia was directly in their path.

# CHAPTER 20

JACOB AND ALDEN PASSED THROUGH the streets of Washington City with a wagon full of gunpowder and a group of militia volunteers. They'd found it surprisingly difficult to gather men for the job as more and more defenders fled their posts after hearing the report of the battle at Bladensburg. Luckily they'd come upon three members of Alden's crew, who had agreed to accompany them.

"The United States needs a strong military." Jacob steered his horse closer to Alden. "The state-supplied militias just aren't effective."

"What? Military training? What a radical thought." Alden rolled his eyes, motioning with his chin toward the president's house, where only a small group of soldiers stood guard. "They won't put up a fight." He shook his head. "Secretary Armstrong and President Madison should have planned for this threat against the capital," he continued. "They should have ordered General Winder to gather an army months ago." He shook his head. "Before she evacuated, I heard Mrs. Madison laid out a fine supper for the president and his generals to celebrate the victory in Bladensburg."

"I'm certain the English officers will eat well, then," Jacob said. He was frustrated that protecting the city had been a last-moment effort brought about only by a bit of news overheard in a servant's closet. Out of habit, he looked toward Elnora's house, only seeing the very tops of the chimneys over the trees and houses.

Alden followed his line of sight. "Should we check at Elnora's? Make certain she and Lydia got to safety?"

Jacob paused for a moment. "They won't be there. Lydia was determined to leave the city, and you know nothing stops that woman once her mind's set." The finality of the words made his heart drop.

"I'm glad the truth came out at last and the two of you were able to reconcile." Alden glanced at Jacob. "You *did* reconcile?"

Jacob pressed his lips together. "Lydia told me she intends to return to her parents' house."

"Well, she was very upset." He nodded. "Of course, you talked her out of it."

Jacob looked ahead toward the naval yard.

"Jake?"

"She wants to leave." Jacob's voice cracked, and he cleared his throat, embarrassed at the emotion that had emerged.

"You hurt her feelings, and she needed reassurance that it wouldn't happen again." Alden reached across and pulled on Hildegard's reins, halting both horses. "I take it you had none to give."

Jacob scowled.

Alden shook his head, his lips tight as if he were holding back a stream of profanities. Which he probably was. "Jacob Steele, how can you be so cursed brilliant about everything else and so absurdly foolish about this?" He rubbed the back of his neck. "Lydia needs what every woman—every person—needs. She needs to feel wanted, safe. You have to ask her to stay. Beg her if you must."

Jacob's throat felt like he'd swallowed sand. "It's too late."

Alden studied him with narrowed eyes. "You want her to go."

"She deserves better." He couldn't meet his friend's gaze, not wanting him to see the hurt in his own.

Alden looked upward as if asking the heavens how his friend could be such an imbecile. "Stop with the martyr business, Jake. There is *nobody* better—for either of you. And you're both too stubborn to see it." He clasped Jacob's arm, squeezing. "Don't let her go, Jake. You'll spend forever regretting it."

Jake studied his friend. "What happened to you?"

Alden released his arm. "This isn't about me. It's about you. I make the mistakes, but you learn from them. Isn't that how we've always done it?" He urged his horse forward, and even from behind, Jacob could see his friend's jaw was tight.

If only reconciliation were as easy as Alden thought it was. Jacob sighed, rubbing his eyes as Hildegard followed.

The shipyard had changed since their time here—barracks and parade grounds replacing workshops and construction sites. But, of course, the harbor remained. The group entered the compound gate, passing the naval monument, a large marble-and-brass tribute erected to honor the officers who'd died in Barbary, and were met by a trio of sailors.

A uniformed man approached Jacob and saluted. "The commodore's been expecting you." He nodded toward one of the buildings—a single family house, by the look of it—where an older man with a round belly stood in the doorway, looking over the harbor.

Jacob approached and stood beside him. "Good afternoon, Commodore."

"Mr. Steele." Commodore Tingey continued to stare at the ships. "You're here because the English are on their way."

"Yes."

The commodore nodded. "I have my orders to burn the place, but only if there is no alternative."

"I'm sorry, sir." His stomach was heavy as he gazed at the magnificent warships. The *USS New York* and *USS Argus* had both fought Barbary pirates in Tripoli, running rescue missions and attacks. Smaller boats bobbed beside the pier, the shine on their decks visible across the distance. Jacob imagined the commodore was familiar with each of the vessels, had read countless reports on their missions, casualties, victories, and damages.

Commodore Tingey had been superintendent of the yard for fourteen years, and its destruction must weigh heavily.

Jacob looked away, giving the commodore a moment of privacy. His gaze fell on the dry dockyard where he'd spent his formative years. The forty-four-gun frigate *Columbia* was still under construction, never to be finished, and Jacob's own throat felt tight.

Commodore Tingey let out a breath, straightened his shoulders, and gave a curt nod. "Let's get to it, then." He called out orders, directing the cannons and cannonballs to be jettisoned. The naval records and family valuables had been removed from the houses and offices, and charges were to be set inside. A man of duty, he apparently intended to follow the orders to destroy the yard quite completely.

Jacob rejoined the group of militia, helping to distribute the barrels of powder through the buildings and ships. The workers went about their duties silently; the work of destruction left none in the mood for chatter or merriment. Adding to the malaise of the operation was the oppressive heat. The summer day was hotter than any Jacob could remember.

The navy worked efficiently, their training and obedience to orders apparent. *If only every harbor in America weren't blockaded,* Jacob thought. *The English would have a fight on their hands.*

Once the charges were set and the yard evacuated, they had only to light the fuses, which the commodore declared he'd not do until he saw the English invaders with his own eyes.

Jacob bid the sailors farewell and went in search of Alden, finding him and his three men on one of the farthest docks. "Time to go."

"I'm taking this one." Alden motioned with his chin toward one of the smaller boats, a single-masted sloop. The small ship was well-crafted, sleek, and not built for battle. Likely the commodore's private boat or a pleasure vessel of one of the captains.

Jacob looked back toward the commodore's house. "I don't think . . ."

"I'll get her down the river and hide her away in a smaller creek. Gordon's warship has probably run aground every quarter of an hour since he entered the Potomac." Alden jumped over the bulwark rail. "He must be at least another day behind. Once he has passed, the way will be clear; I can get us to Annapolis quicker than riding back through Bladensburg. My backside can't take another day in the saddle. And my *Belladonna's* waiting for me."

Jacob considered, and in spite of the fact that Alden was practically giddy over stealing a very expensive and very beautiful boat, his reasoning made sense. "The river will take us past Rosefield."

Alden scowled and motioned his men aboard the vessel.

"I promised her," Jake said.

Alden ignored him and ran his hand over the shining wheel. "Don't worry, Darling. I won't let the English lay a finger on you," he crooned to the sloop.

"I'll take the horses," Jacob said, not believing he was going along with the ridiculous plan. "Where will we meet?"

"Little Hunting Creek." Alden and his crew were already unloading the gunpowder from the ship's hull and setting it onto the dock. "We'll find Elnora and Lydia and get back to this beauty in just a few hours."

Alden untied the sails, and Jake loosened the ropes from the dock's bollards, tossed them aboard, and gave the sloop a shove, wondering why he'd agreed to riding miles through the hot countryside while his friend commandeered an extravagant watercraft. A smile tugged at his mouth. Why should he be surprised?

"We're not taking her home," Alden called, turning the boom to catch the wind.

Jacob sighed and returned to the horses, knowing he was letting his friend down. But he was doing what was best for the woman he loved . . . and crushing his own heart in the process.

# CHAPTER 21

A SERIES OF EXPLOSIONS SHOOK the house, dropping glass ornaments from shelves and making the occupants of Elnora's drawing room cower on the floor.

Lydia held on to the older woman's hand, one arm around her shoulders. Janet did the same on Elnora's other side. Lydia's entire body had erupted in tremors as she wondered if the Hathaway house was the next to be bombed.

The women shared a look. Janet's face was pale, her eyes wide, and Lydia imagined she looked the same.

"The naval yard." Burnett's voice sounded over the heartbeat that thundered in Lydia's ears. "The redcoats must be close."

Lydia and Janet helped Elnora back to the couch, sitting beside her and holding on to her hands. The older woman maintained her composure, but Lydia could feel her hands shaking.

The city was under invasion. A hundred questions moved through Lydia's mind, but she was too frightened to voice any. She watched as Burnett moved around the room, loosening the ties and closing the heavy drapes over the airy fabric beneath. He left the room and returned a few moments later with Elnora's carriage driver. Both men carried a musket and took up a position beside opposite windows, peeking through the crack in the drapes.

The other servants came into the drawing room. Their expressions were fearful as they clustered close to the group. Lydia was glad for their presence. A larger group felt safer.

Guns fired from the direction of the capitol, joined by the booming of cannons. Burnett crossed the room, joining the other carriage driver. They watched through the drapes, but the noise lasted for only a few moments.

"Didn't put up much of a fight," Burnett said, his mouth downturned as he moved to a different window.

Lydia pressed the side of her fist to her mouth, worried she would scream. She felt utterly helpless as the memory of crouching behind the old cradle in the storage building rose up, choking her. The fear of those long moments returned as she waited with the others, praying the next crashes wouldn't come from Elnora's windows.

More shots sounded, accompanied by crashes, shouts, and the shattering of glass. These noises sounded much closer.

"What's happening, Burnett?" Lydia's whisper sounded loud in the tense room.

Burnett shook his head. "I can't see any—" His voice cut off and his eyes widened.

"What is it?" she asked.

He turned toward them and let out a heavy breath. "The capitol is on fire."

Elnora gasped.

Lydia crossed the room to join him. She peeked through the drapes, and her chest ached at the sight of flames engulfing the beautiful unfinished capitol building.

A company of red-coated soldiers marched down the street in front of Elnora's house, and Lydia pulled away from the window. She hurried back to her spot on the sofa.

The noises of destruction continued, sounding irregularly around the city. Burnett reported the government buildings and the president's house were burning as well as the capitol and the naval yard.

His words carried a sense of hopelessness. Beautiful Washington, the capital of their young nation, was in ruins. Defeat felt bitter in Lydia's stomach, and she thought the others felt it too. A few tears were shed as an overall sense of discouragement pressed down like a thick cloud over the darkened room, and Lydia found her fear had ebbed away, leaving behind dismay and fatigue.

The occupants in the room remained quiet, their only communication in whispers. In time, tense shoulders relaxed, and the servants sat on chairs and upon the floor. Lydia didn't blame them at all, glad they felt safe, even though at any other time, the behavior would be quite improper.

The summer day was already hot, but with the heavy curtains closed and the smell of smoke permeating everything, Lydia thought she might be ill. She and Janet took turns fanning Elnora, finding moving air to be slightly cooler. But only slightly.

The marching soldiers passed the house again, their footsteps echoing through the empty streets.

"They're patrolling." Elnora's carriage driver peered through the curtain crack. "To prevent looting."

"That's a relief," Elnora said. "Let's pray the officers can keep their soldiers in check."

Lydia did just that.

A few hours later, Lydia peeked between the heavy drapes, careful not to allow light to escape and give away her presence to anyone who might be watching from outside. Darkness had fallen, but the night was far from peaceful.

The glow of fires burned on all sides, and from her view, it seemed the entire city was aflame. Across the street, another curtain moved, and Lydia imagined another household of frightened people doing the very same thing behind their drapes.

Burnett stood near, holding his musket. As the day had drawn on, the other servants had drifted away, some returning to their duties, as evidenced by the smell of supper that wafted up the stairs. Others were probably peeking through curtains in various rooms throughout the house.

Outside, the night was quiet, which only added to Lydia's unease. Where was Jacob? He'd promised to find her. Had he gone to Elnora's friend's house? If so, he'd have had plenty of time to continue on to Washington City. Her stomach felt rock hard as she considered what may have kept him from keeping his promise.

"You're fretting, dear," Elnora said. "Worry makes time pass slowly."

Lydia returned to the sofa. She knew the older woman meant well, but her words did little to ease the anxiety prickling at Lydia's nerves.

"He'll be here," Elnora said. She leaned close, patting Lydia's arm. "Supper will be ready soon, and the distraction will do you—"

Noises sounded in the hallway below, cutting off Elnora's words.

Burnett crossed the room, lifting his musket.

Lydia started toward the doorway, but before she reached it, the butler, Dawson, entered. The white-haired man's brows were tight. His eyes widened at the sight of the musket, but he turned from Burnett and spoke to Elnora. "If you please, Mrs. Hathaway. You've visitors."

"Visitors?" Elnora said. "Who on earth . . ."

Dawson wrung his hands. "I do not think they mean any harm, madam."

Lydia and Burnett exchanged a look. The man's jaw tightened and he stepped into the corridor.

Lydia followed, staying close behind the carriage driver.

At the top of the staircase, Burnett raised his musket, aiming toward the entryway beneath.

"That is a very unwise decision, man," said a nasally voice from below.

Lydia stepped around the carriage driver, and her skin went cold.

Two English officers stood in the entrance hall.

Both men bowed when they saw her.

"The lady of the house, I presume?" the nasally voiced man said. He lifted his chin and removed a glove. "Colonel Andrews of His Majesty's Army. Lieutenant Reynolds and I have come for supper." He held out his hat and gloves, looking around as if waiting for someone to take them.

"We mean you no harm, madam," the other man said. His voice was much more polite, and his expression pulled in an apologetic grimace.

"Though we may change our minds if your manservant doesn't lower his musket," Colonel Andrews said. "It would take little more than a shout to alert the patrol."

Lydia put her hand on Burnett's arm, pushing it downward. When he met her gaze, she shook her head. "Help Elnora to the dining room, if you please," she said.

She motioned to Dawson and followed him down the stairs, calming her breathing as she went.

The butler took the officers' hats and gloves.

"Colonel Andrews, Lieutenant Reynolds." Lydia curtsied, relaxing her muscles and forcing a natural-looking smile. "Welcome, officers." She took each man's hand, noting the colonel's soft fingers compared to Lieutenant Reynolds's callouses. "Mrs. Lydia Steele. I am a guest here as well."

Burnett led Elnora down the stairs.

Lydia took her arm. "Our hostess, Mrs. Elnora Hathaway."

The men greeted Elnora, and Lydia studied them. Colonel Andrews's lip was curled in a permanent sneer as if the house and everything in it were so far below his position in society as to be repulsive. Even though the army had been marching for weeks, had fought a battle that morning and invaded a city a few hours earlier, he looked well rested and his clothes freshly pressed, which led her to deduce he traveled with servants. The colonel was likely a member of English nobility. Maybe the younger son of a peer.

Lieutenant Reynolds, on the other hand, wore a uniform that had been mended multiple times. Burn marks on the wool of his coat indicated he wore the same uniform he'd fought in. His trousers were wrinkled, and his boots, though polished, were well worn. He was from a different class than the colonel. A gentleman, perhaps, but not a nobleman.

"If you please, officers." Elnora swept her hand toward the far end of the entry hall. "The dining room is this way." She took Colonel Andrews's offered arm, and Lydia took the lieutenant's.

Colonel Andrews sat, very presumptively, at the head of the table, his arrogant expression reminding them that no matter how civil their behavior, the English army still occupied the city.

Elnora did not allow the man's behavior to unsettle her. She sat beside him, next to Lydia. Lieutenant Reynolds took a seat across the table, facing the ladies.

A nervous-looking footman set a bowl of soup before the guests.

Colonel Andrews lifted a spoon, sniffing the soup, then wrinkling his nose. "Mrs. Steele, I believe you mentioned you are a guest here? Where are you from?"

"My husband and I live in Annapolis, but I was raised at my father's plantation in Virginia."

He set the spoon down, his lip curling. "Slave owners. How distasteful."

She didn't allow the insult to change her expression, maintaining her charming smile.

Elnora patted Lydia's knee beneath the table. "And what of you, Colonel? Where is your home, sir?"

"Surrey. My father is Marquess of Hassock. Of course you've heard of him."

Lydia thought it would positively shock the English aristocracy to know how few of their titles Americans were actually familiar with.

"How nice." Elnora dabbed her mouth with her napkin. Her voice sounded strong, even though her hands shook the slightest bit. "And what of you, Lieutenant? Where do you come from?"

"Stropshire, madam. A small town called Whitchurch, close to the Welsh border." The lieutenant's gray eyes softened.

"You miss it," Lydia said. "How long have you been away?"

"Two years," Lieutenant Reynolds said. "Two years of campaigning through Spain, and once we defeated Napoleon and sent him to Elba, we all expected to go home."

"But you were sent here instead."

He nodded.

"I'm sorry," Lydia said, seeing the sadness in the man's face. "You must have been so disappointed."

"Disappointed to be sent to a mosquito-infested swamp to fight uncultured separatists instead of returning to a grand castle?" Colonel Andrews pushed away his bowl, motioning with a flick of his wrist for the footman to remove it. "That's rather an understatement, Mrs. Steele."

"Well, we aren't exactly thrilled to have you here, either," Lydia said.

The colonel glared.

Lieutenant Reynolds laughed. "I imagine not."

"Even France was more civilized than America," Colonel Andrews said. "I have received more insect bites in the past two weeks than the rest of my years combined."

"How very tragic for you," Lydia said. But before he could respond to her sarcasm she turned back to the lieutenant. "Are you married, Lieutenant Reynolds?"

"Yes, madam. Anna and I married a week before I departed for Spain." This time, the sadness in his eyes nearly brought tears to her own.

"And where is *your* husband, Mrs. Steele?" Colonel Andrews asked.

Lydia sat back as the footman delivered a plate of chicken and potatoes. The question caught her off guard, though she should have known to expect it. She swallowed away the lump in her throat. "I don't know." She figured there was no reason not to tell the truth. "He left me here with Elnora and rode to join the flotilla at Upper Marlboro."

"Commodore Barney's flotilla fought at Bladensburg," Lieutenant Reynolds said.

Lydia thought she saw him wince.

"Quite a few Americans left on the ground in Bladensburg, weren't there, Lieutenant?" Colonel Andrews said, cutting into a piece of chicken.

Lydia put a hand over her mouth as coldness hit and spread from her center.

"Really, Colonel," Elnora said. "I took you for a gentleman."

The colonel smirked.

"I truly hope he is well, Mrs. Steele," Lieutenant Reynolds said, his ears reddening. "But take heart, madam. The battle didn't leave too many casualties. Chances are, he retreated or was taken prisoner. If he was injured, he'll be well cared for."

"Thank you, sir."

The colonel motioned for his plate to be removed. He studied Lydia with half-lidded eyes, as if the entire supper was the epitome of boring. "What happened to your cheek, Mrs. Steele? You'd be quite pretty if not for that scar."

A flush burst over Lydia's face, but she only raised a brow, trying to calm the panic at his calling attention to her disfigurement. She knew he hoped to catch her off guard, to embarrass her or make her turn away. But she'd not give him the satisfaction. "An English raiding party plundered my father's plantation, if you must know." She held his gaze as she spoke. "They killed innocent servants and indiscriminately destroyed property. My scar"—she traced the line on her cheek, fixing him with a glare—"was caused by an explosion." She leaned toward the colonel. "I supposed that is what you consider civilized behavior, Colonel Andrews."

He maintained eye contact, though she saw by his scowl that her words had angered him. *Good.*

Colonel Andrews rose. "Come, Lieutenant. I suppose we should oversee the troops. General Ross gave the command that no civilian's property was to be damaged or stolen." He lifted a golden ornament from a side table, studying it, then sniffed, setting it back on the table. "Not that there's anything in this backwoods town worth taking."

The colonel swept from the room.

Lieutenant Reynolds followed but stopped when he reached the women, lifting Elnora's hand and bowing. "Thank you for supper, Mrs. Hathaway. I've not eaten such a delicious meal in years." He released her hand and took Lydia's. "A pleasure to meet you, Mrs. Steele. I quite enjoyed your company."

"And I enjoyed yours, Lieutenant."

Hearing his commander clear his throat, Lieutenant Reynolds inclined his head once more, and the English officers departed.

Dawson closed the door behind them, bolting it.

Lydia and Elnora stared at one another.

"Well, I never . . ." Elnora huffed, sinking back down into her seat at the dining room table. "That pompous windbag."

Lydia sat beside her. "What a horrible man."

"He was very insulting, wasn't he, dear? But his friend was pleasant enough."

The colonel's words about Bladensburg hung heavily over Lydia's thoughts. She tried to smile, for Elnora's sake.

Elnora folded her napkin. "Uncultured separatists," she muttered. "How dare he!"

Lydia squeezed her hand.

"What would Jacob and Alden say?" Elnora asked.

"About what?" Lydia asked.

Elnora shook her head, touching her hand to her brow. "While the pair of them were off fighting, we fed the enemy supper."

# CHAPTER 22

JACOB AND ALDEN LEFT THE sloop with the crewmen in Little Hunting Creek and rode toward Bethesda to find Lydia and Elnora. Avoiding the English army, they stayed well west of Alexandria and crossed the river near Georgetown.

The air was hazy with smoke, making the morning sun appear red. Even from miles away, they could smell the naval yard burning. Jacob hoped that was all that was burning. They'd seen the glow of fires all through the night. As he'd ridden to meet Alden the day before, he'd heard skirmishes but no real battle. The city's defense had fallen in only a matter of moments.

The pair dismounted in the shade near a creek, giving their horses a rest.

Jacob bent forward and then to each side, trying to stretch out the muscles in his back. He'd been in the saddle for days.

Alden pressed his fist into his own back. "Not cut out for the cavalry, are we, Jake?"

"Not at all."

"What's your opinion?" Alden asked, wincing as he bent to hobble the horses. "Will the English occupy the city?"

Jacob crouched down to fill the water flask. "Don't know why they would." He splashed the cool water onto his face then tied a wet kerchief around his neck. "Washington City has no strategic advantage. Its value is the government seat. Capturing the president—*that* would be an enormous advantage."

Alden sat on the grass beside the stream. "The benefit to the English isn't merely strategic." He rested his forearm on his knee. "Striking the heart of America is a blow to morale."

Jacob took a long drink then refilled the flask and handed it to his friend. Alden was right. The emotional impact of the invasion was devastating to the fledgling country. "Do we have any hope of winning this war?" Admitting his doubt felt like a betrayal of the country he loved.

Alden slapped his shoulder. "There's always hope, Jake. No matter what those lobsterbacks think."

Thunder rumbled in the distance, and the two looked up. Dark clouds massed on the horizon.

Jacob rose quickly, knowing better than to underestimate a summer thunderstorm. They needed to locate shelter before the downpour began. "Maybe we can find a barn or—"

Alden snapped his fingers. "Michael Davis's farm is close. And we should pay his family a visit anyway." He untied his horse's reins and swung into the saddle. "See if we can offer any assistance while he's away."

Despite his eagerness to find Lydia and Elnora, Jacob agreed. Michael was a good friend. Checking on his family was the least they could do.

A half of an hour later, they rode onto the Davises' farm. A woman carrying a musket stepped onto the porch, followed by a small black dog. Martha, he assumed, was probably in her late twenties. She wore a mob cap, her sleeves were rolled, and she looked both extremely suspicious and extremely capable of using the weapon.

"Mrs. Davis?" Jacob called, raising his hands.

She scowled. "Who are you?"

Alden raised his hands as well. "Alden Thatcher, madam. And this is Jacob Steele. We're friends of your husband, Mrs. Davis." He dismounted and took a few careful steps forward. "We fought with Michael at Bladensburg."

Her brows pulled together and lifted. She set the butt of the musket down, and leaned on the gun as she began to breathe heavily, pressing a hand to her chest. "Have you come to tell me . . . ?"

"No, no. He's alive. Not to worry, madam," Jacob said quickly. He dismounted as well and glanced at the clouds. The storm would break any moment.

"He was injured, but he'll be well treated by the English," Alden said.

"A prisoner, then," she said.

"Yes." Alden touched her elbow. "Like I said, he'll be well treated."

A young girl stepped out of the house. She carried an infant and looked between her mother and the men. "Mama? Is everything all right?"

The woman turned. "Yes, Sarah. Mr. Thatcher and Mr. Steele are friends of your papa's."

The thunder rumbled, and a few drops hit the ground. "Put your horses in the barn." Mrs. Davis pointed across the farmyard. "Then come inside for lunch."

A few moments later, the men sat at the Davises' dining table while Mrs. Davis prepared their luncheon and rain pounded the roof. The farmhouse was small, but tidy and well cared for, with simple furnishings. But the feel of the place was cozy and orderly.

Jacob ran his hand over the table. Oak. The wood was scrubbed and dented in a few places, but it had been regularly oiled. A child's chair stood at one end, and a vase of flowers decorated the center. He imagined happy memories had taken place around this table, delicious meals, laughter . . . family. An ache grew in Jacob's chest.

The girl Sarah sat on a chair nearby, bouncing the baby and watching two other children. A small boy stacked blocks on the rug, and a girl with golden braids and blue eyes stood close to her sister, holding a toy doll.

Alden waved at the little girl.

She put her thumb in her mouth and watched him with large eyes.

He smiled. "Hello, there. What's your name?"

She pulled out her thumb long enough to say, "Emily," then put it back in.

"And what's your doll's name, Emily?"

"Fanny." She held the doll toward Alden.

He moved from his place at the table and knelt beside the girl, taking the offered doll and holding it carefully in the crook of his arm. He rocked it back and forth, and a moment later, he and the two young children were playing contentedly with the doll and blocks.

*How does he do it?* Jacob wondered again. He'd never known a person to make friends as easily as Alden. Excepting Lydia. She knew exactly how to behave with different people. She was as competent socially as he was insecure.

Mrs. Davis brought bread and soup from the kitchen, serving it into bowls. The black dog followed her back and forth.

Jacob thanked her. "Madam, keeping up the farm must be very difficult without your husband. Do you have need of any assistance while we're here?"

She sat across the table. "Eat while it's warm."

Alden joined them with the children.

The older daughter laid the baby in the cradle and lifted her brother into the child's seat. The little daughter sat beside Alden, her doll on the bench between them.

Once she saw that her children were all served, Mrs. Davis turned to Jacob. "In answer to your question, yes, it is difficult, but my eldest son, Jem, is keeping up with the work."

"Michael said as much," Jacob said. "He's extremely proud of his son—" He looked at the other children and smiled. "And of all of his family."

Alden dipped a slice of bread into his soup. "This is delicious, Mrs. Davis."

"Thank you."

She smiled, and the effect was surprising. Mrs. Davis was a pretty woman, though her responsibilities and exhaustion hid it.

"I believe Michael told me Jem is thirteen?" Jacob asked.

Mrs. Davis nodded.

"And he is working now?"

"He's out in the dairy." She pointed through the window to the farthest building.

The boy would probably remain in the dairy as long as the rain fell, Jacob guessed.

Once the family and their guests finished eating, Alden returned to the rug to play with the children, and Jacob helped Mrs. Davis carry the dishes into the kitchen.

She put a cloth over the bread and a lid on the soup. "I'll leave this for Jem," she said.

They returned to the main room and sat back down at the table, watching as Alden made silly faces that sent the children into fits of giggles.

"Do you have a family, Mr. Steele?" Mrs. Davis asked.

Jacob felt the familiar lump in his throat. "Yes. I have a wife. Lydia."

"And the war's separated the two of you as well." She laced her fingers on the table; her hands were red and calloused, attesting to the difficulty of her daily work.

"Yes."

"When Michael spoke about joining the flotilla, I supported him fully. I wanted to be the perfect loyal wife, sacrifice for America . . ." She sighed. "But having him gone has been . . . difficult. Not only in the management of the farm and caring for the children. But I miss my husband dreadfully. So much it hurts." She rubbed her chest. "I suppose you understand."

"I do," he said, feeling an ache in his own chest.

"I'll be glad—"

The dog barked, and Mrs. Davis jumped. "What is it, Polly?"

The dog whined. In the barn, the horses neighed, and Jacob moved to the window to see what was upsetting the animals.

The rain had stopped, but the wind howled. Trees bent, branches creaked and broke. From the east, a dark column of cloud stretched down into a funnel. A hurricane was headed directly for them. The hairs on Jacob's neck lifted. "Alden . . ."

His friend joined him at the window. "Blast," he muttered.

"Jem is in the dairy," Jacob said.

Alden spun. "Mrs. Davis, do you have a root cellar?"

She came toward them. "Yes, but—"

"Stop there. Keep away from the windows," Jacob said. "Take the children into the cellar."

Alden held the younger children's hands, leading them to their mother.

Jake took his hat from the hook by the door. "We'll go for Jem."

A branch crashed into the window, the sound sending Mrs. Davis into action. She grabbed the small children and called for Sarah to bring the baby.

"Don't forget Fanny," Alden said, handing the doll to Emily.

The farm house door flew inward as soon as Jacob unlatched it. The wind nearly pushed him over, blowing leaves into the house and debris through the yard. Limbs tumbled over the ground; farm tools and supplies were scattered about.

"Careful," Jacob shouted over the gale. "Anything becomes dangerous when it's hurled at that speed."

The hurricane had come from the direction of Washington City. Thank goodness Lydia and Elnora had evacuated.

He and Alden ran across the yard, fighting against the force of the wind. Branches slapped against them, and they held up their arms to keep from being hit in the face. The heavy dairy doors were open and banging against the sides of the building, each slam echoing through the building. Inside, the cows were panicked. They bellowed and snorted, straining to escape their pens as wind blew leaves and dust around them.

"Jem! Jem, are you in here?" Jacob yelled over the ruckus, his voice carried away by the wind.

Alden pulled on Jacob's arm, pointing toward the far corner of the dairy barn. A wide-eyed boy crouched down behind the cattle pens.

The wind blew in a large branch, hitting one of the pens, and a gust lifted up a milk canister and threw it into the wall, spraying milk over the room. The cows bucked, frantic. Jem ducked down, throwing his arms over his head.

"I'll close the doors, you get Jem." Jacob used gestures to get his meaning across since Alden couldn't hear him over the noise.

Alden nodded and started through the building.

Jacob grabbed on to the handle of one of the heavy doors, grunting as he fought the wind to pull it closed. Once the door was in place, he ran for the other. He needed to hurry and latch the doors together before the first blew open again.

Outside, a wagon wheel flew past, and Jacob ducked. The hurricane was right on top of the farm now. He took hold of the door handle.

Something heavy crashed into the wall just above his head, and Jacob closed his eyes to keep splinters from flying into them. He pulled on the door, moving it toward the other, then grabbed on to the first, pulling them together.

A gust threw open the doors, jerking Jacob's arm and launching him off his feet, flinging him into the side of the barn. He hit hard and fell to the ground. He blinked as pain exploded in his arm and shoulder.

Something banged against his side, and he groaned as it pierced through his skin. Keeping his eyes closed against the wind, he moved away from the flapping door and huddled against the base of the barn wall, covering his head with his good arm. The pain in his shoulder was excruciating. White spots flashed in front of his eyes.

*No, I can't fall unconscious.*

The noise of the wind seemed to lessen, but Jacob thought he may have been imagining it. He felt himself being pulled back into the barn, his shoulder flaring in white pain. He certainly wasn't imagining that. The pain increased, as did the flashes of light, until his stomach heaved.

"Jake!" Alden's voice was louder than the wind. He patted Jacob's face. "Jake. Wake up."

Jacob opened his eyes to see Alden and a pale Jem crouched over him.

"Can you hear me?" Alden's voice trembled, which terrified Jacob more than the hurricane had.

"I can hear you." He ground out the words, closing his eyes when the room started to spin. His stomach heaved again.

"Jake, this is bad."

"It's not too bad," Jacob lied.

"Can you ride? We have to get you to a doctor."

The thought of being shaken on a horse made his stomach turn. He opened his eyes to take stock of the situation. His arm was certainly broken, and he thought the shoulder must have been pulled from its socket, based on the pain that seared from it whenever he even thought about that part of his body. But Alden wasn't looking at his arm. He held a cloth pressed to Jacob's side.

When Jacob bent his head forward, he saw the cloth was covered in blood.

"A garden fork," Alden said. His voice was soft and serious. Definitely not a good sign. "Poked straight through. The wound looks really deep, Jake."

Jake wanted to reassure his friend that he'd be fine, but he couldn't even keep his eyes open long enough to speak.

He lay back, only half listening as Alden and Jem discussed his condition.

" . . . wagon is smashed . . . we can't wait . . . get the horses."

Alden squeezed his shoulder. "Don't worry, Jake. I'll get you to a doctor."

"Not to the city. The English . . ." His thoughts spun.

"You need a doctor, Jake. The closest one will be in the city."

Jacob wanted to protest. They needed to find Lydia and Elnora. He opened his mouth to argue, but the pain was finally too much and he slipped into unconsciousness.

# CHAPTER 23

LYDIA PULLED A THIN BLANKET over Elnora, tucking it against her sides. She moved quietly so as not to wake the older woman. The day had been one of the most unbelievable Lydia could remember. Not only was the city occupied and the government buildings burning, but a fierce thunderstorm had poured onto the burning city, followed by a *hurricane*. Luckily none of Elnora's household had been hurt, and the home itself escaped major damage, but Lydia had heard reports from the servants of destruction and loss of life.

Lydia felt drained, her nerves worn out from the events of the past three days. If she'd not seen all of this with her own eyes, she'd never have believed it possible that one city could suffer such terrible fortune in such a short time. She couldn't imagine anything surprising her after the time she'd spent in Washington City.

A knock came at the drawing room door, and Dawson entered.

"Mrs. Hathaway is asleep," Lydia whispered, holding up a finger in front of her mouth.

Dawson's brows were furrowed. His eyes darted to Elnora then to the door behind him. "Mrs. Steele, you should come downstairs."

Lydia's defenses went on alert. The last time she'd seen that worried expression on the butler's face, two enemy soldiers had been in the entry hall. She hurried down the stairs and, following Dawson's nod, entered the downstairs parlor.

Jacob lay on the sofa, his face pale and filthy beneath thick whiskers. Beside him, Burnett knelt on the rug, holding a bloody rag against her husband's side.

"Jacob." Lydia rushed toward them. "Burnett, what . . . ?"

The carriage driver scooted back, giving her room to join him, but kept his hand firmly pressed on Jacob's side. "Mr. Thatcher's gone for a doctor, Mrs. Steele."

She knelt, setting a hand on Jacob's cheek. "Jacob, can you hear me?" She pushed the words through a dry mouth.

"Lydia?" He whispered the word, his eyes flickering.

Relief poured over her. "Yes, I'm here. Don't worry, now; everything will be all right."

Jacob strained, trying to sit up. "My shoulder."

She pushed a hand against his chest. "Lie still." Looking closer, she could see one shoulder was positioned lower than the other. As she studied it, she saw his coat was tight on his arm. "I think your arm is swollen, maybe broken. Help me take off his coat, Burnett."

Jacob winced and sucked in a breath through his teeth when the two shifted him to remove his coat. When she tugged it off his sore arm, he groaned and laid back his head against the armrest.

"I'm sorry." Lydia brushed back the hair from his forehead. His shoulder was definitely out of place, and the arm looked swollen and disfigured, stretching the sleeve. "Burnett, I think we should cut off his shirt. Pulling his arm is too painful."

Lydia called to Janet, sending her for scissors and clean cloths. The maid returned quickly, and they cut the shirt from his arm, moving it as little as possible. The arm was indeed inflamed, and Lydia ordered willow bark tea. When Lydia had injured her wrist as a girl, she remembered the doctor telling her mother the tea helped with swelling and pain.

Burnett kept the rag in place, even while they removed Jacob's shirt. He finally pulled it away to replace it with a clean one. Blood pooled from a deep slash in Jacob's side when the rag was moved.

The sight made Lydia dizzy. "Oh." She gasped, kneeling back onto the floor. She took Jacob's hand, holding it tightly in both of hers, and lay her head on his chest. The sound of his heartbeat, steady and strong in spite of everything calmed her. *This is not the time to fall to pieces. Jacob needs me.*

Janet brought the tea, and Lydia held Jacob's head, helping him drink. "There now, that should help," she said. Using a wet cloth, she wiped the dirt from his face. "Jacob, tell me what happened. Were you hurt in a battle?"

He shook his head, keeping his eyes closed. "Not a battle. The storm. We were helping the boy—Jem. I couldn't hold the door." He motioned toward his side. "A garden fork."

Lydia was relieved the wound wasn't made by a bayonet. "There now," she murmured. "Do you need a drink? What can I do?"

"Just stay," Jacob whispered.

"Don't worry. I'm here." She laid her head back on his chest. "Rest. We'll take care of you."

He curled his arm around her shoulders.

When Alden returned, more than an hour had passed since Dawson had notified Lydia in the upstairs drawing room.

She stood, setting Jacob's arm carefully onto his chest, and moved to the entry hall when she heard Alden speaking to Dawson. Burnett remained in the parlor.

"Alden, thank goodness." She looked behind him. "Where's the doctor?"

Alden tossed his hat onto the entry hall table and rubbed a hand over his face. The man looked terrible. Filthy and unshaven like Jacob, but dark circles hung beneath his eyes and his mouth was pursed in worry. "Not a doctor in this entire city. I searched everywhere." He flipped up his hand then rubbed it over his head as he glanced toward the parlor, his brows drawing together.

Lydia's stomach got tight. "No doctors? But—"

"I know." Alden rubbed his face again, his foot tapping on the floor. "He needs help—from someone who knows what they're doing."

*The English have doctors.* The thought came so suddenly Lydia froze. But she couldn't . . .

"Lydia." Alden turned toward her as if just now realizing whom he was speaking to. "What are you doing here? Jacob said you and Elnora had evacuated."

"We couldn't get out of the city," she said, her mind still turning over the half-formed idea. "Elnora is ill. The government took Jacob's carriage, and the army appropriated Elnora's horses."

Alden nodded. "I'm glad you're here. I didn't know where else to take him."

Lydia took a breath. "I know where to find a doctor." She said the words quickly before she changed her mind.

Alden blinked. "You do?"

"Yes." She turned away before he could see her shaking. "Dawson, if you please, fetch my bonnet and gloves."

Alden clasped her elbow. "I'll go with you."

She considered but dismissed the idea almost immediately. Alden had fought against the English at Bladensburg. She didn't think they'd welcome him into their camp. Perhaps they wouldn't welcome her either, but she thought her chances were much better. They wouldn't consider a woman to be a threat. "Stay with Jacob."

Alden opened his mouth to argue.

"Please. You must trust me."

Dawson returned with her gloves and bonnet.

She thanked him and pulled on her gloves. "Burnett will accompany me, and Janet." She set the bonnet over her hair, tying the ribbons. "If Jacob should wake, one of us should be here."

Alden scratched the skin on his neck, squinting as if he weren't quite pleased with the plan, but in the end, he nodded. "You're right, of course."

"I'll return soon."

The three started off, walking since they had no carriage. Burnett gave an uneasy look when Lydia asked the direction to the English camp. He glanced back toward Elnora's, but he directed her to the northeastern side of the city. As the party walked through the streets, they saw evidence of the storm and hurricane all around. Broken windows, downed trees, carriages in pieces . . .

Outside the city, the devastation seemed to be worse. Farmhouses had been demolished, fences flattened, and debris strewn over fields. As they walked, Lydia's worries lessened and her resolve grew firm. She was determined to do this for Jacob. And she was certain her plan would work. She'd spent the past three days hiding behind curtains while others fought. Now it was her turn. This was something she alone could do. Jacob depended on her, and she wasn't going to let her fear prevent her from acting.

When they neared the British encampment, Lydia turned to her loyal carriage driver. "Wait here, Burnett."

"But, madam." He glanced at the red-coated soldiers standing guard.

"We will be quite safe, Burnett. Helpless women pose no threat." She fluttered her lashes and smirked, hoping to set him at ease.

He gave a reluctant smile. "I don't like it, Mrs. Steele."

"Neither do I," she said. "But I must do it. For Jacob."

Burnett nodded. "Be careful, madam. I don't trust those lobsterbacks."

"I will." She took Janet's arm. "Shall we?"

The maid nodded, but her face was worried. "Very good, Mrs. Steele."

Lydia approached the guards, raising her chin confidently but also putting on her sweetest smile. She gave a slow blink, tipping her head and looking up through her lashes. "Good afternoon, gentlemen. If you please, would you direct me to Lieutenant Reynolds?"

The men looked at one another and one shrugged.

The other nodded. "If you'll follow me, miss."

"Thank you."

She and Janet stepped carefully over the muddy ground as they followed the guard between orderly rows of tents. The soldiers they passed were moving branches and making repairs to property damaged by the hurricane. Lydia guessed the men had found little shelter in their canvas tents, and the sympathy she felt for the enemy surprised her.

A man stepped into their path, and the guard soldier snapped to attention.

Lydia recognized the newcomer at once. "Colonel Andrews." She curtsied.

He raised his brows, his lip curling as he took in the mud on her skirt hem. "Mrs. Steele. This is a surprise."

"I've come to visit Lieutenant Reynolds." She smiled as if visiting an enemy commander was one of her usual errands.

He glanced behind her, shaking his head. "Is this kind of weather typical in your infernal country, Mrs. Steele?"

"Not at all, colonel." She smiled innocently. "I suppose it's God's way of punishing invaders to our beautiful city."

He stepped closer, bending his head down to glare at her. "It's God's way of aiding us to destroy your city." He bared his teeth, standing akimbo as he studied the wreckage around them. "I don't believe I'll ever be so happy as I shall upon leaving this place."

Lydia bit off her retort. Instead of telling the colonel she felt exactly the same, she gave another curtsy. Her husband's life depended on her finding a doctor, and she'd not jeopardize the opportunity by insulting the enemy, though she was very tempted. "It was delightful seeing you again, Colonel. If you'll excuse us . . ."

He looked as if he might protest her dismissal but thought better of it and stomped away.

Their escort widened his eyes when their gazes met, and his mouth pulled to the side the smallest bit. He spun and continued to lead her through the camp.

Upon reaching a particular tent, their escort spoke to the guard outside, and a moment later, the women were shown into the lieutenant's quarters. Lieutenant Reynolds sat at a wooden table, speaking with another man. He stood when they entered, dismissing his companion. "Mrs. Steele. A pleasure to see you. And I must say, a surprise . . ."

"Lieutenant, I am so sorry to disturb you." Lydia's confidence faltered as the challenge of convincing the lieutenant suddenly seemed too great. Tears filled her eyes. "Sir, I need your help."

"Of course, Mrs. Steele." He offered her a handkerchief. "How may I be of service?"

"My husband has been injured—in the storm. He's wounded, and something is wrong with his shoulder. We can't find a doctor anywhere in the city. I hoped . . ." She wiped her eyes as her words choked off. "Do you have a doctor, Lieutenant?"

He studied her and then held his hand toward a chair. "Please sit, Mrs. Steele. And your companion may sit as well."

She shook her head. "There's no time, sir. Jacob is losing blood. He's in so much pain. Lieutenant, I am begging you."

He scratched his cheek, looking toward the door flap. "I have a doctor, Mrs. Steele." He looked back at her. "But this is highly irregular."

"I know. I do not mean to impose on you, but I have no other choice."

Lieutenant Reynolds nodded. "Then we should go."

Lydia thought she would melt with relief. "Thank you," she whispered.

He called to the guard outside the doorway, giving him orders to bring the doctor and prepare an escort detachment.

"Detachment, sir?" Lydia asked, and then she understood. "Oh, because I am an enemy."

"You are one of my favorite enemies." He gave a half smile. "But yes, I must be cautious."

"I understand." Her request did seem very much like a trap.

Five red-coated soldiers marched in formation, accompanying Lydia, Janet, Burnett, Lieutenant Reynolds, and a young doctor with spectacles. Doctor Potter carried a leather satchel and walked quietly beside Janet. Lydia imagined their passing drew curious looks from the residents of the city, but she did not care one bit what people thought of her. Her only concern was making it back to Elnora's in time for the doctor to help Jacob.

As they walked, Lydia described the injuries to the doctor, her throat constricting as she told of the large wound in his side and his pale face. He'd asked a few questions, looking thoughtful as she answered. She wished he'd offer assurances that Jacob's condition didn't sound too grave. But he gave none.

When they arrived at Elnora's house, Lydia hurried inside and rushed to the parlor. Burnett followed directly behind her.

Alden pressed the cloth to Jacob's side, and Elnora sat on a chair beside him.

Jacob's eyes were open but not alert.

Lydia took his hand. "I've brought a doctor."

Alden jumped to his feet when the soldiers entered the room. He bolted toward his musket, but stopped when five redcoats raised their weapons.

Jacob strained to sit up.

Lydia placed a calming hand on Alden's arm. "It's all right. They're here to help."

"Lydia." Alden looked toward his musket but didn't make a move toward it. "What did you do?"

"Lieutenant Reynolds is my friend," Lydia said. "And this is Dr. Potter."

Alden stared at the soldiers, his face tight.

"Please, trust me," Lydia said.

"I trust you." Jacob's voice was raspy.

Alden didn't turn his head. "Jake . . ."

"If Lydia said we can trust them, we can," Jacob said.

Alden folded his arms.

Acting oblivious to the tension in the room, Lieutenant Reynolds removed his hat and lifted Elnora's hand. "Nice to see you again, Mrs. Hathaway."

"And you as well, Lieutenant," she said. "And I cannot thank you enough for bringing a doctor." She motioned to a seat. "Janet, please send for tea."

Not wanting to be in the way, as the room was now very crowded, Lydia sat as well.

Dr. Potter stepped forward, looking nervously at Alden. He set down the satchel beside Jacob. "I take it this is my patient?"

"Yes, sir. This is my husband, Jacob Steele," Lydia said.

Dr. Potter lifted the cloth from Jacob's side.

"Did you sustain this wound in battle?"

"The storm," Jacob said. "A garden fork."

"I've never seen such a storm." The doctor spoke as he inspected Jacob's arm. "Not in Spain or France or the Caribbean . . ." He pulled on Jacob's arm, and Jacob gasped.

Dr. Potter stood up. "The laceration is the most serious injury," he said. "But your shoulder is causing the most pain. Have you had anything to drink?"

"I gave him willow bark tea earlier," Lydia said.

Dr. Potter nodded. "Well done, madam. But he'll want something stronger. Whiskey, perhaps?"

"I have laudanum," Elnora said, motioning to a servant.

"No," Jacob said. "I want my mind clear."

The doctor studied him. "I'd take it, sir. Repositioning a dislocated joint is extremely painful. Opiates are a luxury in war. I unfortunately have none to offer."

Jacob shook his head.

"As you wish, sir." Dr. Potter motioned to one of the soldiers. "Private, please help Mr. Steele to sit up."

"I'll help him," Alden said. He continued to glare at the soldiers as he and Burnett raised Jacob into a sitting position. Alden again pressed the cloth to Jacob's side.

Lydia clasped her hands together. She could see from the tension and paleness in Jacob's face that his pain was excruciating. "Jacob."

Hearing his name, his gaze found hers.

"You'll be all right," Lydia said for his ears only, though of course the entire room could hear.

The doctor directed one man to pull, and another to push as he guided the shoulder into place. Jacob grunted, jaw clenched and sweat standing out on his face as the bone locked into the socket with a sickening sound.

"Oh my," Elnora said.

Lydia's head swam.

Jacob laid his head on the back of the couch.

"Now, how does that feel, Mr. Steele?" Dr. Potter said.

Jacob didn't raise his head. "Much better."

"Very good. We can lay you back down, then."

Janet brought tea, and Lydia set about serving the others. She cut slices of cake for the soldiers, not knowing whether or not an escort detachment was allowed sweets.

Lieutenant Reynolds nodded his approval, and the men ate gratefully.

Once Alden and Burnett helped Jacob lie back down, the doctor bent over Jacob's side, directing Alden to hold a lamp to inspect the wound. He leaned closer, sniffing, and used the cloth to pull the gash open. Lydia put her head into her hands when she became dizzy.

"A clean wound," Dr. Potter said. "Even though it's deep, I don't believe any internal organs are injured." He opened his satchel. "I'll stitch it up and then get to work on the fractured humerus."

Alden left the doctor to his work, moving to sit by Lydia, but keeping a close eye on his friend. Lydia handed him a plate with a slice of cake.

"Mr. Thatcher, may I introduce Lieutenant Reynolds." Lydia motioned to the men on either side of her.

The lieutenant inclined his head. "Mr. Steele is fortunate to have such loyal friend, Mr. Thatcher."

Lydia patted Alden's arm.

Alden inclined his head in return. "Thank you for bringing the doctor," he muttered, sounding like a child who was forced to give a thank-you against his will.

Lieutenant Reynolds turned more fully toward Alden. "I think I saw you at Bladensburg, sir. You were with the flotilla, holding the third line?"

Alden scowled and nodded.

"It was horrible, wasn't it?" Lieutenant Reynold's voice lowered, moving from politeness to a tone filled with pain.

"It was," Alden said. His voice had lost its anger, and in it, Lydia heard the offer of a shared sorrow. "I'm sorry you lost countrymen, Lieutenant."

Lieutenant Reynolds nodded. "Thank you. And my condolences to you as well." He looked around the room, smiling at Elnora and Lydia. "Strange, isn't it? How war makes enemies of people who would in other circumstances be friends?"

"It is indeed." Alden ate quietly for a moment, and then he tipped his head. "Lieutenant, what of the prisoners taken at Bladensburg?"

"They're being well cared for." He took a bite of cake. "I assume the militia will be sent home soon, the regulars as well, I believe, but I'm not the one who makes those decisions."

Alden leaned his forearms on his knees. "I have a friend, Michael Davis. He was shot in the shoulder." Alden tapped his shoulder. "Do you know . . . ?"

Lieutenant Reynolds set his plate onto his lap. "Dr. Potter," he called across the room. "Do you remember a prisoner from Bladensburg, Michael Davis? Shot in the shoulder."

The doctor looked up, chewing on his lip. "Wore a tricorn hat?"

Alden nodded, his eyes tightening. "Is he . . . ?"

"He's mending well. Should be ready to go home in a few days."

For the first time since the Englishmen had arrived, Alden smiled a genuine smile, and seeing it, Lydia couldn't help but smile in return.

Two hours later, Lydia accompanied a tired doctor, a friendly lieutenant, and five redcoats through the entryway.

"He's strong, Mrs. Steele," the doctor said. "If he allows himself to rest, he should make a full recovery in a matter of weeks."

"Thank you." She turned to Lieutenant Reynolds and gave an impudent smirk. "And thank you, sir. I never would have imagined an Englishman would prove to be such a true friend."

The lieutenant laughed. "You are very welcome, Mrs. Steele. If this war ever ends, my wife and I would love a visit in Stropshire from Jacob and Lydia Steele."

She grinned, delighted by the idea. "And we would love a visit as well. I'd be pleased to entertain Mrs. Anna Reynolds. I've no doubt she is a fine woman if she was fortunate enough to win your heart, sir."

"Let us shake on it, then. Make it official."

She giggled as he shook her hand, but became serious again, placing her other over her heart. "Farewell, sir, and my deepest thanks."

She turned to the doctor and took his hand. "Doctor Potter." Her voice choked, and she swallowed hard. "I cannot thank you enough." She pressed a pouch into his palm. "Please accept this, though it is in no way sufficient payment for my husband's life."

"Thank you, madam, but—"

Lydia held up her hand. "No argument, sir. Unless you plan to start another war."

He smiled and gave a bow.

Lydia fished a small bottle from her pocket. "And take this as well. It's laudanum. Even you redcoats shouldn't have to be in pain." She gave a wink to show she was teasing.

Dr. Potter and the lieutenant bid her farewell, and she waved as the company marched away.

Taking slow steps, Lydia returned to the parlor. With Alden's and Burnett's assistance, Jacob had moved to one of the bedchambers. His arm and shoulder were bound, his side sutured. She hoped he would be able to sleep.

Exhaustion made her knees weak, and she sat on the sofa, rubbing her hand over the cushion. She'd nearly lost Jacob. Nearly watched him die right in this spot, and it had terrified her. She thought of how their eyes had met when he'd been in pain, how he'd held her gaze like a lifeline. He'd always watched her intently, even the first day when he'd come upon her at the break in the Rosefield hedge. Like he was seeing past her outside appearance and trying to understand who she was underneath. Lydia sighed. There was no doubt in her mind that she was in love with him.

She rested her forehead in her hands, remembering back to the day in the carriage after they'd argued. She'd told him she was leaving, returning to her parents' house. And he had only nodded. He hadn't argued or asked her to stay. She hadn't admitted it to herself at the time, but that's what she'd wanted. If he'd asked, she would have reversed the plan to leave in a moment. But he hadn't. He didn't want her. And as soon as he was well, he'd deliver her to Rosefield and never look back.

And Lydia feared her heart would never recover.

# Chapter 24

Moonlight and the glow of fireflies shone on the polished wood of the sloop as it approached Rosefield dock. Jacob stared at his hand on the rail, not daring to meet the gaze of Alden or Elnora. Or even Lydia. They were here, and she'd not changed her mind.

Gordon had arrived in Alexandria, and the city had offered no resistance, giving the English the supplies and weapons they demanded. *Cowards,* Jacob had thought, but in truth he didn't blame them. Not after what had happened to Washington.

He and Alden had departed with Elnora and Lydia as soon as they were certain the English ship was secured at Fort Washington. Despite Elnora's protests, they'd all insisted she remain in Annapolis until Washington was safe again.

The English army had departed the night after the hurricane, but Jacob still didn't like the idea of leaving the older woman in a city where the resources were depleted and law enforcement was still struggling for control.

A crewman jumped out, securing the boat, and Jacob closed his eyes, listening to the lapping of the water against the hull and the buzzing of river insects as he fought away the swell of emotion. He could get through this.

He stepped out onto the dock and turned to assist Lydia.

She embraced Alden and Elnora then took his uninjured arm, keeping her face averted from his as she joined him on the dock. She quickly let go of his arm.

Jacob lifted her satchel, glancing up to see Alden standing with his arms folded. Even in the dark, his expression of disappointment was obvious. Jacob sighed and followed his wife along the darkened path toward the plantation house. He was disappointed in himself as well.

Lydia had spoken hardly a word since they'd left Elnora's house that morning. And now she walked ahead, her shoulders tight, and Jacob could feel displeasure coming off her in waves. He should probably say something, tell her he'd send her things and Francine as soon as possible, but such planning seemed trivial at this point.

They crested a hill and saw the house below, the white building standing out against the darkness. The smell of roses filled him, and Jacob was transported back to the first time he'd seen Rosefield early that summer. He'd been frustrated by their assignment, bothered to wear a formal coat in the heat and journey to Virginia to talk with wealthy plantation owners. But as soon as they'd arrived, he'd met a beautiful southern debutante with an untied ribbon and . . .

The ache in his chest expanded until it was an acute pain. "Don't leave me, Lydia." The words came out raspy, and his voice caught. He held his breath as every nerve went on alert, the honesty in his plea making him feel exposed.

Lydia halted. She turned her head, but did not fully face him. "What did you say?"

He braced himself, vulnerability sending his heartbeat into a frenzy and covering his body in a cold sweat. The fear of rejection was nearly over-whelming, but he pushed on. He'd not have another chance.

"You think I married you because your father forced me or persuaded me or paid me, but that isn't true. The choice was mine, Lydia. I came to him. I wanted to marry you."

She tipped her head. The brim of her hat still cast her face in shadow, but at least she was listening.

"Over the past months, I've pondered on the decision, trying to understand for myself why I'd done it." He winced at his honesty, hoping she'd not take offense and that she'd hear him out. "The conclusion I've reached is, the reason I married you isn't the same reason I fell in love with you."

Lydia grew even more still.

"You have the extraordinary ability to understand people, Lydia. To know what they need and how to care for them. You see what others don't. You treat people, all people, with kindness: members of high society, house-hold servants, your father's slaves, enemy soldiers . . ." He paused. "And me, though I do not deserve it."

She still hadn't moved, and his heart got heavy. "The truth is, Lydia, I married you because I thought you needed me, but over the past months, I've come to see it is I who needs you."

Lydia didn't move, nor did she respond. She remained still, facing away from him, with her head turned.

Jacob swallowed hard. His words weren't fancy, and they'd come too late to change anything. He stepped forward and took her elbow. "I understand. Come, I'll take you to the door."

Lydia pulled her arm away and whirled to face him. "Why didn't you ask me to stay?"

"I . . ." He shook his head, not understanding, and taken aback by the suddenness of the question.

"When I said I was returning to Rosefield, you didn't argue at all." He heard tears in her voice. "Why didn't you ask me to stay?"

Jacob had certainly not expected this, and he searched his mind for the right answer. "You were decided," he said. "And I thought you'd be happier . . ." He trailed off as she stepped toward him.

"I told you, Jacob. I tend to change my mind."

He couldn't tell by her tone whether she was reprimanding or teasing or weeping. Panic replaced his other emotions as he scrambled to form a response. "I don't understand. You . . ."

Lydia stomped her foot. "Jacob, you featherhead. I am in love with you. I want to stay with you. I want to be your wife . . ."

He reached out a tentative hand. Her words were affectionate, but they were spoken in anger, and he was utterly confused as to how he should respond. Only one strategy came to mind.

"Lydia." He whispered her name, sliding his hand behind her head and pulling her toward him, then kissing her until her taut muscles softened and she melted against him. She wrapped one arm around his waist but carefully avoided his bound arm and side.

Their lips parted, and she sighed, leaning her head onto his chest. Jacob tightened his arm around her and thought perhaps the right words weren't words at all.

Lydia raised her head, looking up at him. "Jacob, the reasons I married you aren't the reasons I fell in love with you, either. You believe in me—well, aside from when you thought I was an enemy spy."

"I'm so sorr—"

She put a hand to his mouth, stopping the apology, and her lips twisted in a teasing smile. "I do not know another man who would have stood by and let me speak to the secretary of war or put his trust in me when I brought a company of enemy soldiers into the house." She put a hand on his cheek. "I need you too, Jacob."

He did not need an invitation to kiss her again, sealing his lips over hers, and sinking into their softness. The worries of the past months fell away with Lydia in his arms, and he poured his soul into the kiss. A vow to trust and to work each day to make her happy. He'd not let his insecurities come between them any longer.

Lydia pulled back, sliding her hand down to his chest. "Can we start again?"

Moonlight cast a glow over her skin and brightened her eyes, and fireflies danced around her. His wife had never looked more beautiful. "Yes." His chest filled with warmth at the promise of a second chance. He'd do it right this time.

Her bottom lip pouted the slightest bit. "And if I become angry or hurt and tell you I'm leaving, please ask me not to."

He wished he'd understood this rule earlier. "I won't let you go."

She smiled. "I'm sorry I called you a featherhead."

Jacob laughed and pulled her tighter against him. "It is certainly not the worst insult I've received."

She snuggled against his chest. "Now, you silly, stubborn man, will you please take me home?"

*Home.* The word settled around his heart, and the feeling of protector returned. He would do everything in his power to keep this little woman safe. Lydia was his family. He pulled back, tracing his fingers over her cheek. "Soon, but I should like to keep you to myself a few moments longer." He bent for another kiss, and Lydia happily obliged.

Twenty minutes later, the two stepped onto the dock, hand in hand.

Alden flew from the boat and crushed them together in a painful embrace. He kissed Lydia's cheek, then Jacob's, then Lydia's again. "Don't scare me like that again."

Jacob grunted, his arm and side exploding in pain.

"Sorry, Jake." Alden released them, his smile glowing white in the darkness.

Lydia climbed onto the boat and joined Elnora, embracing the older woman. Jacob watched, his heart expanding to the point he feared it might burst.

Alden slapped him on the shoulder. "You had me scared."

"Take us home," Jacob said.

"Nothing would make me happier." Alden slapped him again and jumped onto the deck, and Jacob followed. He took Lydia's hand, and they walked to lean against the rail at the starboard bow.

She slipped under his arm, resting her head beneath his shoulder as he tightened an arm around her. She really did fit perfectly.

A crewman pushed the boat away from the dock, and they started down the Potomac toward the Chesapeake Bay and home.

"Do you know what I'm thankful for?" Lydia said.

"What?" He ran his fingers up and down her back.

She pulled away to face him and touched her cheek. "This scar."

Jacob blinked. That would have been his last answer. "Really? And why is that?"

She took his hand, holding it in both of hers as she leaned back against the rail. "If not for this pink line on my cheek, I'd be married to Jefferson Caraway, and you'd be . . ." She looked up and squinted. "Well, I suppose your life wouldn't be so different."

He cupped her chin, holding her face toward him. "Mrs. Lydia Steele, since I saw your blue eyes in the break in the hedge at Rosefield, nothing about my life has been the same." He kissed her cheek, lingering on the scar. "I'm grateful for it too," he whispered. He pulled back and turned her face to the side, studying the small pink line. "Amazing how a bit of glass could change the course of two lives," he said. "This little scar may have saved America, Lydia." He pulled her against him again as emotion choked his throat. "It definitely saved me."

# EPILOGUE

LYDIA HURRIED TO THE UPSTAIRS rail when she heard Jacob calling for her from the entryway below. She grinned, the sound of his voice setting her heart fluttering, even after three months of marriage. "What are you doing home so early?" she asked, leaning over. "I was going to bring a luncheon to the shipyard."

He climbed the stairs two at a time, a strange smile on his face. "They're leaving! Lydia, the English ships are leaving." He swept her into his arms and spun her around.

Lydia laughed. Spontaneous displays of affection were definitely not typical for her quiet husband. "Careful! Your arm . . ."

"It's been more than a month," he said. "My arm is fine." He took her shoulders, leaning close. "Lydia, did you hear what I said? The English are pulling out of every port. All up and down the coast and the Chesapeake."

Lydia could not believe it. The past month had brought story after story of English attacks. Boston, New York, and two days earlier, they'd lain awake listening to bombs and rockets fired at Fort McHenry as the sky glowed red.

"They didn't take Baltimore." Jacob seemed nearly giddy, as if he might break out in dance. "Twenty-five hours of bombing the fort, and when the sun rose, the American flag still flew above. I heard Admiral Cochrane was so angry, he ordered all the ships to withdraw."

"And where will they go?"

His face grew serious. "Most likely, they're headed for New Orleans. They'll hope to take Louisiana, control the Mississippi."

"Alden . . ." Lydia's stomach went cold. Alden had left Baltimore two weeks earlier in his repaired ship under the cover of darkness, headed back to New Orleans. Though Jacob did not admit it, she knew her husband missed his friend. She missed him as well.

"If there's one man on this earth *not* to worry about, it's Alden Thatcher," Jacob said. "He can take care of himself."

He spoke confidently, but she saw worry in his eyes.

Lydia straightened her husband's lapels. "With the blockade ships gone, you can finish the brigantine."

"True." His eyes took on a playful glint. "But I was thinking more along the lines of sailing the *Gannet*. She's missed the open sea." His smile grew. "Perhaps we could take a voyage up the coast? Visit Boston? Or, if you'd like, we could go south to Charleston."

"Or we could return the boat to the Washington Naval Yard and see Elnora." Lydia missed the older woman ever since she'd left to return home two weeks earlier.

"Or Commodore Barney in Pennsylvania," Jacob offered.

"Or Emmett and Abigail in Canada." Lydia smiled, and then a thought occurred to her, and she jolted. "People will return to the city, now, won't they?"

Jacob nodded.

"There will be balls and garden parties and music performances."

He nodded again, looking a bit less certain at just what she was getting at.

"And shops will carry new gowns." She clasped her hands together. "Finally."

"We shall have to expand your closet." Jacob laughed, pulling her into an embrace. "Perhaps we would do better to remain home for the time being. I know you would miss the Holts if we went away. Especially little Alexander."

Lydia snuggled against him, resting her ear against his chest and listening to his heartbeat. He held her tighter, and warmth flowed through her. She was never happier than when she was in Jacob's arms. "As long as you're with me, I shall be perfectly contented," she said. And nothing had ever felt truer.

# Author's Notes

In researching history, I am often struck by how like us people from times past are, but at the same time, they were so different. Their attitudes toward things such as slavery are repulsive to our modern sensibilities, while their conduct in war was so much more chivalrous. These sorts of contradictions are what make history so fascinating, to me at least.

The story about General Ross calling for a doctor to help Commodore Barney is true. According to Barney's journal, the general saved his life, "treated him like a brother," and assigned his own doctor to care for his enemy in a nearby inn. And sadly General Ross was killed a few weeks later near Baltimore.

Both of these men have become heroes of mine as I've read about their lives. I was familiar with General Ross, but I'd started this series not knowing anything about Commodore Joshua Barney. After reading his journal entries and his biography, I feel a strong admiration for him and wish more people knew what a hero he was. It was difficult to control myself and not make the entire book about him.

General Robert Ross and Captain Harry Smith are heroes of the Napoleonic Wars, and I learned about them quite a lot when I researched for my other series. It was a challenge to figure out just how to reconcile my feelings when they became the bad guys in this war. But what I realized, and why stories about war have such a place in my heart, is the men didn't change. They didn't become good or bad because of which army they fought for.

Soldiers are people, complex individuals, put into horrible situations, sometimes fighting for what they believe in and other times just following orders. And it's important to learn about them, not to just memorize regiments and battle dates, but to humanize people instead of lumping them together as good or evil based on which uniform they wear, especially while our world is in such a precarious state.

The little conversation Lydia has with the colonel after the hurricane is also based on a true account. And I couldn't bear to leave it out of the story. The few sentences tell so much about the attitudes of the times, and the wording is just beautiful. The interchange took place between a British officer and an American woman. I've tried to discover who exactly the man was, but accounts differ.

> *"Great God, Madam! Is this the kind of storm to which YOU are accustomed in this infernal country?"*
>
> *"No, Sir," [the lady] answered, "this is a special interposition of Providence to drive our enemies from our city."*
>
> *"Not so, Madam," [the officer] countered. "It is rather to aid your enemies in the destruction of your city."*[1]

---

1 Anthony S. Pitch. *The Burning of Washington: The British Invasion of 1814*. (Annapolis: Bluejacket Books, 2000), 142.

# ABOUT THE AUTHOR

JENNIFER MOORE IS A PASSIONATE reader and writer of all things romance due to the need to balance the rest of her world, which includes a perpetually traveling husband and four active sons who create heaps of laundry that are anything but romantic. Jennifer has a BA in linguistics from the University of Utah and is a Guitar Hero champion. She lives in northern Utah with her family. You can learn more about her at authorjmoore.com.